THE FOREVER MACHINE

THE FOREVER MACHINE

MARK CLIFTON & FRANK RILEY

Carroll & Graf Publishers, Inc.
New York

Published by arrangement with Frank Riley and the Estate of Mark Clifton.

First Carroll & Graf edition 1992

Carroll & Graf Publishers, Inc.
260 Fifth Avenue
New York, NY 10001

ISBN: 0-88184-842-5

Manufactured in the United States of America

Part I
Crazy Joey

Joey pulled the covers up over his head, trying to shut out the whispers which filled the room. But even with the pillow over his head, their shrill buzz entered up through the roof of his mouth, tasting acrid and bitter, spinning around in his brain. Fingers in his ears simply made the words emerge from a sensation of cutting little lights into words.

"It worries me, Madge, more and more, the way that boy carries on. I was hoping he'd outgrow it, but he don't."

His father's voice was deep and petulant, sounding from the pillow on his side of the bed there in the other room. "Hanging back, all the time. Not playing with the other kids, staying out of school, claiming the teachers don't like him. It ain't natural, Madge. I don't like it."

"Now you're working yourself up again, Bob." His mother's patient voice from her side of the bed cut across the deeper tones. "What good is it going to do you?"

"Did some good when I thrashed him." His father spoke sharply, and a little louder. Joey could hear the buzz of the voice itself coming through the walls. "Stopped him talking about whispers. I tell you I ain't gonna have a kid of mine acting crazy. I passed a bunch of the little brats on the way home tonight. 'There goes Crazy Joey's father,' I heard one of them say. I won't stand for it. Either Joey learns to stand up and be a real boy, or—"

"Or what, Bob?" His mother's voice had both defiance and fear in it.

"Or . . . oh, I don't know what—" His father's voice trailed off in disgust. "Let's go to sleep, Madge. I'm tired."

Joey felt his mother's lift of hope. Perhaps she could keep awake a little longer, waiting for his deep breathing to assure her he was asleep, so she could move from her extreme edge of the bed and be more comfortable—without touching him.

The deep, rasping sensation of his father's weary hopelessness; desire, but not for her. Drab and uninteresting. He was still young enough, still a man; tied down tight to this drab.

The lighter, more delicate thought of his mother. She was still young enough, still hungered for romance. The vision of a green slope of hill, starred with white daisies, the wind blowing through her flowing hair, a young man striding on firm brown legs up the hill toward her, his sloping shoulders swinging with his stride. Tied to this coarse hulk beside her, instead.

The heavier rasp of thought demanded attention. Those girls flouncing down the hallway of the school; looking out of the corners of their eyes at the boys;

8

conscious only of the returning speculative stares; unconscious of the old janitor who was carrying baskets of wastepaper down the hall behind them.

Joey buried his head deeper into the bed beneath his pillow. The visions were worse than the whispers. He did not fully understand them, but was overwhelmed by them, by a deep sense of shame that he had participated in them.

He tried to will his mind to leave the visions, and there leaped, with startling clarity, the vision of his father holding him down on the bed, a terrible rage in his face, shouting at him.

"How come you know how I looked at those two girls in the hall at school? You spying little sneak!" The blows. The horror. The utter confusion.

And the imaginings were worse than the visions. So clear, so intricately clear, they become memories. Memories as sharp and clear as any other reality. Eight-year-old Joey could not yet know the reasoned verbalization: an imaginary experience can have as profound an effect upon personality development as a real one. He knew only that it was so.

But he must never tell about this beating, must never tell anyone. Others wouldn't have any such memory and they would say he was crazy. He must store it away, with all the other things he had stored away. It was hard to keep remembering which were the ones others could remember, and which were his alone. Each was as real as the other, and that was the only distinction.

Sometimes he forgot, and talked about the wrong things. Then they called him a little liar. To keep away from that he always had to go into their minds first, and that was sometimes a terrible and frightening thing; their memories were not the same as his, and often hard to recognize.

Then it was morning. The whispers were all about him again. In half-awake reverie, he shuddered over the imagined beating he had received. He twisted and turned under the covers, trying to escape the also twisting threads of thought between his father and mother in the kitchen. The threads became ropes; gray-green and alive; affection turned resentment coiling and threatening; held back from striking only by hopelessness. He stared into the gray morning light seeping in around the shade at his window. He tried to trace the designs on the wallpaper, but they, too, became twisting worms of despair. And transferred again into the memory of the beating. Involuntarily, a sob escaped his throat, aloud.

"Madge!" This was no whisper, but his father shouting at his mother. "That kid is in there sniveling again. I'll give him something to bawl about." The sudden terrible rage was a dead black smothering blanket.

"Bob!" The sharp fear in his mother's voice stopped the tread of feet across the kitchen floor, changing the rage back to hopelessness.

He felt his father go away from his door, back to his place at the table. He felt the sudden surge of resolution in his father.

"Madge. I'm going to talk to Dr. Ames this morning. He gets in early. He's the head of the psychology department. I'm going to talk to him about Joey."

Joey could feel the shame of his father at such a

revelation. The shame of saying, "Dr. Ames, do you think my son is crazy?"

"What good will that do?" His mother's voice was resentful, fearful; afraid of what the doctor might say.

"I'll tell him all about Joey. He gives loony tests, and I'm going to find out about—"

"Bob! Saying such a thing about your own son. It's—it's sinful!" His mother's voice was high, and her chair creaked as she started to move from her side of the table.

"Take it easy, Madge," his father warned her. "I'm not saying he's crazy, mind you. I just want to get to the bottom of it. I want to know. I want a normal boy." Then, desperately: "Madge, I just want a boy!" The frustration, the disappointment welled over Joey as if it were his own.

"I'll talk to the doctor," his father was continuing, reasoning with her. "I'll try to get him to see Joey. I'm janitor of his building, and he shouldn't charge me anything. Maybe he'll see you and Joey this afternoon. I'll call you on the phone if he will. You be ready to take Joey up there if I should call." The voice was stern, unbending.

"Yes, Bob." His mother recognized the inflexibility of the decision.

"Where's my lunch pail, then?" his father asked. "I'll get to work early, so I can have a talk with Dr. Ames before class time."

"On the sink, Bob. Where it always is," his mother answered patiently.

The sudden rage again. Always is. Always is. That's the trouble, Madge. Everything always is. Just like yesterday, and the day before. That's why it's all so hopeless. But the bitterness switched suddenly to pity.

"Don't worry so, Madge." There was a tone of near affection in his father's voice. Belated consideration. Joey felt his father move around the table, pat his mother awkwardly on the shoulder. But still the little yellow petals of affection were torn and consumed by the gray-green worms of resentment.

"Bob—" His mother spoke to the closing door. The footsteps, heavy, went on down the back steps of their house, each a soundless impact upon Joey's chest.

Joey felt his mother start toward his room. Hastily he took the pillow from over his head, pulled the blanket up under his chin, dropped his chin and jaw, let his mouth open in the relaxation of deep sleep, and breathed slowly. He hoped he could will away the welts of the belt blows before she would see them. With all his might he willed the welts away, and the angry blue bruises of his imagination. All the signs of the terrible consequences of what might have been.

He felt her warm tenderness as she opened his door. Now the lights were warm and shining, clear and beautiful, unmuddied by any resentments. He felt the tenderness flow outward from her, and wrapped it around him to clear away the bruises. He willed back the tears of relief, and lay in apparent deep sleep. He felt her kneel down by his bed, and heard the whispers in her mind.

"My poor little different boy. You're all I've got. I don't care what they say, Joey. I don't care what they say." Joey felt the throb of grief arise in her

12

throat, choked back, the tremendous effort to smile at him, to make her voice light and carefree.

"Wake up, Joey," she called, and shook his shoulder lightly. "It's morning, darling." There was bright play in her voice, the gladness of morning itself. "Time all little fellows were up and doing."

He opened his eyes, and her face was sweet and tender. No one but a Joey could have read the apprehension and dread which lay behind it.

"I sure slept sound," he said boisterously. "I didn't even dream."

"Then you weren't crying a while ago?" she asked in hesitant puzzlement.

"Me, Mom? Me?" he shouted indignantly. "What could there be to cry about?"

The campus of Steiffel University was familiar to Joey from the outside. He knew the winding paths, the stretches of lawn, the green trees, the white benches nestled in shaded nooks. The other kids loved to hide in the bushes at night and listen to the young men and women talking. They snickered about it on the school playground all the time. Joey had tried it once, but had refused to go back again. These were thoughts he did not want to see—tender, urgent thoughts so precious that they belonged to no one else except the people feeling them.

But now walking up the path, leading to the psychology building with his mother, he could feel only her stream of thought.

"Oh I pray, dear God, I pray that the doctor won't find anything wrong with Joey. Dear God . . . dear God . . . don't let them find anything wrong with

13

Joey. They might want to take him away, shut him up somewhere. I couldn't bear it. I couldn't live. Dear God . . . oh dear God—''

Joey's thought darted down another bypath of what might be, opened by his mother's prayer. He willed away the constriction in his throat.

"This is interesting, Mom," he exclaimed happily. "Pop is always talking about it. But I've never been inside the building of a college before. Have you?"

"No, son," she said absently. Thank heaven he doesn't know. "Joey—" she said suddenly, and faltered.

He could read the thought in her mind. Don't let them find anything wrong with you. Try not to talk about whispers, or imagination, or—

"What, Mom?" It was urgent to get her away from her fear again.

"Joey . . . er . . . are you afraid?"

"No, Mom," he answered scornfully. "Course not. It's just another school, that's all. A school for big kids."

He could feel his father watching them through a basement window, waiting for them to start up the steps of the building. Waiting to meet them in the front hall, to take them up to Dr. Ames's study. He could feel the efforts his father was making to be casual and normal about it all; Bob Carter, perhaps only a janitor, but a solid citizen, independently proud. Didn't everyone call him "Mr. Carter?" Recognize his dignity?

Joey's father, with his dignity upon him, met them at the doorway of the building; looked furtively and quickly at the rusty black clothing of his wife, inadvertently comparing the textiles of her old suit to the rich materials the coeds wore with such careless style.

"You look right nice, Madge," he said heavily, to reassure her, and took her arm gallantly. When they had reached the second floor, up the broad stairs, he turned to Joey.

"I've been telling the professors how bright you are, Joey. They want to talk to you." He chuckled agreeably.

Pop, don't laugh like that. I know you're ashamed. But don't lie to me. Pop, I know.

"Just answer all their questions, Joey," his father was saying. "Be truthful." He emphasized the word again, "Truthful, I said."

"Sure, Pop," Joey answered dutifully; knowing his father hoped he wouldn't be truthful—and that his mother might die if he were. He wondered if he might hear the whisperings from the professors' minds. What if he couldn't hear! How would he know how to answer them, if he couldn't hear the whispers! Maybe he couldn't hear, wouldn't know how to answer, and then his mother would die!

His face turned pale, and he felt as if he were numb; in a dull dead trance as they walked down the hall and into a study off one of the big classrooms.

"This here is my wife and my son, Dr. Martin," his father was saying. Then to Joey's mother: "Dr. Martin is Dr. Ames's assistant."

The boy is very frightened. The thought came clearly and distinctly to Joey from the doctor's mind.

"Not any more," Joey said, and didn't realize until

15

it was done that he had exclaimed it aloud in his relief. He could hear!

"I beg your pardon, Joey?" Dr. Martin turned from greeting his mother and looked with quick penetration into Joey's eyes. His own sharp blue eyes had exclamation points in them, accented by his raised blond brows in a round face.

"But of course he is Dr. Ames's assistant," his father corrected him heartily, with an edge behind the words. You little fool, you're starting in to demonstrate already.

That isn't what the boy meant. Dr. Martin was racing the thought through his mind. I had the thought that the boy was frightened, and he immediately said he wasn't. All the pathological symptoms of fright disappeared instantly, too. Yes. Put into the matrix of the telepath, all the things Carter told us this morning about him would fit. I hadn't considered that. And I know that old fool Ames would never consider it.

If there ever was a closed mind against ESP, he's got it. Orthodox psychology?

"We will teach nothing here but orthodox psychology, Dr. Martin," Ames had said. "It is the duty of some of us to insist a theory be proved through time and tradition. We will not rush down every side path, accepting theories as unsubstantial as the tobacco smoke which subsidizes them."

So much for ESP. Well, even Rhine says that the vast body of psychology, in spite of all the evidence, still will not accept the fact of ESP.

But if this kid were a telepath—a true telepath. If by any chance he were . . . If his remark and the disappearance of the fear symptoms were not just coincidence!

But another Ames's admonition dampened his elation. "Our founder, Jacob Steiffel, was a wise man. He believed in progress, Martin, as do I. But progress through conservative proof. Let others play the fool, our job is to preserve the bastions of scientific solidity!"

"Dr. Ames has not arrived yet," he said suddenly to Joey's parents. "He's been called to the office of the university president. But, in the meantime, leave the boy with me. There's preliminary work to do, and I'm competent to do that." He realized the implications of bitterness in his remark, and reassured himself that these people were not so subtle as to catch it.

"I got work to do anyhow," Joey's father said. His relief was apparent, that he would not be required to stand by, and he was using it to play the part of the ever faithful servant.

"Here's a room where you may wait, Mrs. Carter," Dr. Martin said to Joey's mother. He opened a door and showed her in to a small waiting room. "There are magazines. Make yourself quite comfortable. This may take an hour or so."

"Thank you, Doctor." It was the first time she had spoken, and her voice contained the awe and respect she felt. A thread of resentment, too. It wasn't fair; some had so many advantages to get educated. Others—But the resentment was drowned out in the awe and respect. These were not just ordinary doctors. They *taught* doctors!

She sat tentatively on the edge of a wooden chair,

the hardest one in the room. The worn red feather in her hat drooped, but her back remained straight.

Joey felt the doctor thinking, "Relax, woman! We're not going to skin him alive!" But he merely closed the door. Joey could still see her sitting there, through the closed door; not relaxing, not reaching for a magazine. Her lips were pulled tight against her teeth to keep her prayer from showing. "Dear God, oh, dear God—"

Dr. Martin came back over from closing the door, and led Joey to a chair near the bookcase.

"Now, you just sit down there and relax, Joey. We're not going to hurt you. We're just going to visit a little, and ask you some questions." But his mind was darting in and out around his desires. I'd better start in on routine IQ tests, leave the Rorschach for Ames. Now that it's standard, he'll use it. Leave word association for him, too. That's his speed. Maybe I should give the multiphasic; no, better leave that for Ames. He'll discredit it, but it'll make him feel very modern and up-to-date to use it. I mustn't forget I'm just the errand boy around here. I wish I could run the Rhine ESP deck on the boy, but if Ames came in and caught me at it—"

The office phone rang, and Martin picked it up hurriedly. It was the president's office calling.

"Dr. Ames asked me to tell you he will be tied up for almost an hour," the operator said disinterestedly. "The patient will just have to wait."

"Thank you," Martin said slowly. Joey felt his lift of spirit. I can run a few samples of the Rhine cards. I just have to know. I wish I could get away from this place, into a school where there's some latitude for research. I wish Marion weren't so tied down here with her family and that little social group she lords it over. "My husband is assistant to the dean of psychology!" That's much more important to her than any feeling I've got of frustration. If I quit here, and got into a place where I could work, really work, it would mean leaving this town. Marion wouldn't go. She's a big frog in a little puddle here. And still tied to her parents—and I'm tied to Marion. If anybody needs psych help, I do. I wish I had the courage—''

Joey, as frequently with adults, could not comprehend all the words and sentences, but the somatic indecision and despair washed over him, making him gasp for breath.

Martin went over to a desk, with sudden resolution, and from far back in a drawer he pulled out a thin deck of cards.

"We're going to play a little game first, Joey," he said heartily, as he sat down at his desk and pulled a sheet of paper toward him. "There are twenty-five cards here. Five of them have a circle, five a star, a wavy line, a cross, a rectangle. Do you know what a rectangle is, Joey?"

Joey didn't, but the vision of a square leaped into his mind.

"Yes, sir," Joey said. "It's a sort of square."

"That's right," Martin said approvingly, making a mental note that the boy shouldn't have known the word, and did. "Now I'm going to look at a card, one at a time, and then you guess what kind of an image there is on it. I'll write down what the card really shows, and what you say it is, and then we'll see how many you get right."

19

Too short a time! Too short a time! But maybe long enough to be significant. If I should just get a trace. All right, suppose you do? The question was ironic in his mind. He picked up the first card and looked at it, holding it carefully so that Joey would have no chance to see the face of it.

A circle leaped with startling clarity into Joey's mind. And the circle contained the image of Joey's mother, sitting on the edge of her chair in the other room, praying over and over, "Don't let them find anything wrong with him. Don't let them find—"

"Square," Joey said promptly. He felt the tinge of disappointment in Martin's mind as he recorded the true and the false. Not a perfect telepath, anyway.

"All right, Joey," Martin responded verbally. "Next card."

"Did I get that one right?" Joey asked brightly.

"I'm not supposed to tell you," Martin answered. "Not until the end of the game." Well, the boy showed normal curiosity. Didn't seem to show too much anxiety, which sometimes damped down the ESP factor. He picked up the next card. Joey saw it contained a cross.

"Star," he said positively.

"Next card," Martin said.

It was in the nineteenth card that Joey sensed a new thought in Martin's mind. There was a rising excitement. Not one of them had been correct. Rhine says a negative result can be as revealing as a positive one. He should get every fifth card correctly. Five out of the twenty-five to hit the law of averages. Martin picked up the twentieth card and looked at it. It was a wavy line.

"Wavy line," Joey answered. He felt the disappointment again in Martin's mind, this time because he had broken the long run of incorrectness.

The twenty-first card was a star.

"Star," Joey said.

And the next three were equally correct. Joey had called five out of the twenty-five correctly, as the law of averages required. The pattern was a bit strange. What would the laws of chance say to a pattern such as this? Try it again.

"Let's try it again," he suggested.

"You were supposed to tell me how I did at the end of the game," Joey prompted.

"You were correct on five of them, Joey," Martin said, noncommittally.

"Is that pretty good?" Joey asked anxiously.

"Average," Martin said, and threw him a quick look. Wasn't that eagerness to please just a bit overdone? "Just average. Let's try it again."

This time Joey did not make the mistake of waiting until the end of the deck before he called correct cards. The doctor had said every fifth card should be called correctly. Joey did not understand statistical language. Dutifully, he called every fifth card correctly. Four wrong, one right. And again, the rising excitement near the twentieth card. Again, what are the laws of chance that the boy would call four wrong, one right, again and again, in perfect order?

Joey promptly called two of them right together. And felt Martin's disappointment. The pattern had been broken again. And then a rise of excitement, carefully suppressed.

"Let's run them again," Martin said. And he whispered strongly to himself. "This time he must call every other one of them right, in order to pass as just an average boy."

Joey was bewildered. There seemed to be a double thought in Martin's mind, a tenseness he could not understand. He wavered, and then doubtfully, doubting he was doing the right thing, he began to call every other card correctly.

Halfway through the deck Martin laid the cards down. Joey caught the flash of undisguised elation in his mind, and sank back into his own chair in despair. He had done it wrong.

"O.K., Joey," Martin said quietly. There was a smile of tender bitterness around his lips. "I don't know what the idea is. You've got your reasons, and they must be pretty terrible ones. Do you think you could talk to me? Tell me about it?"

"I don't know what you mean, Dr. Martin," Joey lied. Perhaps if he didn't admit anything—

"In trying to avoid a pattern, Joey, you made one. Just as soon as I realized you were setting up an unusual pattern, you immediately changed it. Every time. But that, too, is a pattern." And then he asked, quite dryly, "Or am I talking over your head?"

"Yes, sir," Joey said. "I guess you are." But he had learned. The whole concept of patterned response as against random response leaped from Martin's mind into his. "Maybe if I tried it again?" he asked hopefully. At all costs he must get the idea out of Martin's mind that there was anything exceptional about him. This time, and forever afterwards, he knew he could avoid any kind of a pattern. Just one more chance.

"I don't blame you, Joey," Martin answered sadly. "If you've looked into my mind, well, I don't blame you. Here we are. You're a telepath and afraid to reveal it. I'm a psychologist, supposed to be, and I'm afraid to investigate it. A couple of fellows who caught the tiger by the tail, aren't we, Joey? Looks as if we'd better kind of protect one another, doesn't it?"

"Yes, sir," Joey answered and tried to hold back the tears of relief. "You won't even tell my mother? What about my father?" He already knew that Martin didn't dare tell Ames.

"I won't tell anybody, Joey," Martin answered sadly. "I've got to hang onto my job. And in this wise and mighty institution we believe only in orthodox psychology. What you have, Joey, simply doesn't exist. Dr. Ames says so, and Dr. Ames is always right. No, Joey," he sighed, "I'm not likely to tell anybody."

"Maybe he'll trick me like you did," Joey said doubtfully, but without resentment. "Maybe with that ink-blot thing, or that 'yes' and 'no' pile of little cards."

Martin glanced at him quickly.

"You're quite perfect at it, aren't you?" He framed it a question and made it a statement. "You go beyond the words to the actual thought image itself. No, Joey, in that case I don't think he will. I think you can keep ahead of him."

"I don't know," Joey said doubtfully. "It's all so new. So many new things to think about all at once."

"I'll try to be in the room with you and him," Martin promised. "I'll think of the normal answer each time. He won't look very deep. He never does. He already knows all the answers.''

"Thank you, sir." Joey said, and then, "I won't tell on you, either."

"O.K., Joey. We'd better be finishing the IQ test when he comes in. He's about due now. I suppose you'd better grade around a hundred. And you'd better miss random questions, so as not to show any definite pattern, for him to grab onto. All right, here goes. Tell me what is wrong with this statement—"

The tests were over. Joey sat quietly in his chair watching Dr. Martin grade papers at his desk, watching him trying not to think about Joey. He watched his mother in the waiting room, still sitting on the edge of her chair, where she had been for the last two hours, without moving, her eyes closed, her lips still drawn tight. He watched Dr. Ames, sitting in his own office, absently shuffling papers around, comparing the values of the notes he had taken on Joey's reaction.

But the nearer turmoil in Dr. Martin's mind all but drowned out the fear of his mother, the growing disgust of Dr. Ames.

"It's a choice between Joey and holding my job. No matter how secretly I worked, Ames would find out. Once you're fired from a school, it's almost impossible to get a comparable job. All this subversive business, this fear of investigating anything outside the physical sciences that isn't strictly orthodox. No matter what explanation was given out, they'd suspect me of subversion. Oh Marion, Marion! Why can't I count on you to stand beside me? Or am I just using you as an

24

excuse? Would I have the courage even if there were no Marion?''

He rubbed his hand across his eyes, as if to shut out the vision of a world where there was no Marion. He replaced it with a world where constant fear of becoming grist for some politician's publicity ground all research to a halt. He had quite forgotten that Joey was sitting across the room, and could follow at least the somatics of his thought.

Consciously he shoved the problem into the background, and made himself concentrate on the words of the student's paper before him. The words leaped into startling clarity, for they were a reflection of his own train of thought.

". . . it becomes apparent then that just as physical science varies its techniques from one material to the next to gain maximum result, psychology must obtain an equal willingness to become flexible. I suggest that objective physical science methodology will never permit us to know *a man; that such methodology limits us merely to knowing* about *a man. I suggest that an entirely new science, perhaps through somatics and methodology derived therefrom, must be our approach.''*

Dr. Martin shoved the paper away from him. Must warn that student. His entire train of thought was a violation of orthodox psychology. Ames would crucify the boy if he ever saw this paper. Did he dare warn the boy? Students show so little caution or ethics. He could hear him now down at the milkshake hangout.

"Martin told me to soft-pedal my thinking if I wanted to get a grade."

And the answering chorus from all around the room, the Tannenbaum chant:

"Oh, Steiffel U will stifle you,
We all must think as granddads do!"

Best just to give the student a failing grade on the paper, and let him draw his own conclusion. Got to be orthodox.

With his thumb and fingers he pulled the flesh of his forehead into a heavy crease, grinding it between his fingers, taking pleasure that the pain of the flesh lessened the pain of his spirit. If only the kid had never shown up here!

His thought stream was interrupted in Joey's mind by the scene now taking place in the waiting room. Dr. Ames had taken a chair beside Joey's mother.

"Oh no, no, no, no, Mrs. Carter," he was saying consolingly. "Don't be so frightened. There's absolutely nothing wrong with your boy. Nothing at all— yet. I've never tested a more average boy."

Characteristically, he had overlooked the most vital point, a point also forgotten by Martin when he was thinking of the proper answers for Joey to give—that no boy can possibly be as average as Joey had graded. It never occurred to him that mean average is a statistical concept in psychology, never to be found in one individual.

"Notice I said 'yet,' Mrs. Carter," Ames said heavily. "He's an only child, isn't he?"

"Yes," Joey's mother barely breathed the word. Her fear had not abated. She knew that doctors sometimes did not tell all the truth. In the soap operas they always started out comfortingly, and only gradually let you know the terrible truth.

"I thought so," Ames said with finality. "And as with many one-child families, you've spoiled him. Spoiled him so dreadfully that now you must take stern measures."

"He's all I've got, Doctor," she said hesitantly.

"All the more reason why you want him to grow up into a strong, solid man. A man such as your husband, for example. A child is a peculiar little entity, Mrs. Carter. The more attention you give him, the more he wants."

He continued the development of his theme inexorably.

"Their bodies can be little, but their egos can be enormous. They learn little tricks for getting attention. And then they add to these with others. They're insatiable little monsters. They never get enough. Once they get you under their thumb, they'll ride you to death. They'll try anything, anything at all to get special attention, constant attention. That's what has happened to your Joey."

"I'm not sure I understand, Doctor."

"Well, Mrs. Carter, to put it bluntly, Joey has been pretending, telling lies, deliberately keeping you worried and fearful so that you will give him more attention. He hasn't been able to fool his father so well, so in line with Oedipus complex, he set about to win you away from his father, to come between you. Your

27

husband is a fine man, a good worker; but your son wants to make you turn against your husband so he will get all of your attention.''

He was enjoying the development of his logic, sparing no impact upon her.

''And it could be bad for the boy. Too much attention is like too much candy. It makes them sick.'' He pulled an ancient trick upon her, deliberately confusing her to impress her with the gravity, and his knowledge. ''If this continues, the boy could easily become a catatonic schizophrenic!''

Joey's mother shrank back, her eyes opening wide. The horror of the unknown was worse than the reality might be.

''What is that, Doctor?''

The doctor, gratified by her reaction, pulled another ancient one.

''Well . . . er . . . without the proper background . . . er . . . well, in layman's language, Mrs. Carter, we might roughly define it as an incurable form of insanity.''

''Oh, no, no! Not my Joey!''

The doctor leaned back in his chair. In this changing world of thought anarchy, it was good to see there were some who still retained the proper respect, placed the proper value upon the words of a man of science. These flip kids he got in his classes these days; this younger generation! Without respect, that flip kid he'd had to get expelled.

''Just give us the facts, Doctor, and let us draw our own conclusions. Yours haven't worked so well.''

Yes, it was gratifying to see there were still some who recognized a man of position.

"But you can prevent it, Mrs. Carter." He leaned forward again. "Joey is eight, now. No longer a baby. It is time he began to be a little man. He plays hooky from school, says the teachers don't like him. Why, Mrs. Carter, when I was eight, I got up before daylight, did my farm chores without complaint, and walked two miles through the snow for the wonderful privilege of going to school!

"Now here is what you must do. You must regard this just as you would a medical prescription; with full knowledge of the penalty if you do not use the prescription: You must stop mothering him. Stop catering to him. Pay no attention to his tricks. Let his father take over, Mrs. Carter. The boy needs a strong man's hand.

"He must be forced to play with the other boys. A black eye never hurt a boy, now and then, a real boy. Your boy must get in there and scrap it out with the rest of them, gain his place among them, just as he will have to scrap later to gain his place in society."

A sigh, almost a sob, escaped her. A doctor knows. And this doctor *teaches* doctors. Relief from tension, fear of the terrible words the doctor had said; and then a growing anger, anger at herself, anger at Joey. He had tricked her. Her son had lied to her, betrayed her love, pretended all sorts of terrible things just to worry her. She stood up suddenly, her face white with grief-rage.

"Thank you, Doctor. Thank you so much. I'm sorry we took up your time." Her humiliation was complete.

"No thanks needed, Mrs. Carter. Glad to help.

We've caught it in time. If it had been allowed to go on a little longer—"

He left the phrase hanging in the air, ominously. He patted her arm in a fatherly fashion, and turned absently away, dismissing her.

Joey saw her open the door into the room where he was sitting.

"Come, Joey," she said firmly.

Dr. Martin did not look up from the papers he was now grading with furious speed, furious intensity, slashing angrily with his blue pencil at any thought variant from the orthodox. But even while he checked, circled, questioned, the thought crept into his mind.

"I could write an anonymous letter to Dr. Billings of—yes, that's the thing to do. It's out of my hands then. If Billings chooses to ignore the follow-up, that's his business."

Joey followed his mother out of the room and down the hall. She walked ahead of him, rapidly, her eyes blazing with anger and humiliation, not caring whether he followed her or not.

In one corner of the schoolyard, the boys were playing ball. Joey knew they saw him coming down the sidewalk, alone, but they pointedly paid no attention to him.

He did not try to join them. Even though they were not looking at him, he could hear the hated refrain singing through their minds.

Crazy Joe
Such a schmo!
Hope he falls
And breaks his toe!

30

It was simply their resentment because he was different. Their unconscious wish that he stumble and fall now and then, as they did. He realized that he must learn to do this. Then he shrugged. No, if he carried out his plan, it wouldn't matter.

He walked on down past the fence of the play yard. The boys were concentrating on their ball game.

Without a warning a warmth suffused him, singing sympathy, hope, joy. He stopped, looked about him, and saw no one. Yet the somatic feeling had been near—so very near.

Then he saw it. A dirty, lop-eared dog looking at him quizzically from under a shrub near the playground gate. He thought at the dog, and saw its head come up. They stood and looked at one another, each letting the warmth, the tenderness, affection wash over them. So lonely. Each of them had been so lonely.

Joey knelt down and began to whisper.

"My mother is mad at me right now. So I can't take you home."

The dog cocked his head to one side and looked at him.

"But I'll get food for you," Joey promised. "You can sleep under our back steps and nobody will know if you just keep out of sight."

The dog licked a pink tongue at his face. Joey nuzzled his face in the dirty hair of the dog's neck.

"I was going to die," he whispered. "I was going to die just as soon as my mother got over being mad at me. I was going to wait until then, because I didn't want her to blame herself later. I can do it, you know. I can stop my blood from moving, or my heart from beating; there's a hundred ways. But maybe I won't need to do it now. I won't need to die until you do. And that will be a long time; a long, long time. You see, if I can stop your heart from beating, I can keep it beating, too."

The dog wagged his stumpy tail; and then stiffened in Joey's arms.

"Yes," Joey thought quickly at the dog. "Yes, I know the kids are watching us now. Pretend like—" the thought hurt him, but he said it anyway. "Pretend you don't like me, that you hate me."

Slowly the dog backed away from Joey.

"Here, doggy, doggy!" Joey called.

The dog gave a wavering wag of his stump tail.

"No, no!" Joey thought desperately. "No, don't let them know. They'll want to hurt you if they find out. They're—People are like that."

The dog backed away another step and lifted his lip in a snarl.

"Yah! Yah! Yah!" the kids called out. "Joey can't even make friends with a dog!"

They were standing in a semicircle about him now. Joey stood up and faced them then for a moment. There was no anger or resentment in his face. There never would be now. One just shouldn't get angry at blind and helpless things.

Without a word he started walking down the street, away from them. The dog crouched far back in the corner under the shrub.

"Yah! Yah! Crazy Joey!" the kids called out again.

Joey did not look back. They couldn't see. They couldn't hear. They couldn't know. He felt a rush of pity.

The kids went back to their play, arguing loudly about who was at bat.

The dog waited until their attention was fully on the game again. Then he crept out from under the bush, and started ambling aimlessly down the street in the direction Joey had gone, trotting awkwardly on the bias as some dogs do.

He did not need to sniff for tracks. He knew.

Jonathan Billings, Dean of Psychosomatic Research at Hoxworth University, heard the knock on his study door, and looked up from his work at his desk. But before he could call out an invitation to enter, the door opened.

That would be Mr. Rogan, Resident Investigator. Anyone else would have waited.

Billings watched him without expression as he came through the door—a little man, a negative quantity, who wore heavy silver-rimmed glasses in the hope they would give character to a characterless face. The brief case he carried, too, was heavily decorated with silver, proclaiming its unusual importance. He needed these trappings, and more. He was the kind of man one forgot to introduce, and his whole bearing suggested his determination to command the attention he never quite received.

There was a portentous frown on his gray face, and without any preliminaries of greeting he bustled over and laid a new issue of the college paper on Billings'

35

desk. Billings looked down at the open page, and a cartoon of himself looked slyly back.

That was the trouble of having an old, old face with a thousand wrinkles. Even seventy years had been unkind in putting so many wrinkles there. In a cartoon, and he was often the subject of them throughout the country, those wrinkles could be slanted to make him appear fine and noble, or sly and scheming. It would depend upon which faction of the public the cartoonist wanted to please.

This time, in the cartoon, he was sly; and had his finger held up toward his lips in a cautioning, secretive gesture. There was a caption in bold print beneath the cartoon.

"You were quite wrong, Albert, about the nature of the universe!"

Billings looked up from the cartoon with a slight smile and met the accusing expression in Rogan's washed blue eyes.

"This is highly irregular, doctor," Rogan said firmly, before Billings could comment. "I trust you have not been questioning indisputable facts! I trust you have not been planting disturbing doubts in the minds of our future citizens! I trust you know Congress approved those facts for school textbooks long ago! It would be most subversive, not to mention a waste of time and tax money, to question them now!"

Billings felt a flare of sudden irritation, an emotion he considered quite unworthy of the circumstances. He should be accustomed to this sort of thing by now. For the past thirty years there had been a Resident Investigator, some worse and some not any worse than Rogan; monitoring what the teachers said, the lines of thought they pursued. He remembered a long succession of them who had come through his door; some of them resentful that he was world famous and must be handled with especial care; others seeing in it a golden opportunity for personal publicity if they could catch him in some subversive remark.

Out of the montage of accusations and sly traps written in their collective expressions, one face stood out clearly from all the rest. What was the remark the man had made? Oh, yes, he remembered it now.

"I am completely impartial, Dr. Billings," the man had said. "I merely see to it that you teachers say nothing which might threaten our freedom of speech!"

The memory of that incredible twist of semantics, so characteristic of the early days, cleared the irritation from his mind, and he looked back into Rogan's face with equal firmness. His answering tones were just far enough away from Rogan's speech that he could not be accused of Contempt For An Investigator.

"I trust you know, Mr. Rogan, that my subject is psychosomatics. I trust you are aware that I have no knowledge of approved astronomy courses, and would not feel qualified to comment upon it."

Rogan slapped the cartoon on the desk with the back of his fingers imperatively. He had studied the old films assiduously in an attempt to impart authority into his own attitudes and gestures.

"How do you account for this cartoon, then, doctor?" he asked with the triumphant expression of having scored an irrefutable point. The characteristic puerility of it washed away the final residue of irritation on Billings' mind, and he smiled in genuine amusement.

"Why, I suspect young Tyler, its author, is just having a bit of fun," he said slowly. "He's quite a mischief maker."

Rogan's eyes lighted up with delight at the possibility of a new scent.

"A student, eh?" he asked quickly. "One of these subversive cults probably. Trying to undermine our faith in our institutions."

"The cartoonist is young Raymond Tyler, of Tyler Synthetics," Billings said quietly. "An only son of the family, I believe."

"Ah," Rogan's face smoothed of all suspicion instantly. "Just a boyhood prank then." He was obsequious at the very name of such a powerful industry. "Boys will be boys, eh, doctor?"

"This one in particular," Billings said with a heavy note of irony. "Was that all, Mr. Rogan?" There was a note of unmistakable dismissal in his voice. Even Rogan could not miss it. The little man flushed, and pointedly sat down in a chair as his answer.

"No, doctor, that was just a preliminary," he said. "I have a commission for you from Washington. You are to head up a new line of research."

"I haven't completed my old line of research, Mr. Rogan," Billings reminded him. "Inquiry into the reasons for Citizen Neurosis."

"That's canceled, doctor," Rogan said firmly. "Washington is no longer interested in Civilian Fatigue." He reached out for his ornate brief case, fondled it lovingly as he opened it, and drew from it a thick sheaf of papers in a blue binding.

Billings made an impatient gesture, as if to remonstrate that months of work should not be so easily discarded, and then realized the futility of it. He settled back into his chair again.

"Very well, Mr. Rogan," he said in a resigned voice. "What does Washington instruct me to work on now?"

Even after thirty years of it, he was not yet accustomed to universities being operated on sound businesslike principles, with orders coming from the front office telling the boys in the lab what they should be thinking about today.

Or even more than thirty years. It was impossible to draw a hard line on just when it had happened. Perhaps it was the outgrowth of the practice when he had been a research student and young instructor. The local industry would come to the university with a problem. The university was eager to show its cooperation, its practical place in the industrial life of the nation. They got into the habit of delaying their own lines of research and working on those immediate ones required by industry. The habit grew into a custom. A few universities saw the danger and rebelled. Overnight, custom became a law. To rebel against a law, even a bad one, was subversion.

But he must not let his mind wander into the past. That was the mark of senility, they said. And what was Rogan saying now? And why didn't the man just leave the folder with him? Why did the man have to read it to him, word for word?

The opening pages were filled with gobbledegook, replete with such phrases as "by order of," and "under penalty of." Why did these government agencies always feel they had to threaten citizens? He could not recall any government communication which did not carry a threat of what would happen to him if he failed to comply. Surely after seven thousand years of trying it, governments should have learned that threats and punishment were not the way to accomplish their aims.

His eyes wandered around the room, and scowled at the gray November sky outside the window. The cold light made the dark paneled wood of his walls seem dingy and grimed. The shabby, old-fashioned furniture seemed even more shabby as the little man's voice droned on and on through the phrases.

". . . As revised . . . authorized . . . official . . . top secret . . ." Rogan apparently liked the sound of the governmental jargon, and gave each phase a full measure of expression.

Gradually the sense of the order became dimly apparent through all the legal phrasing. As Billings had feared, it was an old problem, just now coming to light.

That was significant, even though only a few men might recognize it. Not one new principle had come out of the universities in the past thirty years. Not one problem had arisen which hadn't been foreseen then. It was as if something geared to tremendous momentum had had powerful brakes applied. The forward movement seemed to continue satisfactorily; yet it was apparent to anyone who cared to look that it was grinding to a halt.

Odd how the human mind, once it became conscious of the unyielding pressure of limits and restrictions, refused to think constructively. There was a lot of loose talk about the indestructibility of the human will, how it strove onward and upward, overcoming all ob-

40

stacles. But that was just talk, of the most irresponsible kind. Actually the human will to progress was the most delicate mechanism imaginable, and refused to work at all if conditions were not precisely right.

In the half million years man had been on earth, there were only twenty occasions when he had been able to pull himself up beyond the primitive animal level. It was significant, too, that most of these generated their forward momentum in one spurt, and often within one lifetime. Momentum reached its point where rulers became satisfied and clamped down restrictions against any change of the *status quo*. Then began, over and over in each civilization, the slow retrogression and the long night.

In the typical fashion of governmental directives, the order said the same thing over and over, yet never succeeded in saying outright what it meant. Man's inventive techniques had outstripped his reaction time possibilities. A plane, hurtling into an unforeseen disaster, would strike it before the pilot could become aware of the danger and react to avert it.

To protect his own life, man had had to place a limit upon the speed of his vehicles. True, he tried to cope with the situation by inventing servomechanisms, but most of these merely registered their findings upon a dial. The cockpits of ships became a solid wall of dials. No human eye could read all their messages simultaneously and react as they directed.

And, too, the servomechanisms, intricate and marvelous though they might be, were blind and senseless things, capable of following only one design of action.

Only the human mind was sufficiently flexible to vary the patterns of behavior to meet the variation of

41

possible circumstances. But the human mind was too slow, too inefficient, too easily distorted. It was—an understatement—undependable.

Billings watched the unfolding of the inexorable logic in the order with a growing dread which began to mount to the level of horror. For it was clear to him where the logic must lead. Since we did have weapons, the order pursued its line of thinking, which could seek out a target, follow it, strike and destroy it; the work of Hoxworth University was quite simple, and should require little time or tax monies.

The university was simply required to reverse the known mechanical principle and see that a plane, or an automobile, or other moving vehicle, struck nothing!

The order ended with its usual propaganda. Thus the citizens could see that, once again, out of war came great benefits to peace.

Rogan closed the stiff back page of the order and looked up at Billings with an expression of satisfaction at having delivered the government's instructions concisely and completely.

"In other words," Billings said slowly, "they want a servomechanism designed which can foresee the future, and work out a pattern of mechanical operation which will cope with that future at the time it becomes present." He realized his voice showed his incredulity, and that it would displease Rogan. It did.

"I believe the order is quite clear, doctor," Rogan said decisively. "And there is certainly nothing difficult about it, now that Washington has shown you the way to solve it. What a target-finder missile does, you simply have to do in reverse."

"But why did Washington select me, Mr. Rogan?" Billings asked carefully. "I am not a mechanical technician or engineer. I work with the human mind and body, their interaction. I wouldn't know anything about this project at all."

He was sorry he mentioned it, for it could be construed as Unwillingness to Cooperate, a fellow traveler act if not actually subversive. And it was a foolish question to ask, too, since government did not usually take capability into consideration in making an appointment—no more than the people did in electing government. Still, his question did bring him unexpected results.

Rogan hesitated, pulled at his lip, decided not to make anything out of the doctor's slip.

"Washington does not usually have to explain to a citizen," he said, "but I am instructed to answer you. This project is not a new one. It has been assigned before—several times."

"You mean the mechanical engineers have refused it?" Billings asked.

"Those who did are serving their sentences, of course," Rogan said, and his voice implied that Dr. Billings could join them without loss to the world. "But there was one thread of agreement at their trials. They all said that this would be duplicating the work of the human brain, and we'd better go to an expert on the human brain if we wanted to know how that worked.

"So," he finished simply, "here we are."

Billings had thought he was beyond further astonishment, but he had underestimated his own capacity for it.

"Mr. Rogan," he said slowly, trying not to show that he was aghast at the vacuity of such logic. "I do not question Washington's wisdom. But for the sake of the record, I know only a few of the secondary effects of mental action; I do not know how the mind works; I do not know of any human being who does."

He stopped short, for there flashed into his mind the possibility of one who might. Joe Carter, a student— a telepath.

The house where Joe lived was nearly a century old, and did not need the aid of the fog and the dusk to give it an air of grimy neglect. The weather-stained sign which proclaimed light-housekeeping rooms for students seemed almost as old, but at least it did not misrepresent them as being cheery or bright or comfortable.

Billings hesitated briefly at the foot of the steps leading up to its front door, and mentally pictured with dread the two long flights of wooden stairs he must climb to reach Joe's room.

He could have summoned Joe to his office, of course, but tonight that would have been adding insult to injury. And, too, in his own room, the boy seemed to have a little less reserve than in the office or the classrooms.

He started the slow, careful climb up the steps, opened the front door which was never locked for it was obvious that no one here could have anything worth taking, walked across the short hall, and started up the first flight of stairs. He glanced farther down the hall, saw the landlady's door close abruptly, and smiled. It was the same, every time he came to see Joe.

He had known Joe Carter for twelve years. First there had been the letter from Martin at Steiffel University, telling him about an eight-year-old telepath whose parents thought him insane. He, himself, had gone to the small college town and talked with the boy. He had arrived at a bad time. The story, as he got it from others, was that the boy had picked up a stray dog. The boy's parents had turned the dog over to the pound, and it had been destroyed. Joe had become silent, uncommunicative, unresponsive to any of Billings' attempts to draw him out.

Twelve years. From the sidelines he had watched Joe get through primary and secondary schools. He had marveled at the continued, never-breaking concealment the boy practiced in covering his unique talent. But concealment breeds distrust. The boy grew up friendless and alone.

Every year Billings had reviewed the grades which Joe had made. They were uniformly, monotonously, equivalent of C. He was determined to be neither sharp nor dull; determined that he would do nothing to make anyone notice him for any reason. As if his life, itself, depended upon remaining unnoticed.

Both his high school associates and Joe's parents were astonished when Hoxworth University offered him a scholarship. It wasn't much of a scholarship, true, for Joe's parents had no influence and Joe was not an athlete. Since there would be neither prestige nor financial return to the University, it hadn't been easy, but Billings had managed it, and without revealing the reasons for it.

He paused and caught his breath in the hallway at the top of the first flight of stairs, and then resumed his upward climb. They could talk all they pleased about how hale and hearty he was at seventy, but two flights of stairs—

Twelve years. That would make Joe about twenty now. The last three years had been at Hoxworth. And Joe had been as colorless in college as in high school.

Billings had tried, many times, to draw him out, make him flare into life. He had shown infinite patience; he had strived to radiate sympathy and understanding. Joe Carter had remained polite, friendly, appreciative—and closed. Billings had tried to show community of spirit, transcending the fifty years gap in their ages—and Joe had remained respectful, considerate, and aware of the honor of personal friendship from such a famous man. If Joe had known who wheedled a scholarship for him, he had never shown the knowledge.

Tonight Billings would try a different method. Tonight he would sink to the common level of the mean in spirit. He would demand acknowledgment and some repayment for his benefaction.

He hesitated in front of the wooden paneled door, almost withdrew back down the stairs in preference to portraying himself in such a petty light; and then before he could make up his mind to give it up, he knocked.

The door opened, almost immediately, as if Joe had been waiting for the knock. The boy's face was withdrawn and expressionless, as usual. Yet Billings felt there was a greater wariness than usual.

"Come in, doctor," Joe said. "I heard you coming up the stairs. I've just made some coffee."

Two chairs were placed at the pitiful little table; two heavy china cups wreathed vapor. A battered coffeepot sat on a gas plate. The housekeeping was light, indeed.

The two of them sat down in chairs, straight hard chairs and picked up the mugs of coffee.

"I'm in trouble, Joe," Billings began. "I need your help." Somehow he felt that an immediate opening, without preliminary fencing, would be more appreciated. And on this basis, he proceeded into the story of the newest order he had just received that afternoon from Rogan. He made no effort, either, to draw Joe out, to get the boy to acknowledge his talent of telepathy. Billings took it for granted, and became aware as he progressed that Joe was making no effort to deny it.

That, at least, was hopeful. He switched suddenly to a frontal approach, although he knew that young men usually resented it when an older man, particularly a successful one, did it.

"Have you given any thought, Joe, to what you intend to do with your life? Any way you can turn your gift into constructive use?"

"A great deal, of course," Joe answered without hesitation. "In that, at least, I'm no different from the average fellow. You want me to work with you on this synthetic brain, don't you, doctor? You think I may have some understanding you lack? Is that it?"

"Yes, Joe."

"It could destroy the human race, you know," Joe said quietly.

Billings was brought up short. He felt a sudden chill, not entirely due to the bleak and heatless room in which they sat.

"You foresee that, Joe, definitely?" he asked. "Or are you merely speculating?"

"I'm an imperfect," Joe answered quietly. "I often see seconds or minutes ahead. Occasionally I see days or weeks but not accurately. The future isn't fixed. But I'm afraid of this thing. I'm afraid that if we make a machine which can think better than man, mankind wouldn't survive it."

"Do you think man is worth surviving, Joe? After the things he's done?"

Joe fell silent, looking down at the table. Seconds became minutes. The cheap clock on the dresser ticked away a quarter of an hour. The coffee in the cups grew cold. Billings shivered in the damp cold of the unheated room, contrasted it with the animal warren comfort of the dormitories, the luxury of the frat houses. He became suddenly afraid of Joe's answer. He had at least some conception of what it must be like to be alone, the only one of its kind, a man who could see in a world of totally blind without even a concept of sight. How much bitterness did Joe carry over from childhood?

"Do you believe that man has reached his evolutionary peak, doctor?" Joe asked at last, breaking the heavy silence.

"No-o," Billings answered slowly.

"Couldn't the whole psi area be something which is latent, just really beginning to develop as the photo-sensitive cells of primitive life in animals once did? I have the feeling," he paused, and changed his phrasing. "I know that everyone experiences psi phenomena on a subconscious level. Occasionally a freak comes along"—he used the term without bitterness—"who has no barrier to shut it out of the conscious. I . . . I think we're trending toward the psi and not away from it."

"You think man should be given the chance to go on farther, then?" Billings asked.

"Yes," Joe said.

"And you think that if he finds out what the true nature of thought is, at the level he uses it, it would destroy him?"

"It might."

"Why?"

"He's proud, vain, superficial, egotistical, superstitious," Joe said without any emphasis. "This machine, to do what Washington wants, would have to use judgment, determine right from wrong, good from bad. Man has kept a monopoly on that—or thinks he has."

"What do you mean—thinks he has?" Billings asked, and felt he was nearing some door which might open on a new vista.

"Suppose we say that white is good and black is bad," Joe said quietly. "Any photoelectric cell then can tell good from bad. Suppose we say a high number is right and a low number is wrong. Any self-respecting cybernetic machine then can tell right from wrong."

"But those are purely arbitrary values, Joe," Billings objected. "Set up for a specific expediency."

"You're something of a historian, doctor," Joe answered obliquely. "Aren't all of them?"

Billings started to argue along the lines of inherent human nature, instinct for good and right, basic moralities, the things man believed set him apart from the other animals. He realized that he would be talking to a telepath; that he had better stick to the facts.

"At least man has arbitrarily set his own values, Joe," he said. "The photoelectric cell or cybernetic machine can't do that." Yet he caught a glimpse of things beyond the opening door, and became suddenly silent.

"We must emphasize that fact, doctor," Joe said earnestly. "Man must go on, for a while, thinking that; in spite of the contrary evidence which this servo-mechanism will reveal. That shouldn't be too hard to maintain. Man generally believes what he prefers to believe. Most evidence can be twisted to filter through his screen mesh of prejudices and tensions, so that it confirms rather than confounds.

Billings felt a wave of apprehension. He almost wished that he had not come to Joe for help on this project. Yet he felt relief, too. Joe, by the plural pronoun, had indicated that he would work on the project. Relief, because he knew that he had no knowledge whereby the problem could be approached. And he believed Joe did.

The illusion of a door opening remained before his vision. There were dark stirrings beyond.

The work did not progress.

It was not due to lack of organization, or lack of cooperation. The scientists had long ago adapted to the appointment of most anyone as head of a project, and they saw nothing unusual in a specialist in psychoso-

50

matics being assigned to make up a new servomechanism.

The lack of progress stemmed from the fact that their objective was not clearly defined. Through the days that followed, Billings was bothered, more than he cared to admit, by Joe's warning that the semantics of their objective must be kept away from any concept of duplicating the work of the human brain. Yet that was what they were trying to do.

He was helped none, either, by the several incidents, in meetings, when one or the other of the scientists on the project tried to tell him that was what they were trying to do.

"If you want a servomechanism," Gunther, the photoelectric man, said, "which will make the same decisions and take the same actions as a human plane pilot, then you must duplicate that pilot's mental processes."

"If we are trying to duplicate the processes of human thought, why have no psychologists, other than yourself, been assigned to this project?" asked Hoskins, the cybernetic man.

These questions were not easy to parry. Both of these men were first-rate scientists, and in the figurative underground, among friends who could be trusted, they asked questions to which they expected answers. The line which Joe had insisted he adopt did not satisfy them.

"We must not permit ourselves to get confused with arguing the processes of human thought," Billings had replied. "We will bog down in that area and get nowhere. This is simply a machine and must be approached from the mechanical."

Yes, it was unsatisfactory, for it was precisely the same kind of thought control which had blanketed the country. You must solve the problem, but you are not permitted to explore this and this and this avenue in your search for the possible solution.

Joe, too, was a disappointment. Billings had succeeded in getting him appointed as project secretary. No one objected since the job required a great deal of paper work, carried little prestige, and the pay was not enticing. There would be other students assigned later to various phases of production. Billings made a mental note to assign young Tyler to something which sounded particularly impressive. The undercurrents of that cartoon could not go ignored. Joe's appointment, therefore, seemed natural enough, and brought him into the thick of activity.

But Joe did no more than the recording. Billings found himself in the frustrating position of having engineered the situation so that Joe would be there for question on how they should proceed, but Joe gave only vague and evasive answers. The progress reports, turned over to Rogan for forwarding on to Washington, contained a great deal of wordage and little else. That would keep Washington quiet for a while, since their tendency was to measure the worth of a report by its poundage; but it was also dangerous in case anybody felt he was slipping out of the public eye, and began to cast about for some juicy publicity.

One of Joe's typical answers brought typical results.

"We already know enough to build it," Joe had said firmly. "We've got all the basic principles. We can duplicate the action of the human brain, at its present level of thinking, any time we want to. Only if we realize that's what we're doing, we won't want to do it. So, on a mechanical level, we simply have to bring all the principles together and coordinate them.''

That added up to nothing when Billings tried it. Suggestions from various departments, working piecemeal, ranged all the way from pinhead size transistors, to city block long banks of cybernetic machines. Even though they had the knowledge, if they did, to build a separate machine to take care of each possible pattern which might arise in the piloting of a plane, it would create an accumulation large enough to fill the old Empire State building.

In exasperation, Billings called Joe to account in his office. They were alone, and Billings minced no words about the way Joe was dragging his feet.

"Why do you want to build this machine, doctor?" Joe asked abruptly. "You're not afraid of the consequences if you fail?"

Billings had not expected this attack from Joe. As the weeks had passed, he had felt a growing urgency to succeed, but he had not tried to put his feelings into words. To answer Joe, he tried now.

"Every man, who thinks, wants there to be a meaning to his life," he said carefully, for he sensed that this was the critical point. "I've spent my life trying to know, to understand. Everything I've ever learned seems to come together in this one thing. Say I'm looking for a monument, that there should be an apex, a crowning achievement. Every man would like there to be something remaining after him, which says, 'This is the meaning of his life.' ''

Joe was silent, and looked at him steadily. Billings

realized he had expressed only a part of it, perhaps the most insignificant part. He picked up a cigarette, lit it, and took another approach.

"A civilization, too," he said. "Each one of them has produced some one great achievement, one specialty. There're not all the same and with the same goals. But each succeeding civilization seems to adopt what results it can use from past achievements. It synthesizes them into its own special achievement. Our specialty has been technological advance. Never mind that everything else is borrowed and doesn't fit us— we have achieved that. But what we have achieved could be meaningless to some future civilization unless we give it meaning now. Here, again, this thing would sum up and embody in one object the total of our technology.

"If man's advance is toward a broader intellect, it seems we should sum up his intellect to this point—if we can, and in our own language, that of technology. It's the only one we speak without an accent."

Still Joe sat in silence, and picked absently at a frayed thread in the drape which hung near his chair. Though he meant them to be constructive, Billings realized that to Joe such arguments were futile, hopeless, destructive. An old man may think with detachment about thousand-year periods of history, and view with little concern the infinitesimal part his own life plays out of all the trillions of people who may live. But a young man is impatient with such maundering. He wants the answers to his own life, the drive which will give purpose to his own acts. And the purpose was there, too, enough to satisfy even—a Joe.

"No man watches happily," Billings said, "while his civilization passes and sinks back into the Dark Ages. Every man has the tragic feeling that it need not happen; that if some eventual civilization is to endure, then why not his own? True, most civilizations had one spurt which made them shine for a while before they flickered out again. But some had several spurts. Some new thing entered the life of the people. They found the energy to meet the new challenge and solve its problem."

Joe's head came up at this, and he stopped pulling at the string on the curtain.

"According to you, Joe," Billings said in final argument, "this thing may destroy man. It may also bump him up to the next step of evolution."

"You'd be willing to face personal danger for that, doctor?" Joe asked suddenly.

The room grew very still. Billings did not answer lightly, for he suspected Joe saw farther beyond the door than he could.

"Yes," he said firmly. "Of course."

That was the turning point in Joe's attitude toward the project, but it had no effect upon the various scientists, of course. They still operated on the basis of a separate machine for every requirement, and the list of requirements was endless.

Superficially, to anyone who had not thought it through, the problem seemed not too difficult, as Washington had stated. A self-aiming gun, a self-guided missile which fastened upon a distant object, plotted its course to intersect the object, and changed its course to compensate for the change in the fleeing object's maneuvers—these should certainly show the way.

And back of that there had been pilotless radio-controlled planes. And back of that the catapult and the bow and arrow.

But whether it was a self-guided missile, or a spear, there was a human mind back of it which had already predicted, used judgment, set the forces in motion according to that judgment.

Human mind? What about the monkey who threw the coconut from the tree at its enemy? What about the skunk with its own version of the catapult? Well, mind of some kind.

Even the amoeba varied its actions to suit the circumstances. There couldn't be much of a brain in one cell. Yet it did react, within its limits, through variable patterns. Any psychosomaticist knows that every cell has a sort of mind of its own. But certainly a cybernetic machine has capacity for varied patterns, too, according to the circumstances. But preset, man, prechosen! But didn't blind and reasonless environment present and prechoose what an amoeba would do? Need it be a mind, as we think of mind?

Billings was not the only one whose thoughts went around and around in this vein, exploring the possible concepts; not the only one who found a yea for every nay. All the scientists, singly and in groups, inescapably followed the same train of reasoning; and came up against the same futility. In spite of Billings' instructions to keep their concepts mechanical, if they were to duplicate the results of judgment between the best courses of action among the many courses of action a plane or an automobile might take, then they had to think about the processes of judging; and the nature of choosing.

Unfortunately, each of them had had courses in psychology, absorbed its strange conclusions, allowed themselves to be influenced by its influence on man's thinking. They arrived nowhere in their analyses. They made the mistake of judging it by the other sciences, assumed it had its foundation based in fact; and felt it must be their own fault when its results gave them nothing.

Yet Billings remembered that Joe had told him they knew enough to build the machine. Still, what was the use of the finest watch if one had no concept of the measurement of time? One might build endless and complex speculation on the way its metal case flashed in the sun, or how it ticked with a life of its own against the ear, in the way that psychology and philosophy speculated endlessly and built complex structures of pointless word games about the nature of man.

Billings smiled with wry amusement at the position in which he found himself. He was like a student who has been given a knotty problem to solve, knows there must be a solution but can't find it. For he did not doubt the conviction of Joe's statement.

Like the bewildered student, he went to teacher. He was sincere enough and had sufficient stature that he could disregard the disparity of their ages, positions, experience, credentials. He was not too proud to accept knowledge, wherever he may find it.

"It's inability to communicate with each other," Joe answered his question. "It's like the spokes of a

57

wheel, without any bridging rim connecting them. The hub is basic scientific knowledge. Specialized sciences radiate out from that, and in moving outward they build up their own semantics.''

''I've heard the analogy before,'' Billings objected. ''It's not a good one; because, if you think about it, you'll see that none get very far out from the hub without the assistance of the others. The concepts of one must be incorporated into the other before any of them can progress very far.''

''They use one another's products, doctor,'' Joe corrected without emphasis. ''Whether those products be gadgets or ideas, they're still the result of another's specialized thinking. A mechanical engineer uses the product of the petroleum engineer without more than superficially knowing or caring about how its molecules were tailored. Say the product doesn't work. The mechanical engineer doesn't drop everything and spend a dozen years or so trying to find the proper lubricant. He goes back to the petroleum engineer, puts in his beef, describes the conditions which the lubricant must meet. The petroleum engineer goes away, polymerizes and catalyzes some more molecules, brings back a new sample, and now the mechanical engineer can go a little farther out on his spoke. But he doesn't communicate except at the product use level.''

''Then how are we going to get these men to use each other's products, Joe?'' Billings asked impatiently. ''This thing is all out of hand. It isn't taking shape at any point. The more we think about it the less it resolves itself, the more chaotic it becomes.''

He turned to Joe and spoke levelly, almost accusingly.

"You seem to know what needs to be done, but you don't do anything about it, Joe. I counted on you. Maybe I shouldn't have, but I did. It seemed to me that this thing was a solution for you as well as for me. You've never known how to put your talent to use constructively, and you must have wanted that. Well, here's your chance."

He saw Joe's face turn pale, and a mask of no expression settle over it. But his irritation and frustration made Billings plunge in where consideration had held him back before.

"Why can't you do that, Joe?"

"That would mean going into their minds," Joe said slowly, through stiff lips. "Taking over portions of their thinking, directing their actions. I haven't done that since I played around with it as a child, before I realized what I was doing. It isn't right for one human being—and I do think of myself as human—to control another human being."

Billings threw back his head and laughed with sudden relief.

"Joe!" he exclaimed. "You're the living example that special talent or knowledges does not bring with it special wisdom or common sense! Don't you realize that every time we ask somebody to pass the salt at the table, or honk our horn at someone on the street, or buy a pair of socks, or give a lecture, that we are controlling the thought and action of others?"

"It isn't the same," Joe insisted. "You normals are blind and fumbling and crude about it. You just bump into one another in your threshing about. And you can always refuse to obey one another."

"Not really, Joe," Billings said. "How long would a man last in his freedom if he refused to do the million things society required of him? I doubt if there's much essential difference in the kind of pressure you could bring, and the kind which the whole society brings upon a man. You say we fumble, while you could do it expertly. I think I'd rather have an expert work on me than a fumbler. What is the difference in your planting the thought of what these scientists should do, and my sending them a written order? Great Scott, boy, if you can get them to accomplish this thing, then you must go ahead."

"Whatever I think needs to be done to accomplish it, doctor?"

"Whatever the project requires to carry it to completion," Billings defined, "remembering that this thing can be the solution for mankind, push him up to the next evolutionary rung."

Joe was silent for a little while, and then spoke slowly.

"But they mustn't know. Outside of a man's own isolated field of knowledge, he's as superstitious as all the rest. They've got all kinds of the wildest ideas about how dangerous and evil a telepath might be. They mustn't know. You've got to remember that sanity in a person or a civilization is like a small boat on the surface of an ocean. If the subterranean depths get roiled up enough, the boat capsizes and there's nothing but the storming chaos of madness."

"Is that the way we appear to you, Joe?"

"That's the way man is," Joe said simply.

"Then if you can keep from rocking the boat when you direct their thinking on this project, you can depend on me to keep it secret, Joe." Billings said reassuringly.

"It's perfectly ethical, all right, for me to control their thinking on this project, then?"

"Perfectly all right, Joe," Billings said with emphasis. And he thought he meant it.

The door opened wider.

It was Hoskins, in charge of the cybernetic aspects, who put the general feeling into words a few days later.

"I've often observed," Hoskins said to no one in particular, as several of them sat around the general meeting room, "that you'll be faced with a problem which looks completely unsolvable—there's just no point at which you can grab hold of it—then suddenly, for no reason at all, the whole thing smooths out."

Billings darted a quick look at Joe, but that young man, busy at a small table over in the corner of the room, did not look up from his job of assembling various reports into order.

Another, perhaps even more significant piece of evidence became apparent, that the men were incorporating the problem into their thinking normally. The thing acquired a name—Bossy. Suddenly everyone was using it. The animal husbandry department had supplied it.

"Anybody who has ever handled cows knows they can be the most onery, cantankerous, stubborn critters you ever saw one minute, and completely gentle and obedient the next,'' one of the men from that department said.

And that about described their feelings toward Bossy at this time.

Billings had been trying for some time to find a descriptive name, using the familiar method of initials of descriptive words — sensory — apperceptor — indexer — appraiser — comparer — extrapolator — predictor — chooser — activator — He bogged down, not only in that the initials seemed to add up to nothing pronounceable, but the list of terms themselves merely added to the confusion. He, too, called it Bossy. Somehow that was best—for Bossy was, in spite of her contrariness, domesticated, inferior to man, controllable—and gave milk. Quite consciously, he was comforted by the semantics of the name.

Rogan, too, accepted the name. He was a little scandalized and as yet Washington hadn't give any reaction which would guide his attitude, but unless the meat or dairy industry objected, there seemed to be nothing subversive about it.

A third evidence, stronger than the other two, was that everyone began talking about sensory receptors. They reasoned that if a pilot sees and hears and feels the external world about him, even though instruments are measuring these things more accurately than he can determine them, then Bossy must also have the receptors to bring sight and sound and feeling.

First, as a joke, and then no longer kidding about it, they decided to give her taste and smell while they were about it. And then someone spoke out in the commons room and said they were pikers. They'd give her sight that a human pilot couldn't have, such as radar. They'd give her sensitivity such as no human being could feel—like the seismograph. They'd give her gyroscopic balance that would make the inner fluid of the human ear less than mentionable. They'd give her—

The talk of what they would give Bossy, all the delicate ways man has evolved to detect things beyond the range of his crude dull senses, went on far into the night.

Sensory receptors were not too difficult to manage. It was rather astonishing, when one assembled them all together, how widely man had already duplicated human sense receptors. For sight, in the human visual range, there was the electronic camera, the light sensitive film of the photographic plate, the selenium cell, and other. Beyond the normal eye range there was radar, and other infrared and violet-light detectors. There was a wealth of sound-sensitive instruments; and a plethora of touch and feel instruments used by industry in product inspection and analysis. The taste and scent instruments were not so well developed, but there were some, and, approaching it through chemical effect, there could be others.

It was common knowledge, too, that all these instruments converted the external senses to electrical impulse—not too far removed from the way the nerves carry the impact of the sense receptors to the brain.

No one seemed to be bothered about what they would do when they got that far; that an electronic camera could pick up light rays and convert them into electrical impulses until it fogged its lenses, but the picture would have no meaning until the human eye viewed it and gave it meaning.

They went about their job, instead, in the way a skilled artisan goes about his—knowing that problems may arise which he hasn't yet worked out, but also confident that he can handle them when they do arise.

Their work, at this point, was the reduction of size, greater sensitivity, combining the principles of many instruments into one. The human eye contains a hundred and thirty million light sensitive cells. It would be nice if they could get their camera orifices as tidy and sensitive.

Each of the departments put its best students to work on its own problem, until the entire university was coordinated into working on some aspect of the job. The singleness of purpose, the drive for accomplishment was as much as could be asked by any industrialist.

Rogan, too, was caught up in the enthusiasm, and surveyed the activity with a certain approval—for busy hands have no time for mischief. And he found himself with new duties, strange for a Resident Investigator. Hoxworth University did not have all the talent and equipment it needed for this project, not by any means. Rogan found himself assuming the role of a go-between with Washington, requesting, requisitioning, requiring services and specialists not only from other schools, but from industry itself.

Operation Bossy became a familiar term in the administrative offices of Washington, and throughout the industrial and educational life of the nation. As with most other top-secret projects, everybody knew about it and was talking about it. The stories grew with the telling, and Joe's insistence to Billings that it be kept in the mechanical language began to have reason behind it. It was merely another form of the guided missile. No one realized what was really happening, not even the men working at its central core—not even Billings.

Things were happening too fast for that. It was as if the pieces of a giant jigsaw puzzle, cast carelessly upon a table, began to assemble themselves at various places, without much regard for one another, or where each would fit into the whole once the picture was done.

Although no one had thought of synthetic textiles as being more than remotely connected with the project, it was that laboratory which came up with the impulse-storing ribbon. Yet they were the most logical to accomplish this. That field knows probably more than any other how to tailor and alter molecules to suit their purpose. Sound had long been stored on plastic tape; light, too, in photographic plastic.

Without a hitch, Hoskins of cybernetics, began working in the synthetic textiles department, finding in its ability to polymerize and catalyze molecules the ideal opportunity for memory storage units. Again, the elimination of grossness became a major concern, and from the apertures there began to spew a thread, all but invisible, not more than a few molecules in breadth and thickness, with each molecule tailored to pick up and store its own burden of electrical impulse.

Bossy began to take shape, and, oddly enough, the box took on a faint resemblance to a cow. Perhaps this

65

was mainly due to the two eyestalks which sprouted out from near its upper surface, like horns topped with dragonfly eye lenses. None of this poor human vision for their Bossy. The diaphragm for picking up sound on the front of the box was vaguely like the blaze on an animal's face, the apertures for air entrance where scent and taste could be sampled where like nostrils.

It was as if there was an unconscious determination to see that the thing remained Bossy.

A stream of specialized molecules poured past each sense receptor, picked up the electronic vibration, combined to make a thread, in the way that a motion-picture film picks up light and sound, so that when played back they coincide, and stored itself at the bottom of the case.

They had not yet arrived at any point where a new basic principle needed to be found. Although, at this point, they had no more than a superior sense-re-cording machine. The thread could be played back, but that was all. And no one worried about it.

It was music, another unlikely department, who gave the clue to the next step. A note struck on one key of the piano will, through the principle of harmonics, vibrate the strings at octaves above so that they also give off sound. Shouldn't there be a vibronic code signal inherent in each sense stream, so that like things will activate harmonically with other like things? Wasn't that how recognition took place through harmonically awakened association with like experience in the past?

It was.

Outwardly, Bossy ceased to take shape. To codify every sound, every shape, every vibration translated into touch and feel and scent and taste, every degree of light and color density was a monumental task—in terms of detail work, although its organization was not difficult. To translate these into electrical code impulses was difficult. But here again, no new principle was needed. Here again, man had merely the task defining the world in terms of symbol—and symbol in terms of code impulse.

Nor was it too difficult to again tailor the molecules to carry electrical current, which, theoretically, would keep these code impulses vibrating in harmonics with those passing the sense receptor apertures.

And still it was no more than an impulse storage bank. Only in theory was a new impulse activating its counterpart in old impulses. They had no way of testing it in practice. And felt supremely confident that a way would be found.

No one who has not directed a large scale activity, coordinated the work of thousands of people and synthesized their results could fully comprehend the mass of work which fell upon Billings and his immediate staff. Many times he felt he had taken on more than he could handle, that the scope of activity had got out of hand. Yet inquiries and suggestions came from everywhere, and many of them were pertinent and valuable.

It was as if the whole academic life of the nation had been swept up in the same urgency which had compelled him; as if men had something to think about which, for the moment, was unimpeded with restrictions and investigations.

Yet, in spite of the weight of administrative detail, he had the feeling that he had full grasp of everything that was happening, and with a clarity of mind he had never experienced before he was able to see the relation of concepts one to the other.

Perhaps it was this clarity which made him call a halt to the coding as it was developing, scrap much of what had been done, and start over. For it should have been obvious all along that identical things receiving identical codes was not enough. This had been the stumbling block of all cybernetic machines in the past. A tabulating pattern combined only identicals. They could combine the symbols for two apples and six apples correctly into eight apples, but when it came across one apple, it broke this out into a separate category, for the latter symbol differed from the former in that the letter "s" was missing. The cybernetic machines in the past had no sense, were not keyed to vagaries of grammar, spelling mistakes, variations which a child of eight would know were not really variations.

A way must be found to duplicate the dull stupidity of the human mind which could not detect differences unless they were glaring, and yet retain the fine sensitivity of the cybernetic machine.

It became apparent that not only must there be a code impulse for each isolated aspect of the external world, there must also be an interlocking code for activation to bring back the total picture. Remembrances are by association, one thing leads to another.

A symbol of a square must not only activate any previous experience of the symbol of a square but also the circumstances in which that symbol was experienced. Yes, there must be a horizontal interlocking of codes, as well as vertical. For was not that the way decisions were made? In terms of how things, similar things, under similar circumstances, worked out in the past?

Much had been written that the patterns of life duplicate themselves again and again and again; that the intelligent man recognizes this duplication even though it may be in a different guise, while the unintelligent and the machine do not and must solve each thing as if it were new.

While they were setting up the new system of coding, the art department threw the worst curve of all. There was the matter of foreshortening. A square on a card looks square when faced head-on, but looks rectangular if the card is turned at an angle. The human mind learns to make adjustments for foreshortening, so shouldn't Bossy? They asked it blandly, and perhaps a little maliciously, for they had not been consulted up to this point.

Billings was dismayed at this obvious difficulty, and his spirits were not lifted either by the knowledge that it took over three thousand years of art painting for man to move from the side view of the foot, as portrayed by the Egyptians, to the front view, as discovered by the Greeks. And almost another five hundred years to move from the profile of the face to a front view.

It would be difficult to achieve this for Bossy. Still, there was no new principle involved, simply a coding method which would tell Bossy that one object was truly a rectangle seen head-on, and another which appeared to be the same was really a square seen at an angle. It was the same kind of lateral coding which would solve this.

* * *

The key to Bossy's first overt reaction to stimuli came from one of the younger assistant professors one night in the common room. He was ruefully telling how his new baby responded to his wife's hands with contentment and to his hands with fright. The baby was much too young to recognize the difference between mama and papa. It must be familiarity versus unfamiliarity in the manner of touch.

A few days later, safety guards were installed around Bossy. They had long since installed the yes-no principle to be found in other cybernetic machines. There was jubilation and something approaching awe when Bossy demonstrated it could learn—and learn with only one trial. The safety guards were keyed to the reject pattern, but when Hoskins, who installed the guards, depressed the accept key for his own hands, thereafter the machine threw up its guards when approached by alien hands, but left them down for Hoskins' hands. Perhaps it was mass, or shape codes. Perhaps it was color. Perhaps it was scent, for Hoskins had been working around the machine when scent codes were being fed into it. Still Hoskins had no code of his own scent as differing from others. Scent was out, for the machine had no equipment whereby it might do its own coding.

They were not sure just what process had occurred which made Bossy distinguish safe hands from unsafe hands. She had the sense receptors to observe the outside world. She had the codes, a great many and more being added constantly, whereby through keyed harmonics she associated new perception with old. Some moves had been made to key her with similarities and differences. The mechanism was there to compare the new with the old and to determine the identities and the differences. And now she had demonstrated that she could distinguish through the sense perceptors and the established coding.

Further, she had demonstrated that she could take automatic action.

The men cautioned one another, again and again, that they must not fall into the habit of thinking the machine could do anything they hadn't keyed it to do. It had no sense. None at all. Really, this throwing up the bars to keep alien hands out was no more than any selenium cell would do—well, modified by coding.

Even without Joe's warning glance, Billings felt they were reassuring one another on this point perhaps a little too much. He noticed, too, that the gender changed overnight from it to she. But it was several days before he noticed that Gunther had begun to stammer the name to B-b-b-ossy, each time he said it, although the man never stammered on anything else. And Hoskins always hesitated with an audible ''ah'' before saying the name.

The shadows beyond the door began to stir and swell, and seemed to writhe around one another.

Spring came, and then it was June. Commencement exercises were no more than a reluctant interlude from the work. Billings watched Joe throw off his graduating cap and gown, and in almost the same movement start assembling the requests for student deferments from compulsory military service. A summer session extraordinary had been declared that no time be lost in the work on Bossy, and the entire university was humming on a factory schedule.

A new respect had been gained for a baby's mind. Ordinarily adults thought of the newborn baby as just lying there, inert mentally, accomplishing little learning beyond finding out that a cry would summon attention, a nipple placed between its lips would start the reflex of sucking. Now they realized the multitudes of unrelated sense impressions that mind must be storing, the repeated patterns which impressed themselves upon its brain—and prediction of the future.

"If I cry, there will be approaching footsteps. I stop my crying to listen for them. If I do not hear them, I cry again. Soon there will be comforting hands and I will be dry and warm again."

And any young mother knows this is accomplished in a few weeks. One by one the patterns are learned, the sensation relationships repeat themselves, a word is spoken in connection with an object or an action. Always the word and the object appear simultaneously—they are cojoined, one produces the other. Relationships become vaguely apparent. Cause and effect emerge as an expectancy.

If it were not that a baby was human, one might set up certain laws of procedure. An outside world datum makes an impact upon a sensory receptor. This is accompanied by other impacts of other data. There is a relationship of each to the other. And long before there is any concept of self, as an entity, there is a realization of self to the data. Not all the data appear each time and in the same order. But if enough data appear to strike up the harmonics of association with a previous experience—judgment is assumed. Through repetition of patterns of trial and error, some reflex and some calculated, action upon judgment takes place.

But the baby is human, and therefore mysterious, and we may not simplify the awful metaphysics of an awakening human mind into a set of mechanical steps. The human mind is set apart, the human mind could not contemplate itself as being no more than an operation of an understandable process.

But it was different with Bossy. Bossy was a machine, and therefore the processes which would substitute for thought must be approached mechanically. Bossy recognized solely through mechanical indexing—no different in principle from the old-fashioned punched card sorter. This and this and this is the same as that and that and that—therefore these two things have a relationship to one another. Comparison of new data with old data, a feedback process of numerous indexed impulses and these to the external sense receptors and their stream of new impulses—really it was quite trivial.

It was only coincidence that it seemed, here and there, to duplicate the results of an infant mind. Only coincidence that as new experience and new data were being constantly applied, new areas of experience exposed to Bossy, that she should seem to follow the process of the learning child.

Strictly coincidence, and one must not be fooled by coincidence.

As Billings watched Joe assemble the lists of deferments, he wondered about the young man. Since their conversation, when he had asked Joe to use his talents to further the project, they had talked no more than the work required. Billings was no closer to knowing Joe than he had ever been, and Joe volunteered nothing. He did not know what Joe had done to clear away the mental blocks which had prevented the scientists from grasping the problem, he had only the overt evidence that something had been done.

Really this project was all he had claimed it would be. Attempt to reduce it to simplicity though they may, it still remained that all of man's science up to the present had been required to produce it. Bossy's accomplishment was for all time the monument to the triumph of science, the refutation that science exists only through the indifferent tolerance of the average man, the refutation also that man has never used his intellect except to rationalize, justify and decorate with high-sounding phrases the primitive urges he intended to foster anyway. For it had taken intellect to produce Bossy, intellect of a high order, reaching up to—detachment.

"Oh, by the way, doctor," Joe looked up from his work at the desk and interrupted Billings' thinking, "have you been following the articles on witchcraft?"

"Why . . . why no, Joe," Billings answered. "I hadn't noticed. What about them?"

"There's a trend," Joe said. "At first the articles started out faintly deploring, and then explaining. Now there is the current theory that scientists and thinkers generally tend to get off the right track. That there is a mass wisdom for doing the right thing for mankind, embodied in the masses of people. That mankind has proved steadily and progressively he knows what is best for him; and therefore the so-called witchcraft suppression was simply man's way, an instinctive inherent rightness, to keep from being led into the wrong ways of thinking.''

"That is a very common line of thinking," Billings said without much interest. "How are you coming along with that roster of deferments?"

He saw Joe throw him a quick, appraising look, and then turn back to his work again. Probably nothing significant about Joe's remarks. Young men tended to become much too horrified as they realized the terrible stupidity of mankind. As one grows older, one doesn't expect so much; loses some of the idealism of what man should be.

"It's pretty extensive, doctor," Joe said in a colorless voice. "When I think that a similar list is being prepared in every college throughout the country . . . well, the military isn't going to like not being able to harvest its new crop. There'll be an investigation."

Billings hardly heard him. His mind continued along the track of comparison of Bossy and a child. Every day new sensations fed into the child, new admonitions, corrections, approvals, patterns fed into stored accumulation of past sensations and conclusions. Sensations on the order of billions, perhaps trillions—no wonder that thought seemed complex, ungraspable. But as with so many problems the difficulty was size and bulk—and complexity was no more than superimposure of simple upon simple.

But human beings did not learn fast, most of them required many repetitions of a pattern before they grasped it. The man was rare, indeed, who could memorize a book in scanning it once. Really now, a very poor job had been done in tailoring the molecular structure of—

Bossy required only once. Perhaps Joe was right. Perhaps man was still evolving. Perhaps his brain was no more than a rudimentary light-sensitive cell as compared with the eye. Perhaps that was why his brain gave such a poor performance, it had not evolved into its potential.

Billings sat, gazing out of the window at the elm trees and the sky.

"Yes," he murmured, moments later to Joe's comment. "No doubt there will be an investigation." He wondered, vaguely, what there would be an investigation about—but no matter, there were always investigations.

Surely it would have nothing to do with Hoxworth University, or himself. For the assignment had succeeded beyond the wildest imaginings. Perhaps it was immodest, but surely the success of Bossy would be emblazoned across the pages of history for a thousand years—the greatest achievement of all time; and his name would be that of its author.

Man! Know thyself!

"We must not allow ourselves to become fascinated with the sensation mongering of these investigations, Joe," he said chidingly. "We are thinkers, and we have work to do."

Again he felt the quick, questioning look from Joe, but dismissed it and continued with his development of vision. Plainly, Joe still lacked wisdom.

Through the weeks that followed another tension began to assume proportions too great to be ignored. As long as there had been such a recognized thing as science, itself, here had been a controversy concerning one aspect of it. A thing is composed of numerous properties which a theory or an equation must take into account if a satisfactory solution is to be attained. Some of these properties are intangible, but none the less real, such as friction, or gravity. Some are still variable and unpredictable. Thus one of the real and inescapable properties of a thing is—human reaction to it. An automobile could not be called a satisfactory invention if no one would drive it; an electric light could not be called a solution to illuminating darkness if man smashed it in frenzied rage each time he saw it. Since man can know a thing only through the mind of man, then the mind of man is one of its inherent properties. So said a school of philosophy.

This pro school held that human reaction to a thing was as real as gravity or friction; that a scientist who ignored it was like a mechanical engineer who persisted in ignoring the effects of friction, a structural engineer who ignored gravity. On the con side, it was considered that the physical scientist had plenty to do in measuring physical forces and properties; that the force of human reaction, if it existed, belonged in someone else's problem basket.

The pro school held this was not true; that the pharmaceutical chemist did assume responsibility for the effect of his concoctions upon human mind and tissues, the structural engineer did assume some responsibility for the end use of his houses or bridges, the mechanical engineer did assume some responsibility for people using his motor; that no arbitrary line could be drawn separating responsibility from nonresponsibility.

The con school, in the vast majority because it is

easier to evade responsibility than to assume it, still passed the buck.

And because this real property of things continued to be ignored, the gap between the scientist and the man in the street widened, and widened, and stretched out farther and farther. Any physical scientist knows that regardless of theory, there is a practical limit to the elasticity of a material. There is also a limit to the elasticity of human reaction to a science it can not understand, and therefore fears.

It became also apparent, in these weeks, that there was a serious leak of details on the progress of Bossy. No project as widespread as the work on Bossy could be kept entirely under security. Even where trained scientists possess only scraps and portions of the whole knowledge, misconceptions will occur. And multitudes of those working on some phase of Bossy were not yet trained scientists. They were students. Students, for all the grave respect they hold for the weight and importance of their knowledge, are notorious for misconceptions. There is a dividing line between effective scientist and student, but it has nothing to do with graduation exercises. Too many remain students, multiplying misconception upon misconception. An astonishing number of these, unable to make their way in the laboratory, turn to teaching for their living. The gap between science and superstition widens.

Beyond a serious central leak, which was becoming apparent, there were widespread rumors and bits of information leaking out. Each, in itself, was perhaps a harmless thing—if properly weighed and stripped of its exaggerations and misinterpretations. But human beings, generally, are not noted for their ability to weigh judiciously, discount exaggerations, and allow for possible misunderstanding. People like sensationalism, and in the telling add their bit to it.

Bossy, at first ignored as being the business of the scientists and having no relationship to bread and bed, suddenly became a topic of conversation everywhere. Everyone found he had an opinion. Ready-made opinions by the score poured through the news columns and over video. Bossy began to assume proportions of concern, dread, then outright fear.

When you stop to think of it, some of the more articulate would say, the most inefficient, unpredictable, costly and exasperating machine used in industry is the human being. The only advantage it has over other machines, the only reason an industrialist uses it, is its wide flexibility of adaptation to numerous conditions, the ease of replacement if it doesn't function properly.

But now there was Bossy.

It did not take long for the sensationalists to predict manless factories, manless shops and stores, manless utility and transportation services. Once the coals were breathed into flame, it did not take long for the fire to gather fuel and spread in white heat. And like a gasoline poured into the flames was the wholesale student deferment.

Some of this reaction trickled, much diffused, into the ivory towers. Billings tried to offset it. He made a personal appearance on a national hook-up, but he mistook fire for water and poured oil on the waves to quiet them.

"There is nothing to fear," he said. "The brain of

79

Bossy is no more than a compound of synthetic proteins, colloids, enzymes, metallic salts, fatty acids—each molecule designed and shaped to do a specific task, picking up codified impulse charges to complete their structure, and then combining into a threadlike substance for storage and release."

If he had spoken in Hottentot, it would have been as comprehensible and less dangerous. For without conveying the slightest understanding, and even in his attempts to show this thing was not human, he heightened the dread.

Bossy was truly a machine, a synthetic thing. Its inventor, the famous Billings, had said so, himself. Had it been alive, man might have understood it better, even though alien and inimical it would have shared with him the mystery of life and thought.

As he droned on and on through his talk, as he described the lenses, the diaphragms, the metallic, glassite, plastic receptors, showing how they saw and felt and tasted and heard, he confirmed all the rumors. Bossy *was* capable of replacing man.

And Bossy had no soul.

Letters by the thousands, the hundreds of thousands, poured into Congress. Congress, far more receptive to the will of the people than is generally realized, tried to act. But it was the Administrative Department who had cut the orders for work on Bossy. The Administrative Department unfortunately chose this issue as a battle arena to show Congress it could no longer be shoved around so easily. The resultant conflict, the raw tempers which flared into print and over national hookups, served merely to heighten the tension throughout the country. There was something to it!

80

The quiet and doubtful words of the mollifiers, the advocates of let's wait and see, the admonishers of you're not hurt yet, their voices were lost in the angry outpourings of revolt against this manufacture of a soulless machine to replace man, this deferment of favored young men, these irresponsible scientists—science itself.

In damning the very idea of science, it never occurred to most that they were using the products of science to get their message into every corner of the land, into every mind.

The first overt move came from a small band of men who chose to have a parade of protest. It was national news. They fed upon the publicity. The parade regrouped and formed into a march—a march across two states toward Hoxworth University. The ranks of the marchers swelled. Other marchers started.

And in the village of Hoxworth, near the university, the residents decided they did not need to be reminded of their duty by people from other communities.

There sprang from the mind of a fanatic, and couched in the lyrical language so often used by the psychotic, a huge placard that was set up at the corner of the library park one night. In one corner of it, there was a copy of young Tyler's cartoon of Billings. And in bold lettering:

HIDE! HIDE! WITCH! THE GOOD FOLK COME TO BURN THEE!

All day there was a crowd around it. In the strange manner of disturbed people, some stood for hours just looking at it, letting its message seep into the bottom fibers of their beings—awakening ancestral memories.

But during the small hours of the night, some student, perhaps equally psychotic in his bitterness against such medieval reaction, added another placard below with these scornful words:

THEIR KEEN ENJOYMENT HID BENEATH THE GOTHIC MASK OF DUTY!

It was a most unfortunate thing, for it struck deep into the roots of guilt, and even where some had hung back, now they raged and stormed with the rest when it was discovered the next morning.

A pall of quietness, inactivity, hung over Hoxworth University. A miasma of gloom, apprehension, like the somatics within a prison, filled the grounds and seeped through the halls. Classes were sparsely attended, and instructors found themselves straying away from the subject of their lectures. Most of the students had gone home in the weeks before.

All work on Bossy had ceased at the orders of the Board of Governors of the University. She had been dismantled and her parts stored away. The activated brain floes had been carefully lifted out of its case and folded into a thin aluminum box. No one was sure what damage even this handling might do, and no one had the urge to test and experiment to find out.

"I tried to warn you, Dr. Billings," Joe said once, in the dean's office.

"But if you knew this, Joe!" Billings exclaimed. "Why didn't you tell us?"

"Each time I tried, doctor," Joe said quietly, "you told me to mind my own business, that I lacked wisdom. I didn't know for sure what would happen, or I'd have forced you to listen. I knew only that men of science have failed to bring the people along with them, that human beings are capable of terrible things when they are terrified. You told me, many times, that scientists are not concerned with these things; that scientists don't want to hear about doom consequences; that scientists are quite certain everything will be all right if they're just permitted to do as they please."

"People have predicted doom at every single advance of science, Joe," Billings admonished him. "Look at all the doom written around the time of atomic discovery. It never happened."

"I know," Joe said. "It's case of 'Wolf, wolf' being cried too often, isn't it? Too bad. But your history should tell you, doctor, there always comes a time when the wolf really does come."

There wasn't any more conversation along this line. There wasn't anything more that either of them could say. Joe went back to his work at his desk in the corner of the room, trying to fill in the new batch of questionnaires Rogan had received from Washington. Rogan had taken them from his silver incrusted brief case, wordlessly, and laid them on Joe's desk. Rogan was as grim and apprehensive as all the rest. He had followed orders all the way, but it had gone wrong. Rogan could see only one thing; he would be blamed for it all—and yet he had merely followed orders.

Billings was a little glad when Joe finished his work and left the room. He realized he had been stupid. He had had an instrument at his hand, a delicately tuned instrument capable of picking up facts far beyond the range of his own senses, Joe, a telepath, and he had chosen to ignore the readings of the instrument, to depend upon his own crude and dull senses. The guilt of his stupidity weighed heavily upon him. He was glad that Joe did not like to look into the mind of a normal. He hoped Joe had not looked too deeply into his. The vague discomfort he felt when Joe was around was heightened now.

He sat behind his desk, alone, and reflected with profound disappointment upon scientists, collectively and individually, himself included. They could tear apart the atom and milk it of its strength, they could reconstruct the molecules of nature and improve upon them, they could design instruments far beyond the range of man's senses, solve the riddles of the universe, and, yes, reconstruct the very processes of thought.

Yet they were powerless against the most ignorant of men. Against the most primitive flares of superstition and dread of the unknown, they had no defense. Weakly, in such a situation, they would try to explain, to reason, to appeal to rationality and logic—against minds preset against all explanations, never having learned reason, alien to rationality and logic.

Was this intelligence? To use against one's most bitter foe a weapon which they knew, in advance, would not touch him?

And knowing that, knowing the potential of it which is always present, still they said with impatient superiority, "Spell us no evil consequences of our acts. We are tired of hearing about doom."

A fresh newspaper, a regular city daily, had been laid on his desk. He pulled it toward him, flipped open its pages, and looked at another cartoon of himself.

Yes, it was signed by young Tyler—but a glance showed it had not been drawn by him.

And suddenly he knew where the central leak had been. Young Tyler had been in the thick of everything; but young Tyler was a violent and arrogant young man. He seemed to thrive on trouble, to generate it, to know that in mischief or crime itself his father would rescue him. Billings had been blind to that potential, too.

The central figure in the cartoon, himself, was drawn in massive impressiveness, almost Michelangelo in treatment, dressed in classical flowing robes, holding Bossy up in one hand, and surrounded by a glowing nimbus. The cartoon needed no title nor identification.

Every expert line of it was innuendo—Billings' pretense at nobility, transcendency. Every expert line revealed the blasphemy. In it was the age-old message that it was forbidden to eat of the tree of knowledge, to reach for the stars. In it was the stern admonitions driven into the innermost fiber of almost every child's being.

"You're too young to know! Keep your hands off of that! Mother and Daddy know best! That's none of your business! That's over your head! Wait till you're older! That's too deep for you to understand!"

The message of defeat, weakness, dependency upon higher authority, driven in day by day and hour by hour into the child's basic structure of reaction. And to offset that solid bedrock, a few mumbling teachers said occasionally that the child should think for himself.

It was no wonder that there was a suppressed desire in most small boys' hearts to burn down the schoolhouse which tried to make them learn, when their whole world and all that was safe in it had been composed of not learning. When the very act of knowing, meant punishment. "You *know* better than to do a thing like that, young man!" And the obvious conclusion drawn by the child, "If I didn't know better, I wouldn't be punished."

What could be done when the very act of knowing brought penalty?

In anger, Billings crumbled the paper and threw it in the wastebasket. It occurred to him that, in like manner, he had just crumpled his whole life and thrown that, too, in the wastebasket. He leaned forward and flipped on his desk radio. He listened, almost without comprehension, to a trained and professional rabble-rouser shouting into a microphone, down in the village below.

". . . Torn stone from stone . . . so that we may wipe out this evil from our midst . . . Let us not wait for others to show us our duty . . . let us march upon it . . . now . . ."

"What a miserable string of worn-out clichés," Billings murmured in amusement. Then he realized, with a shock, they were talking about Hoxworth University.

He flipped off the switch, cupped his chin in his fingers, and stared at the wall.

Well, let them come. It didn't matter. Nothing mattered. He smiled in self-scorn when he realized he could say this because he was quite sure they would not come, that reason would prevail, always prevail.

How unrealistic can a man get? What guarantee was there that they would not come? Had man's basic nature changed since yesterday? What had happened before would happen again, in endless repetition. The cycle would repeat itself.

Primitive man, who knows no step taken beyond that of his father's—the bright and courageous dawn of reason—the rise to a comprehension beyond that of his father's—the brief hesitation at the height of the cycle when sanity and rationality soared—the beginning of the downward curve of revolt against sanity and rationality—the retrogression of comprehension—the final dying embers of reason—and, again, the primitive man who knows no step taken beyond that of his father's.

The circle was endless, enduring on and on for a million years now since dawn man emerged. It would endure on and on for—

How long?

Was there no solution? Was man doomed to follow in the circle endlessly, like a two-dimensional animal bounded by a carelessly thrown thread, unable to conceive of a third dimension whereby it might change direction and crawl *upward*?

Was Joe's idea the right one? That man was just biding his time, slowly evolving, that psionics would mark the next stage, that it was a spiral and not a circle? He must talk further with Joe about this. Now, for the first time, perhaps, he was prepared to listen to something he had not thought of himself. Had he been like the kind of scientist he scorned, refusing to listen to anything which did not fit in with his already formed conceptions?

Outside his windows, the elm trees rustled in the rising breeze of night. It had grown quite dark. Yet, there in the distance down the hill, was the glow of a light. It was a flickering, leaping, orange light, in the direction of the library park. The light grew brighter in the darkness—as if flames were mounting. Faintly, on the rising wind, there came the murmur of a crowd noise.

He wondered, idly, what the occasion was among the villagers, what they were celebrating, what was the reason for such a huge bonfire. For some strange reason, the placard lines leaped into his consciousness. He connected the lines, the bonfire, with the radio speech.

His head slumped forward on the desk.

He did not hear the door open, or see Joe's grin fade to quick concern. Quickly Joe darted across the room, felt Billings' pulse, put his ear to Billings' chest and heard the heart still beat.

"Just fainted," Joe said to Hoskins, who had come in behind him. "We'll have to carry him. We can't wait any longer."

"Fool thing to delay this long," Hoskins grumbled. "Don't know why you stalled, Joe."

"He had to grow up," Joe said cryptically, and began massaging the flesh at the back of Billing's neck.

Billings came out of his shock coma at the handling, and stiffened his head.

"That's better," Joe grinned. "Come on. Let's get him out of here. We've got work to do. Science isn't licked yet, not by any means." He turned to Hoskins. "You sure you've smuggled all of Bossy's parts out of here safely?"

"Sure, I'm sure," Hoskins grinned back at him. "You sure you've got a safe hiding place for us?"

"Sure, I'm sure," Joe said.

Billings stood up then, and suddenly he was quite strong.

"All right, Joe." Billings shook his head dazedly. "Making a mistake isn't too bad, I guess—if you live long enough to learn from it, and do something about it. Science has had a lot of knowledge, but mighty little understanding.

"Let's go find out what *that* is."

Part II
"Bossy"

CHAPTER I

J ust ahead, on Third Street, the massive facade of San Francisco's Southern Pacific depot loomed, half hidden in the swirling fog and January twilight. Joe Carter pulled his rented pickup truck to the now deserted curb, and squinted appraisingly into the gloom. The warning had come, the usual tingling up and down his spine, the drawing sensation at the nape of his neck.

He sent an expanding wave-field ahead of him, a telepathic inquiry, but there were too many people around the depot for him to sort out the specific source of danger without first knowledge of a focal point. The static of general anxiety, grief and gladness, which always seems to hang over a depot like a pall of smoke, prevented him from finding any menace directed toward himself.

And on the outside of the depot the scene was quite normal. The blurred yellow lights of a taxi pulled out of its reserved section and turned down Townsend Street toward the Embarcadero. The muffled rumble of traffic on the long overhead approach to the Bay Bridge was an audible accompaniment to the esper hum of half vocalized words and phrases picked up from the minds of the people all about the area.

He watched a police car cruise slowly by and disappear into the fog. He sampled the stream of consciousness of the two officers. Their casual glance has registered him in their minds: male truck driver, white, about twenty-two, no obvious disfigurements, not breaking any law at the moment. But there was no recognition.

He swept the street again with his physical eyes, and almost passed over the skid-row wino who had drifted a little far south of the usual haunts. The fellow had stopped in the chill shelter of a darkened store front, and was apparently drinking with desperate thirst from a wine bottle held in a paper sack. It was so usual, so completely in character, that Joe very nearly made the mistake of not penetrating. But even as he started to flick his eyes onward, his nape muscles contracted more sharply, heightening the awareness of danger.

Still doubting that the somatic price he must pay for sharing the wino's hopelessness and dejection would be worth some bit of factual information drenched in it, Joe pierced.

He got a series of photographs, sharp and clear.

The Federal agent's disguise was near perfection. Joe chuckled silently, with genuine amusement. In rinsing the wine in his mouth to give him a breath, just in case some other bum stumbled up to him, the agent had inadvertently swallowed a slug of the cheap stuff.

With him, and as clearly, Joe felt the somatic effect of the wine in the man's nose, mouth, throat and stomach.

But the agent's disgust did not wash out the dominant picture in his mind. He had recently been briefed, and his upper stream of consciousness still carried the conceptual images.

Two more agents were inside the depot; one of them standing near the line of people waiting to get tickets validated; the other reading a newspaper over near the hallway which led to the rest rooms.

Within easy vision of both sat their quarry, Professors Billings and Hoskins. Billings had been recognized at the depot in St. Louis where he was changing trains in his flight across the country. Hoskins had not been discovered at all until he had joined Billings less than half an hour ago. There was elation in the agent's mind over the meeting, for it might mean that the end of the long trail was near. Obviously, the two men were now waiting for someone else to join them.

And when someone joined them, it was possible, unsuspectingly, they might lead the agents directly to Bossy.

Up until now there had been absolutely no indication of where the synthetic brain had been hidden. There was disgust and contempt in the agent's mind that during all the years that Hoxworth and other universities had been experimenting in the building of the cybernetic marvel, subsidized with government funds, Washington bureaucracy had not realized the significance of it. It had taken an uprising of the people, themselves, to drive home to Washington how man would react to the destruction of all his previous concepts on how the human mind worked and the values it assumed were absolute.

Someone had said then that this machine was more important than the atomic bomb had been forty years ago; that the implosion of its significance upon man's psyche might do what the atomic bombs could not do; that man has a way of surviving physical destruction, but there was a large question of whether he could survive self-knowledge.

"You are so right," Joe murmured, and lit a cigarette to heighten the impression that he had stopped to rest his shoulders and neck from arduous driving.

The agents' orders were quite clear. Professors Hoskins and Billings were the central figures in developing the synthetic mind. The trail of these two men, sooner or later, would lead to Bossy. Until then, they were to keep the two professors under unsuspected surveillance; were not to concentrate enough agents to arouse suspicion; were to make an arrest only if the actions of the two men forced their hand.

Joe drew on his cigarette, and probed to a deeper level. He found what he wanted. The agent was tired, and he was chilled. He doubted that his stakeout position was necessary. The reports were that old Professor Billings, at least seventy-two, was as naive as a child; that he couldn't elude the typical Junior G-Man, age six. And the agent's stomach was beginning to feel queasy from the raw wine he had swallowed.

He was tired, he was chilled, he was queasy. Joe tied himself into the somatic discomfort, intensified it in himself, fed back the intensified dissatisfaction; picked it up again; oscillated it back and forth between them on feedback principle, stepped up each time—

in the way he had watched mob reactions heighten far beyond the capacity of any isolated individual—and waited.

The man began to look down the street toward a small restaurant. He was growing ill. Perhaps the wine had poisoned him. There was the fleeting glimpse of wonder if he would be included on the roster of those killed in pursuit of duty. There was the rational denial of the urge of self-pity. There was the compromise to get a cup of coffee first, to see if that would break the chill, rest him, settle his stomach. But, undoubtedly, this was that extreme situation which would justify his leaving his post of duty.

By the time Joe had meshed the gears of his truck to pull away from the curb, the agent was already halfway down the block, hurrying to the restaurant, still clutching the neck of the wine bottle in the paper sack. In case he did die, it might be valuable evidence.

Without more care than an ordinary truck driver would show, Joe drove the pickup into one of the loading docks on the far side of the station. He willed away the last sympathetic waves of nausea from his own stomach, and climbed nimbly up on the ramp. He strolled, without appearing to be in any hurry, through the door marked with the sign of Railway Express.

The clerk looked him over, took in the greasy leather jacket, the oil-stained jeans, the crumpled cap with the cracked visor.

"Yeah?" the clerk challenged. "What do you want?"

"Pickup for Brown Appliance Company," Joe answered easily. "Crate of television parts." No flash of alertness, suspicion, was evident in the clerk's mind. It was confirmation that no one knew of Bossy. He handed the clerk the shipping bill he had obtained when he forwarded the parts of Bossy from a town a hundred miles away from Hoxworth.

"No such package here," the clerk said automatically. There was no real animosity in his voice or his mind. It was the simple desire to obstruct found in everyone, and often expressed where there is no fear of retaliation.

"Boss called the day crew," Joe said dryly. "They said it was here. Suppose you get the lead out and find it."

The clerk looked at him levelly and curled his lip in a slight sneer. If this punk's boss had called and got the manager during the day, there might be a stink. He decided to cooperate. He found the crate in the back room, slipped the blade of the hand truck beneath its edge, grumbled at how heavy and bulky it was, and wheeled it out on the loading dock. To his own surprise, he found himself helping Joe load it carefully into the bed of the pickup.

Joe walked back into the office with the clerk.

"Boss wants me to get a ticket to L.A.," Joe said. "Where do I do that?"

"In there," the clerk said and jabbed a finger toward the door leading to the waiting room of the depot. "You want me to lead you by the hand?"

"No," Joe answered. "Don't like to get my hand dirty."

He walked on through the door and down the corridor which led to the depot waiting room. He knew that the clerk was standing behind his counter with his jaw hanging down and his mouth open. The clerk's shock of being bested at his own game gave Joe the somatic hook he needed to blur the image of himself in the clerk's mind. In spite of the repartee, he would not be remembered. As any courtroom knows, emotional disturbance can call up wildly inaccurate descriptions. Already the clerk was remembering him as a hulking brute of a truck driver with coarse black hair, wide flaring ears and tobacco juice stains on his chin.

At the corridor entrance to the waiting room, Joe paused, and with both psionic and visual sight picked out the two professors. Their disguises were simple, and still intact. The seventy-two-year-old Billings had had the distinguishing mane of white hair cut short and dyed black. The elaborate gold pince-nez on the flowing black ribbon had been replaced with garden variety horn rims. His clothes were cheap and nondescript. But far more than such superficialities, Joe had counted on the change in the man's bearing to keep his identity secret. Gone was the assurance of the world-famous figure, known to every child through picture, cartoon, newsreel, the renowned Dean of Psychosomatic Medicine at Hoxworth University. In its place was hurt, bewilderment, incredulity—a lost and tired old man. Even so, he had been recognized and followed here.

Professor Hoskins, at forty, with even less change in his appearance had not been recognized before joining Billings.

The two of them sat there now, according to plan, waiting for Joe to join them, to tell them what they must do next.

And with the wino agent's mentations as a focal

guide, Joe had no difficulty in picking out their two watchers. These two were also nondescript in appearance. They waited patiently, as might well-domesticated husbands waiting for wives, without either calling attention to themselves, or avoiding it.

Joe's lips twitched in a smile, and he took advantage of their natural wish to relieve their boredom. The one with the newspaper signaled the other with his eyes that a conference was necessary. Aimlessly, they drifted together near the entrance to the depot. One followed the other out the door, and together they walked up the street toward a restaurant.

With no suprise at all, they joined their fellow agent in the wino disguise, and the three of them sat discussing their quarry, speculating on who was to contact the professors, and when the trail might lead to Bossy. The wino agent had recovered his feeling of well-being with astonishing rapidity, concluded he had just been momentarily chilled. He didn't bother to mention why they had found him there, and it did not occur to them to ask.

For a full half hour, long after he had got the two professors and Bossy safely away from the depot, Joe kept them in the mental framework of considering their quiet discussion there at the restaurant counter a perfectly normal part of their duties.

Then, since Joe was not above a certain sense of humor, he allowed it to occur to each of them, simultaneously, that they had wandered away and left their quarry unobserved. They looked at one another, suddenly wild eyed with consternation, and sprang away from the counter as if it had burned them.

100

They ran pell-mell down the street to the depot. They searched the place from cellar to roof. Throwing aside all precautions, they questioned everyone. No one remembered having noticed the two men at all.

They drew together out near the loading docks and began to rationalize and justify their behavior after they had realized the futility of trying to fix the blame each on the others. They were well experienced in devising stories which would convince judge and jury, but their superior had come up through the ranks and would not be so gullible.

Their attempts to account for their decisions and actions grew marvelously ingenious, didactic, logical. Their story began to approach the infallibility of conclusions found in scientific textbooks.

The simple and factual explanation of what had happened was completely outside the potential of their real world framework. And had anyone suggested it, they would have considered him mad.

CHAPTER II

The Deluxe Hotel, in the heart of skid row, tried to live up to its name by running wooden partitions breast-high between the cubicles before they finished off to the ceiling with the usual chicken wire. It was both a sop to a higher standard of modesty, and slightly more discouraging to pilfering. They changed the sheets on cots between guests, as required by the Board of Health, with a little less than the customary reluctance; but there was no difference at all in the ever present smell of vermin repellant.

Jonathan Billings sat on the edge of his cot with his head in his hands, his elbows propped on bony knees—a tired old man shorn of dignity, sureness, confidence; completely at a loss in these strange surroundings.

He looked over at his companion, Duane Hoskins, formerly Professor of Cybernetics at Hoxworth, who now sat in much the same position on his own cot, and reflected with astonishment that there was nothing in their outward appearance to distinguish them from other bums, winos and bos who lived in this section of San Francisco. Or, how did Joe express it: Men who were on the short line.

"Three days is a long wait," Billings murmured softly, conscious that anything louder could be overheard. "I wish Joe would get things resolved."

Hoskins looked up from his own reflections, his face a study in puzzlement and growing resolution.

"I've been thinking, Dr. Billings," he said obliquely. It was characteristic of the two men, even in these surroundings, that they would maintain university protocol and formality. "I've been thinking that we are a pair of fools. What are we running from? Why are we—" He broke off the sentence, but his eyes swept the small cubicle which contained their two cots and a small stand, and indicated by his expression he meant the flop house itself, skid row, San Francisco.

"We are under Federal indictment, you know, doctor," Billings reminded him austerely.

"All right!" Hoskins exploded, without realizing the loudness of his voice.

"Break it off, you two!" a voice grumbled thickly from beyond the partition. "Either talk loud enough so I can hear, or be quiet so I can sleep."

Both men turned and looked at the partition resentfully, and then at one another warningly.

"All right," Hoskins repeated, and kept his voice to little more than a whisper. "So we're under indictment. But running and hiding like this makes it worse, not better. We didn't do anything wrong. Our conscience is clear. The thing for us to do is face it, get it cleared up. I can't understand why we bolted in a panic, like crazed animals in a burning stable."

104

He paused, reflected, and added an emphasis significantly.

"There's a great deal about this I do not understand." He looked at Billings questioningly, almost in a challenge.

Billings looked back at him over his glasses. He was tempted now to tell Hoskins that Joe was a telepath; that Joe knew what he was doing; that if he, himself, had paid sufficient attention to Joe in the past things might be different now. Back at the university he had had no difficulty in keeping Joe's secret. There he had been in his own element, and ethical silence was natural. But now things had changed.

He lifted his hands from his knees and massaged the knuckles of one in the palm of the other. He opened his mouth, to speak, and closed it again. Even now, needing the cooperation and comprehension from Hoskins as he did, he could not break confidence. He said nothing.

"Perhaps there's something to the old wheeze about absent-minded professors, doctor," Hoskins attempted a wan smile. "We do tend to get wrapped up in our own work, lose touch with what the layman calls reality. But these weeks of running, hiding—and now this. I ask myself why?"

He paused, seaching for a comparison.

"It's like an amateur play, where the actors are doing and saying completely unnatural things; where a bad director is shoving the cast into completely false situations. I'm one of those actors who suddenly realizes just how false the whole position is, how impossible it is to maintain it. Or—I'm that absent-minded professor who comes out of his woolgathering long enough to realize he isn't lame at all. He just has one foot in the gutter.'' He grinned wryly at the unexpected aptness of his metaphor.

"Conceivable, doctor," Billings remonstrated in a whisper, and did not realize the incongruity of his concept forms in these surroundings, "your new apperception of reality may be as untenable as the one you wish to avoid." Then a broken, almost sobbing, sigh escaped him, inadvertently. "There is nothing in the world so terrible as a mob of enraged human beings," he murmured.

He quickly lowered his eyes to his knees again, to conceal the pain in them, to conceal his broken faith in the innate goodness of man, the profound despair of realization that reason might not after all triumph over ignorance.

"Perhaps," he murmured aloud, "to believe in the inevitable triumph of rationality might, in itself, be no more than another expression of those same superstitions which we deplore in the ignorant. It is apparently an occupational disease, perhaps a fatal one, for the scientist to be too sanguine about eventual rule by reason. There is so little evidence—"

An impatient creaking of cot springs in the next room broke him off, and kept Hoskins from answering. Both men became silent, and stared down at the cold linoleum on the floor. Simultaneously, and along parallel lines, their thoughts went back over the events of the last year or two.

First there had been orders from Washington, transmitted, as usual, through the Resident Investigator. The orders were to construct a servomechanism, along

106

the principles of the guided missile, which would prevent one plane from crashing into another, or crashing into a mountainside, to land it always safely, uncontrolled throughout by human pilot or ground crew. A servomechanism, in short, which could foresee the outcome of any probability pattern when necessary.

Apparently the phrases had been tacked on, one after another, by the bright boys there in Washington, without any realization of what they were asking. There was some dim realization that this might be a psychological problem, so Billings had been designated to head the project. The penalty, as usual, for failure was a public whipping by investigation, and imprisonment for contempt if he answered back.

And something strange had happened. It was as if the pressure of human originality, stultified for forty years through opinion control, had burst out of bounds.

Bossy, nicknamed from the machine's faint resemblance to the head of a cow, became more than an ordinary servomechanism.

The fever of original thinking spread beyond the departments of Hoxworth. The suppressed hunger to think was like an epidemic. Every academic institution, even some industrial laboratories, caught the fire of enthusiasm, contributed to the work. It was as if the scientists were resolved Bossy would be empowered to think in areas where they were forbidden to go. It was as if they felt secure in their obvious defense.

"But this is only a machine," they would say. "It cannot be held morally responsible for arriving at the only logical answers possible; even though such answers do not support your political bias. Logical rationality is neither subversive nor nonsubversive. It is simply a statement of fact. You may destroy the machine, but your verbal public whippings and pillories cannot incurably damage its psyche. It is only a machine.''

Consciously, and subconsciously, Bossy was the answer of science to the stultification of opinion control.

The news of what Bossy had become leaked out to the public. There was enough truth in the misinterpretations to disturb the public with profound unrest. Bossy could take over any job and do it better than a man. Bossy could replace even management and boards of directors. Bossy's decisions would be accurate, her judgement unclouded by personal tensions.

Bossy could tell right from wrong!

It was perhaps misinterpretation of this last faculty which shook man off the narrow ledge of reason, and sent him plunging into the depths of blind, superstitious fear. Certainly it was the hook used by the rabble rousers, whose monopoly of moral interpretation might be challenged.

Opinion control had answered the gauntlet of science.

In the last minutes, before the frenzied mob had broken down the doors of the university, the three last remaining men, Billings, Hoskins and Joe Carter had escaped. Later, Billings learned that Joe and Hoskins, long anticipating this move, had crated and shipped Bossy out of the area.

They had fled in panic.

They had continued to flee, sustained by some vague dream of a quiet sanctuary where they could continue

108

work on Bossy uninterrupted. Typical of their kind, they had no concept of where this might be; or how this new sanctuary might nullify the pressures of mass reaction to their work; or how continued work, even daily living, might be financed. Their whole life had been in the ivory tower. It had never occurred either to Hoskins or Billings that there could be any other kind.

And now they were hiding out in a flop house on skid row. Even more incredible, to Hoskins, they were totally dependent for their next move on a youngster barely twenty-two years old.

"Incredible," Hoskins said aloud, in disbelief.

"I wonder when Joe will be back?" Billings asked plaintively.

Hoskins looked at him, impatiently, and didn't answer.

The two of them sat facing one another on the edges of their cots, and endured the waiting. Hoskins reached over and took another sandwich from the supply the hotel clerk had brought them at Joe's orders. Billings wondered if he might safely make the trip down the hall to the community shower and bathe again. He smiled, ruefully, at his apparent compulsion to bathe again and again, a protest against his surroundings. He put the thought out of his mind. The fewer people who saw them, the safer they were.

Joe had told him that the word had gone out along skid row that nobody, and it meant nobody, was to talk to anybody, and it meant anybody, about Joe and those two buddies of his holed up in the Deluxe Hotel. It was a command, a group more. But there were still those with craving for a drink or a snifter of dope, always available for stoolies who might break the taboo.

Billings' self-analysis took him back to the consequences of opinion control, the same consequences which had occurred again and again throughout history. There had been many times when man had been forced to adopt the only right opinion. Each time man's forward thrust had slackened, vegetated, and died. Once, through the dark ages, the period had lasted almost a thousand years.

There was an odd peculiarity to the scientific mind. Block off an area where it may not go for speculative consideration, and immediately every line of research seems to lead into that area.

A small boy may sometimes survive for hours with no thought for the cookie jar, but forbid him to touch it and he can think of nothing else.

"Such a pity that it happened this time," Billings said, and did not realize that he was speaking aloud. "The clue was there in front of us all the time, too. Had we realized Einstein's coordinate systems were adaptable to all fields of science, not just physics, man would have gone even beyond his own dreams. Why, in the field of sociology alone—"

There was a loud, protesting creak of bedsprings through the thin wall. It was more than a man merely turning over in bed. There was the slither of hands being slid up the wooden partition. Fingers rached the top and slid through the chicken wire to grasp support. They tensed, showed strain, and there was the sliding noise of a heavier body being pulled up the wall.

The head of hair was first to show, matted and

yellow gray. Eyes followed, rheumy and blinking. The shapeless red nose, and then the mouth. The mouth smiled in an expression which the face apparently thought was friendly. It was the placating, conciliatory smile of the long habitual alcoholic.

"Would you really attempt to apply physical quantum laws of space-time continua to sociology?" the mouth asked. The words were blurred; the flaccid lips had long since forgotten how to form crisp, incisive speech.

Billings and Hoskins had been watching the apparition arise, above the partition. Billings was first to recover himself. The question restored his position in the academic world.

"Unquestionably, it should be considered," he answered.

The eyes closed. The whiter lids accentuated the grime on the face. They opened again.

"I wonder now," the mouth asked, "why that possibility had never occurred to me in my reflections? Perhaps I may blame it on the times we live in. Yes, certainly worth considering."

The head began to disappear behind the partition again, then came up. The face had an eager expression this time.

"I would offer you gentlemen a nightcap—if I had one," the mouth said hopefully.

"I'm afraid we don't have any spirits either," Billings said regretfully.

The eyes regarded them, searching their expressions for truth. Apparently the face grew satisfied that they were not selfishly hoarding.

"Then you, also, are broke," the mouth said with

111

a twist of philosophic humor. "Distressing, isn't it? But thank you, gentlemen, for a new idea. It amply repays me for this disturbance of my rest."

The head sank quickly out of sight, and this time it did not reappear. In a few minutes there were gentle snores coming through the partition, an accompaniment to the louder ones from down the hall.

"Imagine that," Hoskins whispered finally. "Imagine finding a mind like that in a place like this."

"My good Dr. Hoskins," Billings whispered back with asperity, "we're here, aren't we?"

CHAPTER III

It was three o'clock in the morning when Joe checked them out of the Deluxe Hotel. He had paid for their room in advance, of course, and checking out meant no more than dropping their cubicle key at the desk. The night clerk picked it up without question, without comment, without speculation. He had seen everything in his time and had lost all curiosity about men on the short line. Guided by the grapevine command, it was easy for him not to notice that this was an old geezer, a middle-aged bum, and a young punk.

The lobby was discreetly darker than the street outside. At the door, before stepping out, Joe touched Hoskins on the elbow and spoke in a low voice.

"I'll go first. You follow a quarter of a block behind. Hang onto one another, as if you'd had too much wine, but don't overdo it."

Hoskins started to speak and then nodded grimly.

"What about police?" Billings asked softly. "Aren't we in danger?"

Joe looked the two men over critically, and smiled.

"You look too seedy to be able to pay a fine, so the locals probably won't bother you. The Federals have had a shake-up in the last couple of days. Seems some of their men were derelict in their duty. And they're still working the better-class sections. It's too early in the normal pattern for you to have come as far down as skid row, yet. Just follow along behind me."

Out on Third Street, the wind off the harbor was chill and sharp. The fog was so heavy it was like fine rain. A few gray shadows of men wandered aimlessly up and down the sidewalk, looming up out of the fog a half block away and then disappearing again.

Joe hunched his shoulders and shuffled toward the corner of Howard Street. He waited there until he saw the two familiar figures lurching along behind. He steeled himself against the somatic effects of dejection and misery, and sampled the minds of those men still out on the street. Everything seemed to be normal. Some of the men were drunk; others, lacking the price of a flop house, were drugged with weariness and lack of sleep. A pair of cops were working the street two blocks up, routing such men out of doorways or alley corners where they were trying to sleep. But they were already beyond Joe's destination.

He waited again at the entrance to an alley, until the professors were almost up to him. They were doing very well with their act, and when they followed him into the alley it might have been no more than the act of any normal human being seeking food from a garbage can, or hunting redeemable bottles thrown away by some more fortunate wino.

Joe stood in the darkness of the alley, waiting until they had come up to him. He made a quick survey of

114

the minds in the vicinity and detected no evidence that any of them had been noticed. He took a key from his pocket and opened a door. He led them down some steps, cautioning them to feel their way carefully in the blackness. He took another key and opened another door at the bottom of the steps.

He led them into the even deeper blackness of a room, closed the door behind them, heard the click of the latch, and snapped on a light. After the darkness, the light dazzled all of them for a moment, and then they began to see. They were in a small and neatly furnished living room.

In front of them there stood a slight little man who stared unwinkingly at Joe. Heightened by flared up eyebrows, the eyes might have been those of an owl.

"I see you made it, kid," he said in a dry, brittle voice. He turned and called into another room, "Mable, they're here."

The side door to the room opened, and a huge woman waddled in. Her hair had been dyed a flaring crimson, but showed a full two inches of gray at the roots. Her face appeared to be coated with varicolored enamels.

"Quick trip, son," she said approvingly. "Coffee isn't even ready yet."

"Mabel . . . Doc Carney . . . meet my friends, Professor Billings and Professor Hoskins." It never occurred to him to fumble for Mabel's last name, or that Doc Carney might have any other. It never occurred to anybody. Their identities were complete and understood.

He watched both Hoskins and Billings bow slightly

in the direction of Mabel. Here, in a more familiar kind of habitation, some of their dignity came back to them, and they wore it well.

"Sa-a-ay," Mabel boomed at them in her hoarse voice, "you're people."

Joe was pleased to see a look of comprehension, orientation, come into Hoskins' eyes. Perhaps that ivory tower had not been so sheltering, after all. Naturally he had never looked in to see, since that aspect of Hoskins was none of his concern. But Billings was completely bewildered. His expression seemed to say that naturally they were people.

"The word 'people'," Joe instructed in a dry, didactic manner, "used in this context at this ethnological stratum contains a specialized semantic content, signifying respect, approval, classifying you as superior in the humanities attitudes."

Thus translated into simple English, Billings grasped the idea quickly. He took a step forward and held out his hand.

"You're people, too," he murmured. "That is not difficult to apprehend."

"My-y," she bridled in admiration, and shook his hand up and down heartily.

"You're entirely right about that . . . er . . . professor," Doc Carney said with approval. "Mabel was a hundred-dollars-a-night girl in her day. She's real class."

"You don't say," Billings murmured, without any comprehension at all.

Mabel threw him a quick look, then flicked her glance suspiciously at Hoskins. Hoskins gave her a broad grin, and with a wink indicated that Billings was

116

not wise to the life. Mabel took it then as it was meant, a compliment. Joe hurried quickly, before he burst into laughter, into the adjoining kitchenette where the coffee had begun to percolate. The somatics in the room were wonderful. He hadn't needed to supplement with broadcasted reassurance at all.

"And did I understand that you were introduced as Doctor?" Billings turned toward Carney after they were all seated and asked. "What field, may I ask?"

Joe heard the question and came to the doorway with the percolator in his hand.

"Doc is an honorary title," he told Billings. "He's a carney."

"I beg your pardon, Joe?" Billings asked.

"Doc Carney was a practicing psychologist" Joe explained. "A mentalist at traveling carnivals. He had an act. From the stage he told you things about yourself. I was his shill in the audience one summer while I was on vacation. That's how I got to know him. We rolled 'em in the aisles."

"Never saw anybody pick up the codes faster than Joe," Carney commented. "Tried to get him to stick with me, we'd have made barrels of money."

Mabel was in her element. It had been a long time since gentlemen had sat around in her parlor, talking in high-class voices. She sat in an elegant pose in her old red sweater, and surreptitiously glanced at a wall mirror to see if her bright orange face powder and flaming lipstick were wearing well. In a provocative gesture of old, she flicked her long jet earring back and forth at the side of her cheek with her finger, and tried to shrink her broad and shapeless thighs into something like seductiveness. With the forefinger of her other hand she scraped idly and futiley at a dirt spot on her old black skirt.

The room fell suddenly silent, and all of them welcomed the steaming cups of coffee Joe carried in on a tray. All of them sipped slowly, appreciatively. Mabel alternately straightened her little finger and tucked it in again, unable to remember which was considered the more fashionable. It had been a long time since she was a hundred-dollars-a-night girl. A very long time.

"Now to business," Joe said crisply, and set his cup down on an end table beside his chair.

Hoskins and Billings were past any stage of astonishment. It seemed quite natural to them that Mabel was their landlady; that she owned half of the property on the short line; that she had documents, letters, inscribed jewelry, and memories of former days which protected her against shake-down and blackmail.

"I could tell you plenty about these sanctimonious old geezers who tell the rest of the world how to be good," she boomed. "But I leave them alone and they're glad to leave me alone. It's the same with my tenants. As long as you boys treat me fair, pay your bills, and don't get me mixed up in your troubles, I leave you alone. I don't know what you're doing here. I don't want to know. It's none of my business. I don't pry and snoop. I don't have to. I've already seen everything."

"She means it, too," Joe said. "Mabel doesn't pretend to be respectable, you know. So she doesn't need to get her kicks out of peeking and spying and being scandalized and righteously indignant."

118

Mabel turned and looked at him with shrewd eyes.

"What would you now about it, son?" she asked. "You're not even dry behind the ears yet."

Joe winked at her and pulled his mouth into an expression of self-mockery.

"Why, Mabel," he said, teasing her, "you've heard about this terrible younger generation. I might even be able to tell you a few things."

She threw back her head and roared with a hearty laughter. They went back to business.

Doc Carney was to be their outside contact man, buying all their supplies for them. Hoskins and Billings wouldn't need to go outside at all. There was a big room, beyond the bedrooms to this apartment, which could be fitted into their workshop. Long ago power lines had been cut into the trunks under the street. It was never exactly mentioned, but it gradually became clear that the former tenants, who had paved the way for them, were counterfeiters.

It became apparent also, as Joe had planned, that Mabel and Carney assumed they were also counterfeiters. Obviously Billings was the engraver, no doubt some old renegade who had once worked for the Treasury. Hoskins must be the mechanic, the handy man, the chemist. Joe was the front for the outfit. And now that Mabel and Carney had seen them all, Joe was probably the brains of the outfit, too. These other two were putting on a good show at being college teachers, but it wasn't all show. they really were out of this world, and didn't know enough to come in out of the rain.

When they began listing some of the things they needed, Carney's suspicions were confirmed, although his eyes opened wide at the list of electronic and chemical equipment they felt they might need. His expression indicated he thought these boys were really going first-class.

"You can't buy this stuff with queer money," he said at one point coming right out into the open with his suspicions. "I can get all this stuff cheap. The boys heist it from warehouses, or highjack it, or lift it from labs and plants. Most of this stuff is hard to dispose of, so it'll be cheap. They got no sense about what will move fast. Their fingers stick to everything. Still, you got to play fair with them. Pay them with queer, and you cut off your own nose."

"The money will be good, Carney," Joe reassured him. "This is a square deal all around."

"That's all I want to know," Carney answered with relief. "How you pass the stuff and get good money for it to pay the boys is your business."

"I haven't said I was going to pass any queer," Joe reminded him.

"That's right, son," Mabel interrupted. "Never tell anything."

"But just how will we get the money?" Hoskins asked. "It will take a great deal. And we're not working on subsidy now."

"It won't take as much as you think," Joe said. "We're almost through. Just a few additions and conversions to be made now. I've been playing the races for it. I've got a system."

Carney looked at him with admiration. The kid thought of everything. That would answer any questions about where the money came from. It was an old blind, but a good one. He threw back his head and laughed.

Mabel thought Joe was kidding them, and laughed along with Carney. Anybody knows that systems are for the lambs who want to be fleeced. Hoskins considered that Joe had rebuked him for discussing it in front of strangers. He laughed to cover his *faux pas*.

"I am not certain that one can be assured of winning on such wagers," Billings said doubtfully, seriously.

They all laughed then.

"Don't worry about it," Joe said. "Any of you. That's my job."

"Just keep your nose clean, son," Mabel boomed.

Everyone sat and admired everyone else. Everyone was quite certain he understood everyone else. And Joe knew none of them understood anything at all.

For he had not yet told Billings and Hoskins what he intended to do with Bossy. Their realization had not yet come that he had been using them this last year; using the facilities of Hoxworth; the facilities of all the institutions who had helped on Project Bossy; using the subsidies from Washington. He had been using them selfishly, with determination, with practical application of psychology to serve his own purpose.

He had no sense of guilt about this. It was certainly normal and well-established practice for individuals to divert tax monies to their own advancement. It was one of the many survivals of savage custom working in modern society. The tribesmen paid their tithes to the chieftains, the elders, the witchdoctors—as always.

And, without even attempting to rationalize it into the end justifying the means, it was an obvious bargain for both sides. For the human race there was now a thinking machine, one which could use discrimination and judgment, and act. When the troglodytes got over their superstitious fear of flame, they would find fire quite useful.

And for him, it was deliverance.

For him the long loneliness would be ended. He was already quite clear on how the psychosomatic therapy knowledge of Billings could be incorporated in the machine, how the machine could interact with a human being to get down to the bedrock of every fixation, inhibition, repression of a person. How these would be supplanted with orderly rationalization.

From the machine, in due course, a man or a woman would emerge—a real man or woman; not the twisted warped, pitiful deformity which passes as human.

And, if his reasoning were correct—another telepath.

CHAPTER IV

For a week, almost day and night, Duane Hoskins worked on the reassembly of Bossy. Now that the parts were in his hands again, and he had a place to work undisturbed, he pushed conflict with his circumstances into the background and gave all of his thought to the task of bringing Bossy back to her original state of function. He assured himself that when his job was done, then he would attempt to get a more realistic approach to his relationships with government and other people.

The reassembly took all of his thought. He started out on the task as if it were no more than a routine nuisance which he must endure, since he had been all over this ground in the first assembly. But as the subassemblies began to accumulate into their proper relationships again, he grew more and more excited.

Guided as he was by a rigid intellectual honesty, that one faculty which makes the scientist differ from any other calling, he found himself freely acknowledging that Bossy was not his creation. Bossy was not even a true product of cybernetics—at least not as that science had been conceived before the start of this project.

Somewhere, somehow, they had surmounted the thin and narrow conceptions of their predecessors. Only now, with the accomplished fact before him, did he realize just how thin and self-restricting those concepts had been.

More important, and more incomprehensible, they had surmounted the sterility of opinion control. Although, in the narrow sense, his field was far from the dangerous social sciences; early in his career Hoskins had realized that no field of science is remote from the affairs of men, that there is a sociological implication inherent even in the simple act of screwing a nut on a bolt.

Of course he had never expressed this in a classroom. Outwardly he had held to the prevalent opinion that the physical scientist has no responsibility to man for what he achieves. As with all other instructors, he knew that in each class there were bound to be at least two or three students who, in preparation for careers to come, had set themselves up as the supra analysts of what was the only right opinion. These were diligent in reporting to pressure groups, or directly to Resident Investigators.

The consequence was that even the brightest of students were becoming no more than cookbook engineers. This had always been regrettably true of ninety-five per cent of engineering students. But before opinion control there had been at least five per cent whose minds were fertile enough to conceive a variant idea.

Now, for almost half a century, there had been nothing new. There was an apparent progress, of course. The cookbook engineers were still able to mix up new batches from old ingredients. There was still enough gadgetry invention to confound any criticism. But there was no exploration of new areas, hunting for new frontiers.

In his own field of cybernetics, he had studied the mid-century experiments with ultra high-speed computers, the automatic chess players, the visible speech mechanisms, and the like. He had discovered how close the followers of Baggage and Vannevar Bush had come to their dream of the second industrial revolution. But here, in the closing decade of the century, cybernetics was still playing mechanical games with the same concepts.

Only Bossy was different.

As he continued with the reassembly, Hoskins grew deeply troubled. At times he felt as if he were on the verge of some vast concept not quite grasped; as if he caught hazy glimpses of an outline of a totally unknown continent where, always before, all science had assumed there were only empty seas. He cursed the sterility, the rote memorization which passed for learning. He bitterly accused his own mind of being like a wasted muscle, long unused, now incapable of a task which should be accomplished with ease.

Not that he was failing in the reassembly. Complex as it was, he remembered each step in perfect order. And, laid out before him as it was, he knew the theory and purpose of each part. What he failed to grasp was how it had been conceived in the first place.

He recalled well, in the early days of the project, the consternation, the blank incomprehension between

125

one department of science and another. The legendary Tower of Babel was a miracle of understanding by comparison. As is to be expected when men are deeply disturbed by a sense of inadequacy, each branch of science had withdrawn into itself, become more and more esoteric, more ritualistic. As the inadequate man looks for and seizes upon differences so as to establish his superiority, so each science had moved farther from the common purpose of science—which is to know. And that was the way this project had begun, in spirit and in practice, back there at Hoxworth.

Then, suddenly, for no apparent reason, men understood one another; problems were solved; old jealousies forgotten; prejudices discarded. Everywhere in the university the departments were caught up in the spirit usually known only to a few men—the desire to go beyond apparent differences, to understand what is really meant, to regard with pitying impatience those who would still value personal ascendency over comprehension.

And, most astonishing of all, everyone took it for granted. No one seemed to have realized what had happened or much less why. He, himself, had not realized it until now; when the act of reassembling Bossy forced him into a minute review of each stage of the work. Only in its totality did it reveal its logical impossibility.

He tried to question Billings during the afternoon when they were working together installing the random synaptic selectors which would respond to sensory code patterns.

"Dr. Billings," he said carefully "while it is apparent that no individual part of Bossy was unknown to science, even fifty years ago, the blending of the parts, and, above all our concept of what happens in the process of thought, is new. How did we manage it? You were the head of the project. You ought to know.''

He saw the same hesitancy, the same film of concealment that usually came over Billings' candid blue eyes when this topic had been discussed before back at Hoxworth.

''Probably no more than fortuitous circumstance,'' Billings answered evasively.

''I don't believe that, and neither do you,'' Hoskins stated bluntly. He pointed to the hydrogen ion concentrators, to the wave-field harmonics receptors. ''These are accident?'' he questioned with disbelief amounting to derision. ''It was accident that the Department of Music was able to give us the clue to search activators in pattern selection? That the department of Synthetic Textiles was able to show us how to polymerize and catalyze strings of molecules into the material which became Bossy's concept storage unit?''

In nervous tension, he paced up and down the room, and puffed at his cigarette as if in agony.

''That Bossy is able to take part patterns,'' he continued in the same incredulous voice, ''and fill in the missing pieces from probability selection through her proprioceptors? That we were able to recognize this as the treasured and mysterious process of reasoning?''

He stopped his pacing and pounded softly and slowly on the edge of the work bench with the heel of his hand.

''Above all,'' and now his voice was almost querulous, ''it was sheer accident that we were able to under-

127

stand one another, go beyond sematic differences to the real core of meaning—when, as you know, our usual pattern was a gleeful destruction of the other fellow's attempts at comprehension? Dr. Billings, I am neither a child nor a fool. I cannot accept the theory of fortuitous circumstance!''

''We did it,'' Billings answered shortly, and wondered why Joe had permitted this question to arise in Hoskins' mind at this time. Joe should have told him, should have cued him on what to do. This was conflict, and Bossy was not yet completely assembled. ''We did it,'' he repeated futilely. ''Isn't that the only important thing?''

Hoskins glared around the room, at the bare pinewood floor, the stained cement walls of the basement room, the harsh overhead lights, the door to their bedrooms which was the only source of fresh air.

''What am I?'' he asked hoarsely. ''No more than a handy man? Is that why I've placed myself in jeopardy, taken all these risks; just to hold a job as subordinate mechanic—without pay? Are we working as a team, doctor? Do we have one another's confidence; or don't we?''

''I don't know how to answer you, Duane,'' Billings said slowly, and Hoskins noticed that his first name had been used in their conversations for the first time. ''I don't know why you've been permitted to think of these things.''

''Permitted to think of them!'' Hoskins exploded.

Billings fluttered his hands in the air, as if to ward off violence.

''You will have to ask Joe,'' he said weakly.

CHAPTER V

The three men sat in the small living room of their basement quarters, having a late sandwich before going to bed. The somatics in the room were tense.

Hoskins pored over the schematic of the multiple feedback system, alternately fretting over whether Carney would be able to find the right tube for the torque amplifier, which had been cracked in transit, and stewing over the indignity of having been referred to Joe for the answers he felt he must have.

Billings mused over the problem, given to him by Joe days before, on how automatic psychosomatic therapy mechanisms could be installed in Bossy, what the most effective electrode contact with human subjects might be, and how reverie reviews could be taken down to cellular level, as Joe had insisted they must.

Joe worked at the small desk, extending the probabilities of his system to the end of the Tanforan meet, to tailor his bets to the amount of money they would need until the next racing season. The system was imperfect in that jockeys sometimes changed their minds in the heat of the race, extended their horse when they were not supposed to, won when they were not supposed to win. Reserves had to be set aside to cover a streak of these. Still, it was the safest method of getting enough money without calling attention to himself.

The scene was much the same as it had been back at Hoxworth, when he was secretary on Project Bossy; but the circumstances, both overt and somatic, were different.

He was aware that Hoskins was facing a crisis, one which had been maturing for the past two weeks, that if he let it go on, Bossy, herself, might be threatened. He could have avoided it, of course, just as he had avoided it all those months at Hoxworth. Delicately, he could have implanted the right impulses in Hoskins, so that revealment would come as no shock. But he had a sound reason for doing otherwise. Hoskins had a first-rate brain, and Joe had come to realize that blind acceptance of his extrasensory perceptions would give him no clue as to how the same gifts might be installed in Bossy. It was necessary that Hoskins fight it out on a cerebration level.

Further, he felt the same loyalty toward Hoskins that he felt toward Billings. And he wanted Hoskins to have the full benefit which Bossy could eventually give. That meant Hoskins had to grow up, willingly, of his own volition.

At that moment Hoskins reached over to the stand beside his chair and picked up another of the sandwiches. He glanced at Joe obliquely, his curiosity almost overcoming his resentment. Joe chose this moment to look up from his own work.

"Every man surrounds his mind with a framework of screen mesh." Joe said conversationally, "composed of his prejudgments, preconceptions of what is acceptable to him. Everything he receives must filter throught it."

Hoskins glared at him impatiently, as if a precocious child, age five, had tried to be profound about man and woman in marriage. He flared in sudden anger, and his mind formed the sentence, "What would a young punk like you know about it?" but he was too courteous to say the words.

"So it seems to you," he spoke flatly.

"So it is, doctor," Joe said, without deferment. "The first strands of the screen are strung very early. 'Don't do this! That's bad! Now that's mother's good little boy! That's nasty, shame on you! You're too little to do that alone! That's over your head, wait until you're older! Always tell mother when the children are bad to you!' On and on with things like that."

"So?" Hoskins questioned with a shrug.

"So a pattern of standards is formed. Everything is judged in relation to that pattern. The stream of commands, admonishments, casual remarks are buttressed, ingrained, and enforced with emotional impact, sometimes with physical shock treatment administered with the flat of the hand where it will do the most good."

"Then education comes along," Hoskins debated with a smile, "and tears your screen to pieces."

"In theory only," Joe said. "But not in practice.

Even then everything received is modified by the screen. Oh maybe there's a hole punched here and there, and rewoven with new strands. But new strands are woven, that's the point. The filtering goes on just the same. Even if a new idea pushes against the screen with such force that it must be considered, it is usually so distorted by the time it has been 'rationalized through the screen' that it means just what the receiver wants it to mean.''

"The prime purpose of education, Joe," Hoskins instructed, "is to insure an open mind, the ability to consider an idea on its own merits, to accept reality without distortion.

You've been wondering, lately, how Bossy came into being," Joe said abruptly.

Hoskins looked at him curiously, and then over at Billings accusingly. Billings had had no right to discuss their conversation with this immature boy.

"I'm a telepath," Joe said simply.

"Nuts!" Hoskins exploded disgustedly.

Joe threw back his head and laughed freely.

"You see what I mean, doctor?" he chuckled.

"I see I've got enough problems on my hands already, without having you spring a lot of wild-hair notions on me." Hoskins snapped. Then pityingly, "Joe, I've always thought you were a diligent and fair student. I never suspected you harbored ideas about that superstitious guff. Joe! That's for the credulous, the wild-eyed! It's . . . it's beneath the notice of rational men.''

"Dr. Rhine didn't think so," Joe answered.

"That's different. That was scientific research under laboratory conditions. However, it is significant that Dr. Rhine never found, nor claimed to have found, a true telepath."

"Neither have I," Joe said quietly. He kept his voice normal, not revealing the dark loneliness of life-long solitary confinement, such as might be known by a human who was never once permitted to communicate with one of his own kind.

"At best," Hoskins continued forcefully, "all he found was some phenomena which exceeded the laws of probabilities. That might mean some trace elements, true. But it could also mean that our notions of the laws of probabilities could stand revision."

"And your screen mesh prefers the latter," Joe laughed.

Billings looked over his glasses, and cleared his throat.

"I have known about Joe," he said hesitantly, "since he was eight years old. Dr. Martin of Steiffel University wrote me. That's why I brought Joe to Hoxworth. There was sufficient evidence, Duane. I could not deny it. And . . . I, too . . . tried."

"You've been the victim of some elaborate hoax, Dr. Billings," Hoskins said harshly.

Joe looked at Hoskins, undismayed.

"Professor," he asked, "what was it Algazzali wrote about the 'fourth stage of intellectual development'?"

Instantly, like a man reciting a bit of poetry learned in high school, Hoskins quoted:

" . . . When another eye is opened by which man

perceives things hidden in others . . . perceives all that will be . . . perceives things that escape the perceptions of reason—"

"You didn't know you remembered that, did you, professor?"

Hoskins shrugged.

"It means nothing," he said. "Neither the drivel nor the fact that I remembered it. A young college student absorbs a lot of such guff before he gets down to serious work. You've run across it somewhere, Joe. It was a safe assumption that I would have, also."

"But how clearly you recalled it!" Billings teased. "And after all these years, too."

"That, too, means nothing. We've shown in Bossy how a concept may lay idle, never be called into use, until the right harmonics stimulate a pattern where it is required."

Joe reached over, took a piece of paper and pencil, scribbled a note, folded it, and handed it to Billings. At that moment Hoskins started up from his chair.

"Excuse me." he murmured in a stricken voice and headed for the bath.

In a few moments he came back into the room. His eyes were watery, his cheeks pale, his nostrils drawn.

"Don't eat any more of those sandwiches" he said. "The meat must be tainted. At least in that one I got."

At Joe's motion, Billings handed the note to Hoskins. Curiously, Hoskins opened the note and read it.

"Professor Hoskins will need to vomit in less than one minute," the note said.

Hoskins crumpled the note and threw it in the wastebasket in disgust.

"That's telepathy?" he asked derisively. "Probably

134

saw me turning green around the gills. Jumped to conclusions again.''

''Even before you felt any discomfort, professor?'' Joe laughed. ''And how many of these conclusions do I have to jump to before the evidence will penetrate your screen.''

''A great many more,'' Hoskins snapped. ''I—''

There was a sudden urgent rap on the door.

''Another demonstration, professor,'' Joe said dryly, as he got up to open it. ''That'll be Carney. He'll have Mabel with him. He's very disturbed. Incidentally, he has your torque amplifier tube. And, gentlemen, he has found out who we are. This is a showdown, so let me handle it.''

When he opened the door, Carney and Mabel stepped through, and Carney shut the door quickly, as if he were being pursued. The old reprobate's eyes were flashing anger. Mabel's usually generous friendliness was replaced by a mask of curiosity, wariness. Although Carney had much to say, he seemed at a loss how to begin now that he was here.

''I got the tube,'' he opened accusingly, obliquely. ''This stuff is real hot. The Feds and local boys have passed the word along to watch for anybody buying it. They're paying big stoolie dough, too. You guys are hot, too hot!''

He turned to Joe, his voice a compound of anger and disappointment.

''You tricked me,'' he burst out with what was really bothering him. ''I didn't know you guys was Brains. I didn't know you was them three from that eastern college the whole country is looking for.''

135

Billings and Hoskins looked at him curiously, and then at Joe who stood easily beside the closed door and said nothing.

Carney turned to Mabel.

"I swear, Mabel," he said apologetically, "I didn't know these guys was Brains when I asked you to rent them this place. I just thought they were in a counterfeiting racket or something." Then he added bitterly, "But I guess I ought to have known. The way Joe picked up the code when he worked with me in the act. I just thought maybe he was psychic or something. I didn't know he was a Brain."

Joe glanced at Hoskins with a suppressed smile.

"See what I mean about prejudice screens, doctor?" he asked. "Now it would be all right with Carney if I were merely psychic. But to have a trained mind—that's something to arouse antagonism."

"But you're not our kind of people at all," Carney argued, his anger arising again. "You don't belong with us. And you tricked me."

Help came from an unexpected source, and without any effort from Joe.

"Who are we, Carney," Mabel asked slowly, "to point the finger at anybody?"

"But these guys are the ones who invented that machine which is gonna blow up the world, Mabel," Carney shouted. "They're the ones that thought out that thing which is gonna make slaves of all the people when it takes over the world and runs it. They built Bossy!" He cast a fearful look toward the back room.

"I'll bet it's that Bossy thing they've got in that back room, not a counterfeit press at all! These guys

136

want to wipe humans off the face of the earth, and we're helping them!''

Both Hoskins and Billings started to protest the string of cliches picked up from yellow journalism, but Joe silenced them with a warning look. Let the boil-over run its course. You couldn't get into a man's mind with reason while it was inflamed with anger; the prejudice screen was at its very strongest then. It was the old clash of ignorance without learning and ignorance with it.

Only Mabel seemed able to surmount the conflict.

''I've always said,'' she commented, ''that a person does what he has to do. Maybe Joe and the professors can't help being what they are—any more than you and I could help being what we were.''

Joe watched her intently. He knew now that she could qualify for his intended use of Bossy, as he had suspected she might. He had been wise in choosing skid row. Only here, among these broken by accusation, could be found those unwilling to accuse. Only here, among the victims of a too narrow sense of right could be found those who were not fatuously confident of their special endowments for defining it. The same conclusion had been reached once before, two thousand years ago.

''It's not for us to say, Carney,'' Mabel added firmly.

She stood there, a shapeless hulk in her old red sweater and black skirt. Her swollen feet were planted far apart. The red joints of her rheumatic fingers opened and closed painfully. The mask make-up on her face, meant to conceal the age and pain lines, could not conceal her quality. Mabel was—people.

CHAPTER VI

For almost a week Joe avoided everyone as much as possible, allowing the change of status to settle itself into acceptable relationships. He knew that Billings and Hoskins were having many long conversations about his psionic ability, that Hoskins was gradually rationalizing the idea that Billings had not been hoaxed after all.

"I mean," Billings said at one point in their conversations, "we must be willing to go beyond the present frontiers of physics to understand Joe's psionic traits. We must get a notch above the concept that for a thing to be scientific it must have visible wheels."

"The frontiers of physics—." The phrase appealed to Hoskins, helped him to view this dark trait with something nearer acceptance.

"I have no doubt," Billings pressed his advantage, "that the answer lies in some order of energetics not yet explored. We do have to go beyond the mere parroting of the words of Einstein's coordinate systems and think in terms of genuine practical application."

139

"I'm not sure I see how that can be done here," Hoskins objected.

"The eye is no more than a cellular mechanism activated by the wave field of energy we call light," Billings reasoned. "The encephalograph reveals the brain generates its own wave field of energy. Some obscure area of Joe's brain has taken a mutant leap and is activated by that wave field, so that he can perceive thought directly, as the eye perceives light. Such an area might be present in every brain, but rudimentary in the way of light sensitive cells in primitive life."

It was not the complete theory which Joe held, but it served to orient Hoskins to the idea that Joe was no more than an eugenic mutant. It brought the idea out of the areas of metaphysics into the realms of physics.

But even with such rationalization, the emotional implications of living in the presence of a telepath were too much for Hoskins to accept immediately. Man, even the most brilliant of men, is not all intellect. No man is without skeletons in his closet, those little quirks, those dark little actions and mean motives, shameful little things which he does not even reveal to his doctor, his confessor, his psychoanalyst.

Hoskins resolutely faced such things in himself, and as resolutely turned away from them. His mind refused the idea that Joe could see them clearly.

"How could you continue to respect me if you knew these things about me?"

He had not yet arrived at the knowledge that Joe would have seen thousands of carbon copies of such traits in others, would have grown up with them, accepting them from the first as being no more than normal to any human being. That in the balance scale of a man's life, achievement was even more splendid because it did gain ascendency over the furtive quirks; that man was even nobler in that, at the same time, he was so reprehensible.

Hoskins would arrive there, but it would take time.

Carney progressed in his own adjustments much more easily. His resentment changed to admiration, partly helped by Joe's unsuspected somatic assurances, partly through the example set by Mabel. The tenderloin stratum has an almost universal contempt for the organized hypocrisy of society. Unable to accept it, become a part of it, they are broken by it. They seldom become enough detached to see it is this very pretense of man to be better than he is which drives him to convert his pretense to reality.

Carney was delighted, after his first shock, to find that Brains sometimes find themselves in the same boat as shortline outcasts.

Somehow the word had leaked out that the two professors had been found, and lost, in the San Francisco area. The search, which had been spread over the nation, now concentrated itself in the San Francisco area. And the area was ideal for the search. Surrounded on three sides by water, San Francisco has almost the status of an island and the traffic flows are concentrated ideally for thorough search.

The newspapers and communication channels which had been regretting a lack of world crises at the moment, revived the entire issue with enthusiasm. All the lurid misconceptions were rehashed, improved upon, spun into the most sensational stories the fertile minds of reporters could conceive. The witch hunt was on in full force, and Carney kept himself busy collecting commentary. Although the danger was great, he was almost beside himself with pride that he was on the inside, that a word from him could blast the whole thing wide open. For the first time, he felt revenged upon society. It was within his power to withhold the very information society craved. And, at this point, that knowledge was sufficient satisfaction.

Half a century previously there would have been many champions rising to argue both sides of the question of Bossy; many to defend the right of these professors to push the frontiers of knowledge ahead. But forty years of effective opinion control had ingrained the habit of instant agreement with official opinion, regardless of how often that official position might change sides or contradict itself.

Still, one man did have the courage to call for a calm and rational consideration of the issues.

Howard Kennedy released his editorialized interview through one of the newspapers where he owned the controlling stock shares. He cited, calmly, the historical precedents where mass reaction had been violently antagonistic to other scientific discoveries; anaesthesia, steam power, electrical power, Newton's laws of motion, Galileo's concept of the solar system, a long list which, upon analysis, was seen to contain almost every advance man had made in his long climb from savagery. He related all this to the question of Bossy, and left the question hanging as to whether this might prove to be another such instance of misguided opposition.

It was a daring thing to do, for it ran counter to popular opinion. Apparently he felt his millions, his position of power, his well popularized philanthropies, his liberal attitudes toward labor, would protect him.

Billings and Hoskins found in the article divergent rays of hope. Billings saw in it the possibility that man might once again capture the rational point of view. Hoskins, fretting under the conditions of the dark basement, the lack of competent assistants, the pressure of knowing he was hunted by government, saw a protector, a subsidizer, a return to the respectability of an ivory tower.

Joe, too, got a lift out of the article. The work on Bossy was almost finished. Billings had spent the necessary hours feeding the concepts of psychosomatics into Bossy's storage unit. Bossy had found the concepts consistent with the carefully screened factual information which had been fed into her at Hoxworth. She had not thrown out psychosomatics as being a tissue of unsupported theory. Her acceptance was all the more impressive because she had refused most of the theoretical structures of orthodox psychology on the grounds that such structures had little or no relation to observable data.

Joe had no intention of keeping Bossy to himself once he had accomplished his aim. He, too, would need someone with courage and influence, such as Howard Kennedy. But not so naive as the two professors, he resolved to find out what went on in Kennedy's mind before they responded to Kennedy's obvious bid for their confidence. The man did not take the risk of public boycott simply to speak his piece. His motive was obviously to make contact. Beyond that, Joe could not go, not until he could get close to the man, see him, obtain some object which Kennedy had handled, some focalizing channel. It was one of Joe's limitations on his ability that he could not use it in the way some of the totally untalented normals imagined the trait would work.

But of all the adjustments, that of Mabel was most important. And when Billings told him that there was nothing further to be done with the therapy mechanisms of Bossy until that already installed could be tested and adjusted, Joe knew it was time to talk with Mabel.

There literally wasn't anyone else qualified. Hoskins was needed for his understanding of the mechanical principles. Billings must work in tandem with Bossy, man and machine coordinating to the utmost in the therapy while Bossy learned it. Aside from the fact that Joe was their only protection against the outer world, his psionic ability was too valuable to risk as a test case. Carney was openly cooperative, but Joe knew there was a hard core of hidden antagonism and suspicion. Further, Carney was quite satisfied with himself as he was, and no system of psychotherapy can make more than a temporary indentation against a basic unwillingness to change.

That left only Mabel. Mabel was obvious for an overt reason. She suffered painfully from a complex of rheumatism and arthritis, aggravated by fat. If Bossy was to prove effective at all, improvements in these would be most observable. At least these were the arguments Joe used to Billings and Hoskins. His plans went far deeper.

He went to see Mabel in her apartment on the floor above them.

She received him matter-of-factly, without question, without apology for some fancied untidiness of her apartment. Of the long list she might have been justified in having, Mabel retained only one small vanity, and that a harmless one. Mabel had never been a respectable woman.

As he seated himself in her best chair, Joe smiled inwardly, and tenderly, at her little vanity. Even in this, she was intensely human, for she chose to be vain on a point where there was no justification for it. Her mind was too simple and direct, her honesty was too innate, she lacked the hard-eyed viciousness which comes from forcing the psyche into deformities unnatural to it. No, even if she had tried, Mabel lacked the basic characteristics which would have qualified for her respectability.

Not that she lacked inner conflicts. Her complex of arthritis and her fat were sufficient evidence that she had not been free from these.

Even her considerable wealth was not a result of calculated avarice, but was the accidental result of an odd whimsy. In her younger days, some of the important men, finding in her qualities they could not find at home, seemed to receive some defiant pleasure out of freely giving her the things which their wives schemed and trapped and blustered to gain. In that small boy mischievousness of males, they built up a solid fortune for her in a mood of perverse gratitude.

Ordinarily it is only the blackmailers and shakedown

artists of the police who grow rich from her profession, but as the influence of her clientele grew her numerous arrests ceased, and she no longer found it necessary to turn over all surplus monies as the price of being let alone.

Instantaneously, her life flashed through Joe's mind as he settled back in his chair.

"We need your help, Mabel," he said, without hedging on the purpose of his visit.

"In what way, son?" she asked, and her booming voice was quieter than usual.

He told her, briefly, the facts about Bossy, how they had come to build the machine, some of the things they expected from it. She made only one comment.

"It ain't the first time the newspapers have got things all twisted up."

He went on then to tell her how they hoped to make Bossy into a machine which would cure the ailments of man, such as her arthritis. Billings was a genuine medical doctor, and if she had paid any attention at all she would know he had a world-wide reputation.

Mabel nodded that she did know. She asked the obvious question.

"Why could a machine do things a doctor couldn't?"

"Doctors are human," Joe answered, "and, there-fore, limited. The secret of any psychotherapy is that the doctor should be less twisted than the patient. This is seldom possible. True, he may be twisted in some other way, but if he simply substitutes one twist for another he has gained nothing. The greatest care was used, when Bossy was being educated, to feed in only

146

absolutely proved and undeniable fact. Bossy did her own interpreting. She rejected unfounded opinion, or prejudice built on false premises. She is more capable of unbiased therapy than any man could be."

"I don't think I understand what you're talking about, Joe," Mabel said frankly.

He developed for her the basics of psychosomatic therapy. To bring it into her own experience, he recalled how her stomach would be upset if she tried to eat when she was acutely worried.

"The cell," he said, "is like the stomach. It refuses to function properly when such things as repressions, inhibitions, suppressions and the like affect it. Before long it gets twisted out of its healthy pattern into an unhealthy one. The idea of all the psychotherapies is to lift these suppressors so that the human can function again. Most of the psychologists work with some mysterious thing they call mind. The psychosomatic men work directly with the body cells. Not only in the brain but all over the body, each cell seems to have a mind and memory of its own. Each one is capable of getting its own twists of inhibitions and repressions. The idea is to go clear down to the cellular level and take the load off of each cell so it can stretch and grow and function again."

"Like being in a strait jacket and getting out," Mabel commented. "I got me a general idea, son. I guess, being ignorant, that's all I can hope for."

"We don't know how Bossy is going to work," Joe told her frankly. "I don't see how it can hurt you. The worst that can happen is that you won't get cured. And, of course, you won't get cured if you hang on to the ideas which caused the trouble. That's the toughest part, Mabel, to be willing to admit that you might not know what is right and what is wrong."

She threw back her head and laughed her free, booming laughter. "Son," she said heartily, "I never did know that."

"You might be changed—a lot," he warned her. "You might not want to go on living here as you do now. You might . . . anything might happen. It's a chance you would have to be willing to take. Nobody has ever had a look at reality except through smoked glasses. We haven't got any idea of what it's really like without them. You'd be the first."

She looked down at her broad thighs, her old black skirt. She lifted her wrinkled hand with its enlarged knuckles.

"What good am I, like this?" she asked.

"I don't know for sure, Mabel," Joe said simply, "but I think you'll be giving a lot to mankind."

CHAPTER VII

It was not to be expected that the psychosomatic therapy would go smoothly. Carney greeted the announcement that Mabel would undergo the test with flatfooted opposition. His suspicion and resentment came close to the surface and showed itself in alternating sulks, in his forbidding Mabel to have anything to do with Bossy, and then in actual threats to do his plain civic duty and turn them all in to the Feds.

He seemed determined to demonstrate the old truism again: that the only enemy man has is man. The universe does not care whether man unlocks its secrets or leaves them closed. Water does not care whether man bathes in it or drowns in it; whether it waters his fields or washes them away. If man masters its laws and utilizes his knowledge, water becomes a force in his favor. But enemy or servant, water does not care.

Of all the forces, only man seems determined that man shall not master the universe.

Carney paid lip service only to the boon of health which Bossy might bring to Mabel and to all mankind.

He could react only that Mabel had deserted him, had gone over to these men from the other side of the tracks. It was a bitter realization that his long friendship with her counted for so little.

More than knowledge or enlightenment or understanding, man values his ascendency over something or someone. The fate of mankind is of little consequence to him if he must lose his command in the process. Carney felt alone and deserted. It took a great deal of somatic comforting from Joe, and Mabel's stern commands for him to mind his own business, to settle him down.

The second hitch came from Bossy.

There had been a considerable argument from Hoskins that inasmuch as the hunt for them had concentrated in San Francisco, and discovery was inevitable, their best course was to initiate contact with the government, turn themselves in and hope for the best. Or as an alternative, they should make contact with Howard Kennedy, whose interview had been so liberal, and let that industrialist negotiate for them. Joe had countered these arguments with the fact that the public was still bitterly fanatic on the subject of Bossy, and that government would not dare go against the will of the people and their blood thirst.

He pointed out, however, that if they could demonstrate, with an accomplished fact, Bossy was a master healer, then Kennedy would have something to work with to make the public change its mind about Bossy. Hoskins agreed, reluctantly.

Almost day and night for the past week, Billings had fed his lifetime of knowledge into Bossy on every facet of psychosomatic therapy. And his knowledge

150

represented the accumulated knowledge of the world. It was, therefore, a bitter disappointment that their first question to Bossy for an estimate of time required for the therapy on Mabel should cause an instant flashback of an unwanted answer.

"Insufficient data."

It was the old familiar phrase which, even back at Hoxworth, they sometimes viewed with impatience. A human being is seldom bothered with insufficient data; often the less he has the more willing he is to give a firm opinion; and man prefers some answer, even a wrong one, to the requirement that he dig deeper and find out the facts.

Here, under the pressure of time, knowing they might be discovered any day, Bossy's bland reply, flashed on her screen, made them sick at heart. Yet, without even a survey of the problem, what else could they expect?

The problem had not been Mabel, herself. She had been more than cooperative. In view of the situation, Billings had decided to make the therapy continuous, and Mabel had willingly arranged her affairs with her attorney for a ten-day absence. As willingly, she had fitted herself into the network of electrodes and lay on the couch with complete confidence. Her last words, before Billings began to induce the hypnosis, were to Carney who had watched the preparations with hostile eyes.

"Don't be an old fool," she said, "give me a chance to get well again."

For the first four hours Billings, in tandem with Bossy, played her memories back and forth, trying to uncover the central tensions which were the source of her troubles. At the end of the fourth hour, while she was in a rambling, repetitious incident of her childhood, Billings again put the question to Bossy for a time estimate.

"Insufficient data," Bossy flashed back again.

"What data do you need?" Hoskins snapped at Bossy irritably.

"A complete survey of every cell memory to determine the quantum of repressors." Bossy flashed.

Joe, who had been hovering in the background, stepped forward.

"Based on techniques now in use," he asked, "how long would that take?"

"Insufficient data," Bossy's screen said.

"What do you need to get the data?"

"Cessation of interference," Bossy said. "By verbal methods now used, a survey would take years, or never be accomplished. The past failure of psychosomatic therapy is not in theory but in technique. A human mind is too slow, reactions are too gross. The best the human can accomplish is a few obvious snarls."

"If left alone, how would you accomplish it?" Billings asked curiously.

"It is simple," Bossy said, "for me to use the principles of the electroencephalogram. I would run all combinations of my entire storage unit against the patient. Any disturbance to the alpharhythms would indicate the source of a tension in the patient—on the order of the lie-detector principle. All such tensions could be released by replacing fallacy with understanding."

"How long would that take?" Hoskins asked.

"Insufficient data," Bossy answered.

"It makes sense, though," Billings said. "We've always known that time was our greatest enemy; that even in months we could only uncover a few of the most obvious. Bossy can operate on a thousands per second review of her storage units."

"What would be the effect of the tension release?" Joe asked Bossy.

"When the repressors are removed from the cells," Bossy answered, "they can again function normally, restoring themselves."

"Which would mean that health is restored, obviously," Billings said.

"Any objections to Bossy taking over, gentlemen?"

"You're the doctor," Hoskins said.

And it was not until a week later, a week of constant watching, intravenous feeding, physical body care, while Mabel lay on the couch in an apparent coma, that they saw any change.

It was on the morning of the seventh day, after Hoskins had spent his vigil through the night sitting beside Mabel, that they saw how startling a change had occurred. It was as if accumulated releases were, all at once, showing their affect.

The puffiness was disappearing from her cheeks, the deep pouches under her eyes were less swollen, the roll of fat around her neck had shrunk. Slowly, like a face emerging from a sculptor's shapeless blob of clay, there was another Mabel—a younger Mabel.

It was more than a skin health and tautness, than the relaxation of rest, than the disappearance of wrinkles, than the reduction of swelling in the joints.

153

The three men stood looking down at her recumbent form on the couch. They stared at her with wide, incredulous eyes. Mabel was growing young again!

The faint hum of Bossy, working at top level speed, buzzed in their ears.

CHAPTER VIII

I t was not a miracle.

The regeneration and rejuvenation of Mabel was no more than the end result of completely applied psychosomatic therapy. Yet it was a result which a human therapist, unassisted by Bossy, could never attain. However he may strive for detachment from bias, no man can grow to maturity without at least something of a framework of prejudice; and the therapist, in removing the warping deformations of one matrix, unconsciously supplies another.

Further, thousands of hours or verbal therapy were reduced to seconds by Bossy. Never before had anyone known what a complete therapy could produce. And they did not know now. Dr. Billings, Professor Hoskins, Joe Carter, the three men stood looking down at Mabel who lay on the couch, the center of a network of conduits connecting her to Bossy, and marveled.

They did not understand the obvious reformation of Mabel's body. But they were witnessing it.

It was characteristic of Billings that even in the

moments of astonishment he remembered to check the gross aids of therapy. To his surprise, the last drops of the synthetic plasma, fed from the suspended tank to Mabel's veins, were running out of the container. He had put on a fresh bottle the night before, and at her low threshold of activity, it should have lasted for two more days.

Almost instantly, as the last drops ran down the transparent tube, Mabel's lips began to move.

"Hungry," she muttered. "Hungry, hungry, hungry, HUNGRY!"

Bossy's screen was flashing on and off in emergency signals.

"Cells cannot regenerate without food," the machine said, over and over. The statement of fact seemed, to the men, to carry a connotation of contemptuous impatience, as if these human beings should be expected to know at least that much.

Quickly Billings ran across the room, grabbed up one of the few remaining bottles of plasma, broke the seal on his way back, and replaced the empty bottle with the full one. As the liquid began to flow down the tube, Mabel's mutterings ceased, and she lay still and quiet again. Almost visibly, Joe, Dr. Billings and Professor Hoskins could see the changes in her appearance taking place, and wondered what mental changes could account for them.

Joe tried to follow, but the thought-patterns were so rapid and so varied it was like trying to pick up and follow one spoke in the blur of a speeding wheel.

"Hunger creates tensions to act as cell repressants, hindering therapy," Bossy volunteered a flash on her screen, as if to reproach them and warn them not to let it happen again. In the pattern of human beings generally, they had given her a job to do, and then followed a procedure to hamstring her and prevent her from doing it. As with human beings generally, they did not intend to thwart her, they merely let their lack of comprehension do it for them.

Perceptibly the level in the bottle was lowering. At this rate the supply, expected to last for another two days, would be gone in two hours. And they had only one more bottle in reserve.

Synthetic fortified plasma cannot be cooked up in the ordinary apartment kitchen, and none of them were sufficient biochemists to attempt it. The only alternative to halting the therapy, and none of them would consider that, was to obtain more plasma quickly, within the four hours their total supply would last. And even that time was a rough estimate, the consumption of the supply might be progressively accelerated.

They called Carney into their living room.

He had been hanging around the outskirts of the experiment for a week, since it had started; not admitted to the workroom, nor asking to be admitted since Mabel, herself, had told him to stay out. His sulks and belligerence had disappeared, replaced by anxiety. His anxiety was mitigated by confidence. He realized that inasmuch as Mabel had made the decision and had stuck to it, she could not be in better hands.

But their reports to him did create some doubts. They were all identical, and to him they were vague and unsatisfactory.

"Mabel is resting naturally and progressing normally."

He had not had much real experience with hospitals.

157

His concepts of what probably went on was drawn from motion picture script writers' efforts to knock themselves out with drama piled upon drama, one near-fatal crisis after another, ever trying with the same old tricks to excite a public long since immune to further emotional response. Yet, without it, something seemed lacking to Carney.

His reaction, when Joe told him that more plasma must be obtained at once, was one more nearly relief than alarm. This was more like it. As with the script writers, it did not occur to him that crisis piled upon crisis is usually a sign of inefficiency and bungling. It did not occur to him to ask the very normal question of why this need for further plasma had not been foreseen, or what change had occurred in Mabel to make their estimates fall short.

Actually, he was flooded with a sense of satisfaction. He would be of some use after all, Mabel's life depended upon him. He, Carney, was as important to her as these Brains.

He was cooperative. That is, he wanted to be.

"But I don't know where I could buy that stuff on short notice," he blurted. "I had plenty of warning on the last and put out the word I could use it. In a few days the word came back that it was ready. You got to be careful on things like that. It's different from tools and electrical stuff."

Billings, standing beside Joe, was visibly shaken.

"We simply have to get more," he insisted. "Our present supply will last less than four hours. Mabel can't be cured without it. It's dangerous to try."

Carney blanched. His fingers shook as he tried to light a cigarette.

158

"If I had more time," he muttered, "but four hours, and in broad daylight."

Joe glanced at his wristwatch.

"It's nine o'clock now. That means we must be back by noon, to give us margin. Where's the nearest big hospital?"

"There's an emergency just a couple of blocks over," Carney said.

"An emergency hospital wouldn't have enough," Joe said. "I want a place that would have a big supply."

"I don't know," Carney said hesitantly. "There's Memorial, I guess. Down off Protrero."

"I want a doctor's whites," Joe said crisply. "Where can I get them?"

"I can do that," Carney said with relief. "It'll take me five minutes." He turned and almost ran out of the room.

He was back in less than five minutes. The uniform was complete, even to a little black bag.

"The boys' fingers do stick to everything, don't they?" Joe smiled.

Carney grinned.

They were almost over to the interurban depot, where taxis were plentiful, before Carney asked any questions.

"What're you gonna do, Joe?" he asked between puffs of breath as they walked rapidly down the street.

"Steal it," Joe said tersely. "There are times when the ethics of esperance must be secondary."

Carney nodded, sagely, without any comprehension of the phrase.

"In broad daylight!" he gulped. He sighed and squared his thin shoulders. "But I'll try anything for Mabel," he added, slipping easily into the improbable valence of a movie plot.

When the cab pulled up in the broad circular driveway in front of the hospital, Joe paid the fare and gave the driver a tip.

"If you'll wait," Joe said, "we'll be going back in about ten minutes." His words were casual, but he beamed a sense of high drama into the driver's mind.

"I'll wait," the cabbie promised, as if he were taking an oath.

Joe took the steps, two at a time, with Carney panting behind him.

In the lobby, Joe smiled at the young nurse behind the information window, and beamed a strong field of reassurance at her.

"Where can I find the head nurse, please?" His eyes told her that, after having seen her, he was in no way interested in the old battle-axe of a head nurse.

The girl returned his smile, while she automatically evaluated him for age, possible marital status, financial prospects. She was already confident of his susceptibility. It was the normal and expected thought process. Joe tied himself into it, and pushed it farther by gently projecting the image of a young intern backed by wealthy parents.

The nurse's eyes sparkled, and she inhaled to give Joe a better appraisal of the merchandise.

"Do you mean our Day Supervisor?" she twinkled. "Shall I get her on the phone?" Her tones, and her thought-patterns, pleaded with him not to be in such a hurry to part company.

To the image of the wealthy young intern, unmarried, Joe fed the picture of a shining blue convertible, upholstered in red leather, and followed that with a picture of bowing head waiters in a dining room with soft lights.

"She's so busy this time of day," the nurse said doubtfully. "If I could help you—?"

"Well, I'm really heading for the Blood Bank," Joe said easily. "I'm borrowing a supply for St. Luke's—" The picture crystallized into a long evening of dancing at the Venetian Room at the Fairmont, so much less touristy than the Top of the Mark.

"Oh, that," the now utterly vivacious young woman trilled. "I'll be happy to show you the way, Dr.—?"

"Dr. Carter . . . soon, anyway . . . I hope," said Joe, with a wink.

The nurse turned to the non-uniformed girl at the typewriter behind her.

"I'll be right back, darling," she cooed. "If anyone asks where I am—"

"I know," the girl said with a bored tone. "You're powdering your nose." These nurses with their airs!

None of them paid any attention at all to Carney. Obviously, in the hierarchy of the hospital caste, a system which puts India's to shame, he was an Untouchable, lower, probably, than even an Orderly. As Joe and the nurse walked down the corridor, her heels clicking smartly, Joe knew that Carney, following behind, was staring at his back with an awe bordering on reverence.

During the course of the short trip to the second floor, rear, Joe dutifully went through the protocol of finding out the young nurse's name, hours on and off duty, the telephone number at the adjoining nurse's residence.

When they reached the Blood Storage Room, the nurse spoke crisply, and fraternally, to the intern in charge.

"This is Dr. Carter, from St. Luke's—"

The intern, obviously not backed by wealthy parents or a blue convertible, regarded Joe enviously.

"I wish I could make St. Luke's," he said. "How long have you got?"

"Two more months," replied Joe, with a sidelong glance at the nurse. "Sometime come over and get acquainted. Glad to introduce you around."

"Well, thanks! I'd sure like to!" The intern offered his hand. "Harry Vedder," he said, "Cal—"

"Harvard Medical," murmured Joe. The intern blinked with respect, and thawed even more. His guess had been right. This was one of those wealthy boys; probably been money in the family so long that he didn't even think about it; all this equality was the real thing, not an affectation. A real guy! The nurse was all but ready to take off and fly.

"A couple dozen botttles will be enough," Joe said, bringing their thoughts back down to his errand.

"Surgery ran short. Called your administrator. Guess you got the release. We're returning it in the morning."

His words were innocuous enough, but his face showed them what he thought of a hospital administration who could let surgery run short of a vital supply. The nurse and intern picked up the expression, and suppressed smiles. As with any subordinate under a hard taskmaster, they were delighted to see their bosses slip.

"No, the order didn't come through," the intern said.

Joe grinned knowingly. Everybody, all along the line, was slipping.

"Maybe you'd better call the front office and get confirmation," he said easily. He heard a subdued gasp behind him from Carney.

"Not me," the intern said instantly. "Maybe over at St. Luke's—but here at Memorial we don't remind our heads that they've slipped. Just take along what you need, and I'll check it out when the order does come through."

They all grinned then, the nurse turning hers into a charming, provocative smile.

In another two minutes, Carney was staggering down the corridor under the load of heavy cartons. To the astonishment of the intern and the nurse, Joe, himself, hoisted the last remaining box on his own shoulder. The astonishment gave way to satisfaction. This was a real guy, indeed, thoughtful enough not to make the old man take two trips, secure enough in his position that he didn't have to make a show of it.

With his free hand, Joe again shook hands with the intern. The nurse twinkled along beside him down the corridor, as if he were her special property. She escorted him to the front door, to save him the trouble of being stopped and questioned should any official notice the two men carrying out cartons of plasma.

"Don't forget," she whispered as she held open the heavy door for him.

Joe laughed, a laugh which promised a great deal.

The taxi driver came halfway up the steps and relieved Carney of part of the load. By the time he had driven ten blocks he had convinced himself this was a very important mission; and by the time he helped them unload their boxes in front of the emergency hospital, he was certain he had been an important part of high drama. When they refused his help in carrying the cartons into the emergency hospital, he knew beyond all doubt that secrecy on his part was of highest importance. He drove away, his long dormant scout's honor keeping him from even looking back through his rear-view mirror.

"Kid," Carney puffed, as they let themselves in through the door to their own basement quarters, "if you can stay out of jail, you'll con a million." He was filled with admiration, almost ready to forgive Joe for being a Brain.

Joe stopped the old man in their living room, unwilling to let him go on into the workroom, to see what was happening to Mabel.

"This will be enough to last us a couple of days, anyway," Joe said. "But you'd better send out the word for more plasma through your usual channels."

"Sure takes a lot," Carney answered curiously.

"Always does," Joe shrugged, as if it had all been perfectly normal. "Think you can get more?"

"Sure," Carney answered easily, "now that I've got time."

Carney went away satisfied, comfortable in his mind for the first time in more than week. He had something to do, he was important again.

* * *

164

Inside the workroom, Billings and Hoskins were still standing near Mabel, watching her. Somehow, probably in an absent-minded daze, Hoskins had brewed their morning coffee, and, equally absently, they were drinking it.

A quick probe of Billings' stream of rationalizing satisfied Joe that the first astonishment had lessened and was being replaced by a new evaluation of the tenets of psychosomatic therapy. Billings was trying to talk this out to Hoskins, to verbalize his thoughts into coherency.

"This is all quite understandable," he was saying slowly, carefully, "if we draw an analogy between the cell and a bullet shot from a gun. At first there is a given momentum of like force, strong enough to rise in an ordered projectory. The cells renew themselves with healthy vigor. Like the amoeba, barring accident, they are immortal—that is, they have the potential of immortality through continued self renewal."

"But air resistance, or the resistance of heavier materials, and the pull of gravity gradually overcomes the bullet, drags on its momentum, so that the bullet reaches a balance, then gradually sinks to earth, inert," Hoskins said.

"Exactly," Billings agreed, "as do the cells. They renew and multiply through the growth of the child to its maturity. But gradually the accumulation of mistakes, repressions, frustrations, disappointments, tensions of all kinds, overcome the momentum of the initial life force. The cells cannot keep up their renewal production as against all these depressants. They slow down, more and more, until finally some organ—or complex of organs—is too weakened to function. We call it disease, old age, death."

"Would gravity, itself, have any effect, doctor?" Joe asked, as he stepped up to them and poured himself some coffee. "It seems to me that the constant pull of gravity against the cells would tend to slow them down, just as it does the bullet. If cells have a form of memory, as you contend, then the memory of weariness would be passed from the old cell to the new one, and be added to in the experience of the new cell. The accrued memories of weariness, alone, might be sufficient to account for old age."

Billings looked up at him.

"It could be," he agreed.

"Let's ask Bossy," Hoskins said, instantly.

He flipped open the communications key, and Billings put the question.

"Is gravity a factor in cell renewal?" he asked.

"Yes," the machine answered instantly. "The most basic. All living cells, whatever the organism, accumulate such memory of weight as to destroy their potential for renewal."

"Did you eliminate such cellular memory in the patient?" Joe asked.

"Naturally," Bossy answered. "My instructions, regarding therapy, were to find all tensions of any nature and remove them."

Billings and Hoskins settled back in their chairs.

"And the result is that the organism is allowed to continue on at the rate of its peak," Billings said.

"Let's face it, doctor," Hoskins said harshly. "The result, in effect at least, is—immortality!"

"Well now," Billings said hesitantly. "New repressions, new weariness memories, new suppressants can accumulate—''

''And again be wiped out by treatment,'' Hoskins said, pounding his fist into the palm of the other hand. ''Immortality—it brings up some powerful ethical questions, doctor.''

''More than you know,'' Joe answered with a smile. ''You've both overlooked one thing. Mabel was willing. Who else would be?''

''Anybody! Everybody!'' Hoskins said at once. ''Everybody wants to be immortal.''

''Duh . . . I wanna be immortal!'' Joe parodied a famous comic, who parodies a vast portion of mankind. ''You haven't yet considered the price, Professor Hoskins.''

''I'm not sure I know what you mean, Joe,'' Billings asked curiously.

''The patient must be willing to be relieved of all tensions,'' Joe said.

''Yes,'' Billings agreed.

''A firm belief in anything acts as a tension, in that it disallows the opposite of that belief. The admission ticket to immortality is the willingness to divorce oneself from all frameworks of preconception and prejudice.''

''Would that be so difficult?'' Hoskins asked, with a challenge in his voice.

''I think so,'' Joe said quietly. ''I think, gentlemen, you will find that they'd rather be right—and die.''

CHAPTER IX

For two more days the three men watched the progress of Mabel. They hardly slept at all, and ate only in snatched mouthfuls. The fascination was beyond anything they had ever experienced.

It was like watching the minute hand of a small watch. No, it was more like the unfolding of some fabulous blossom. Staring intently, the eye could not quite catch any change from microsecond to microsecond. Yet if one looked away and looked back again, the development was apparent. And over the two-day period, the change was incredible.

There had been some alarm about her hair. It had come out in matted gray masses on the pad which supported her head; and for a while they feared she would be completely bald. Then a fine mist of hair began to show, and now her head was covered in a helmet of gold mahogany ringlets. Her face, smoothed to clean and classic form, took on the simplicity of a child, the serenity of a sage.

During the early stages of therapy, Hoskins had

attempted to keep her body covered with a sheet. Typical of man, he reasoned that this was a concession to Joe's youth and inexperience. Actually, he was obeying the compulsions of his own tensions. Billings had finally, and rather irritably, reminded him that theirs should be a clinical attitude. Joe, concealing his amusement, reminded him that when one, from earliest childhood, could see directly into the thought streams of others, clothes lost their utility as a modesty mechanism for individuals.

Hoskins, a little angry at himself for feeling foolish, dispensed with the sheet; and had resolutely maintained a clinical attitude.

Mabel lay in a position faintly suggestive of the foetal curl; or like a dancer of perfect body relaxed and fallen asleep on a casual couch. She breathed slowly and deeply, and only now and then showed a flicker of expression on her face as Bossy touched some deeply buried memory of pain, some formula of prejudice which had no basis in fact, and erased them.

It was still impossible for Joe to get through to her mind. For the first time in his life, he found himself blanked out of another's thoughts, emotions, motives. For the first time, he got a taste of what it must be like to have a normal mind.

He had always pitied others because they were psionically blind; now he marveled at them. How had man managed to live with man at all, unable to see one another truly? No wonder they fumbled awkwardly in their dealings, and made incredible mistakes of misunderstanding!

The human race was like a universe of material bodies, each with its own eccentric orbit, blindly crashing into one another, caroming off, senselessly changing direction as a consequence of random contact. The miracle was that even rudiments of order, on a few occasions of history, had somehow been achieved.

For the first time, he gained a little respect for cane tapping.

He had likened them to blind people, feeling their way along, tapping their canes ahead of them in total darkness. Their science was a tabulation of how many cane taps it took to get from here to there. Their lore was the measurement of exteriors. He had understood, abstractly, why it was they so often substituted measurement for meaning. But it had taken this inability to get through to Mabel to give him a real appreciation of their problem.

Suddenly Joe felt the need to get out and walk. The two days had left him feeling cramped and stifled. He was restless with his inability to get through to Mabel, his inability to find out if Bossy, in clearing away all the debris of prejudice screens, had opened a window through which she might see—psionically.

His question to Billings on whether there was anything he could do received a negative answer. His question to Bossy on whether any complications were anticipated drew an equal negative. Hoskins murmured that he, himself, was going to catch some sleep and would relieve Billings who watched at Mabel's side. Joe gladly escaped the confines of the room.

Outside, on the street, the dark and fog enveloped him as he headed away from Third and Howard toward Mark Street. It was a night for walking. And it was a

171

city which calls to stranger and old resident alike for exploration. Years may pass but one never becomes quite accustomed to the magic mystery of San Francisco at night.

And Joe was at that period of growth when a young man walks down the streets of a strange city in the darkness, looking at the absorbing activities of all the little people about him from a mile-high vantage. Escaped, at last, from encircling arms, from the protections of childhood, a youth grows tall, taller than the buildings, broader than the city, swifter than the wind in his face.

He is filled with an all encompassing love for mankind, with pity and compassion. Out of his sudden enormous strength he would do great things of purpose and import. He knows his debt for all the things civilization has given him, and he feels an overwhelming obligation to repay that debt. He must strive to lift man from his despair and purposelessness into realms of great achievement, enlightenment. Nothing less would be good enough for mankind.

And for Joe the purpose of Bossy was to give, at last, psionic sight to man. How else could man take the evolutionary step necessary to lift him from the blind circling rut which, time after time through ensuing civilizations, returned man to his starting point?

He had been sure that his own psionic ability could be put to such use. Along with a few others, he felt his obligation to use his total capacity for helping mankind.

He crossed Market Street, conscious of being confined by the traffic cop's angry whistle to their painted white lines, seeing in that the symbolism of cane tapping, and began to climb the hills of Powell Street.

He had held the theory that since psionic rudiments were more apparent in lower animals and in children than in human adults, if all the debris of false training could be cleared away the esperance might develop. He did not know. He had never been able to discuss it with anyone—feel it with anyone, share comprehensive speculation.

For communication implies shared comprehension. It was not only that they lacked vocabulary—they did not even know they lacked it. To a race of totally deaf would the musical instrument and the complex art of music develop? Even if they gained an abstract comprehension that there could be communication through tone modulation, what ridiculous developments would derive from their attempts to realize it! Logical and rational to them, perhaps, but ridiculous to one who could hear music.

Strangely enough, they had the beginning tools. Einstein had given them the coordinate system, where truth was relative to its own framework but need not apply outside. But instead of being able to use that tool intimately and familiarly in daily life, they relegated it to some theoretical abstraction of light speed and universe size. Instead of seeing meaning, they saw only measurement.

Their mathematics contained many valued calculi of symbolic logic, and, incredibly, they did not see how it could possibly apply to an understanding of one another, but rationalized it out of existence, useful only to some totally alien form of thought.

They were like two-dimensional creatures who had achieved the mathematical symbolism of height, but who, by the very nature of their limitations, could see no way it might apply to their own world reality, and, therefore, denied it except as a plaything of abstraction.

To one whose horizon was bounded by what he could touch with his outstretched cane, where was the vocabulary to give the picture of tumbling mountains piled back and back of one another, farther and farther away, blue and bluer to deep purple in the distance? If there were no organ to respond to light of any nature, how could one build up the concepts of modulation in color? Was it possible to communicate a symphony to a science which could only measure vibrations per second?

Yet, in Bossy, the cane tapping proved valuable. He could not have built Bossy himself. He did not have the training. He might have accomplished other things through his psionic sight, but he could not have communicated them, and they would, therefore, have been valueless.

To deal with the blind, Bossy had to be of the essence of the blind. To move a two-dimensional creature into a third dimension, there must be at least a two-dimensional entry. It is insufficient to scorn or rant at a two-dimensional creature because he cannot understand the concept of "pinnacle." If his entire world—and all he values—is two-dimensional, what would be the value of a pinnacle to him, even if he could conceive it?

In a nonpsi world he may speculate on the abstraction of the psi, but would he be willing to throw aside

174

his cane tapping to gain it? Wouldn't he regard all talk about it from the two-dimensional point of view, his scorn for the nonsense of height being his greatest handicap in reaching it?

Bossy contained the two-dimensional entry. Bossy contained the most enticing of all baits—immortality!

Was the exit three-dimensional? He did not know.

What would a mind be like, governed solely by rational relationships of facts, free from all the debris of precedent, undeformed by pain, punishment, grief, repression—

Suddenly Joe stopped in his tracks, appalled!

What a terrible oversight!

Man does not live by logic. He does not live according to the patterns of fact applied to fact. He does not live according to rationality, not even according to reason.

He turned and started running swiftly down the hill. Frantically, he sent his probe ahead of him into the basement room, but he could sense nothing of its contents. Billings had fallen asleep in his chair, and in his mind there was only the residue of random impression that everything was all right. Naturally, or he wouldn't have fallen asleep!

What a terrible oversight! Bossy had been filled only with proved fact. Any conclusions drawn were carefully labeled as suspect, to be considered only as possibilities. All prejudice, assumption, fallacy had been carefully screened out by checking and double checking of the finest minds in the country over the past two years of her building back at Hoxworth.

And everything had been fitted into the framework

of material for a machine's thinking. In submitting Mabel to the machine, they had overlooked the fact that a machine's approach might not necessarily be the wisest for a human. A previous sentence flashed on Bossy's screen returned to Joe's memory.

"My instruction, regarding therapy, were to find all tensions of any nature, and remove them."

That was what Bossy had done.

Joe groaned aloud at their stupidity in giving such an order. He was passing St. Francis Hotel now, and had to slow his speed to keep from attracting attention. There were taxis, of course, but a taxi pulling into skid row at this time of night would surely attract too much attention. One does not take taxis to get to a two-bit flophouse.

And it was only a few more blocks. As usual, the slum and the palace were closely adjacent, the one seeming to require the other.

Again and again he sent his thoughts ahead, trying to wake the sleeping Billings through the urgency of his thought. But the old man's weariness and two days of sleeplessness defeated him. He tried again to contact Mabel's mind and found it no more responsive than Bossy.

That was it, of course! Mabel's mind, at this stage, was reacting in the valence of a machine.

At Mission and New Montgomery, he turned south toward skid row. Ahead of him there was the stir of unusual activity. Although it was near two in the morning, there was a crowd of people gathered in a spot of light which streamed out from the open doors of a saloon. A squad car was parked nearby, but the two policmen standing beside it made no move to interfere in the excitement. This, in itself, was strange, for only the toughest were assigned to the skidrow beats, and they did enjoy using their clubs whether called for or not.

Cautiously, Joe stepped into the shadow of an alleyway, and sent an exploratory wave field ahead. At first there seemed to be little pattern in the jumble of impressions and stirred emotions. Then bit by bit, principally from the thoughts of a pair of young sailors, supplemented by the knowledge of the officers, Joe put the elements of the story together.

The wagon had just carted off a woman to the City Jail. That, in itself, would have caused no more than passing interest on the shortline. But the woman had been very young. She had been beautiful. Even allowing for normal exaggeration in the sailors' minds, she was the most beautiful thing they had ever seen.

And she had been stark naked.

She had come strolling off Howard Street. The sailors had just been coming out of the door, and the streaming light had caught her like a spotlight on a dark stage. They had been too stunned even to whistle. A cruising squad car, coming by at that moment, had almost crashed into a fire hydrant before it skidded to an astonished stop.

One of the officers had thrown his own coat about her while they stood waiting for the wagon. She hadn't spoken a word. She just stood there, looking from face to face, and smiling her strange, sweet smile.

The wagon appeared shortly, and whisked her away. It was all routine. Yet the two officers did not climb back into their car. They stood there, watching the crowd, apparently waiting for it to disperse or grow unruly. But their expressions were far away. It was not the nudeness, as such, which remained in their minds. It was as if they, too, were still stunned at having seen, all at once, too much beauty.

Even as Joe ran down the alley toward their basement quarters, he knew, with near certainty, it had been Mabel.

At the foot of the stairwell, leading down from the street level, the outer door was open and swinging. He snapped its lock behind him, and ran through their living quarters into the workroom. Mabel's couch was empty. Billings still sat in his chair beside the bed, his head slumped forward in sound sleep.

Bossy was lighted, but silent. Her screen showed two words.

"Problem solved."

CHAPTER X

Dr. Eustace Fairfax, Consulting Psychiatrist to the San Francisco Police Department, gazed down his thin nose and transfixed the lieutenant with a glare, heightened by polished glasses, in which anger and incredulity were fiercely blended.

"Do you mean to say," he demanded, "that I have been called at this fantastic hour of the night to examine a . . . a . . . a routine case for the psycho ward?"

"But this isn't a routine case," the harried lieutenant insisted. His own disbelief made him weak in his protestations.

"Bah!" Dr. Fairfax tossed the police blotter across the desk. "I have never seen a more routine report: '. . . Nude young woman arrested, corner of Howard and New Montgomery—' And you wake me up at three o'clock in the morning! The commissioner will hear of this!"

"Wait, sir," pleaded the lieutenant. "You don't understand—" It was an unfortunate choice of words, for one does not tell a consulting psychiatrist that he does not understand.

Dr. Fairfax, who had turned away and was starting out the door, whirled around.

"And what is it I am incapable of understanding?" he asked, his words as brittle as flake ice.

"This young woman isn't really young," the lieutenant began hesitantly. Then, overcoming his own doubts, he rushed on. "You see, according to the fingerprint records, this woman, Mabel Monohan, is actually sixty-eight years old!"

"Then why in heaven's name do you book her as a young woman?" the psychiatrist asked in extreme exasperation.

"Well, the fact is . . . the Booking Officer thought . . . we all swear she wasn't a day over twenty-one!"

"Then you've made a mistake, that's all."

"No sir, we didn't make a mistake. The fingerprints checked in every particular, not just one print but all of them. We wired the prints to the FBI in Washington. They check there, too."

"Then the mistake was made when the prints were taken before."

The lieutenant began to get a little heated now. The efficiency of his department was being questioned.

"Mabel Monohan," he said firmly, "has been in and out of this jail for the last fifty years. She has been printed countless times. We called in some of the old-timers. They swear this girl looks like the Mabel they knew forty years ago, ah . . . from seeing her in jail, of course."

"That does it! I'll call the commissioner the first thing in the morning. You may need the professional

180

services of a psychiatrist around here, but not to examine the prisoners!"

Dr. Fairfax's ordinarily nasal voice had risen to a high whine under the stress of extreme anger. He was often angry at people because they contrarily refused to fit in nicely with his theories. And, of course, it was the people who were wrong. The theories had been advanced by the most Eminent Authorities, and proved by carefully selected case histories. His one satisfaction in life was that so many of the laws he had advocated to make people conform to these theories had been passed—despite strong opposition.

Apparently more laws were needed. He jammed his hat on his head and stalked toward the door. The lieutenant hurried around the desk and caught him by the arm. And was shaken off.

"Please, doctor," the lieutenant begged, desperation bringing sudden firmness to his voice. "I think it is necessary you examine this woman tonight. I couldn't reach the commissioner, he's been on a three-day . . . he's unavailable, but when he learns the facts I'm sure he'll agree."

Apparently it broke through the psychiatrist's indignation.

"All right," he agreed, as if he were following rule three and humoring a psychotic patient. "Inasmuch as I'm here, I might as well examine her. But it's a clear case of fraud, or incompetence. I don't need to see the prisoner to determine that!"

He began to get a certain glow of anticipation. Apparently the girl was cleverly pulling some new stunt, and it would be his pleasure to expose her. Laymen simply didn't understand these things; but it was always possible to rationalize symbolisms until one found them fitting into theory. He grew almost pleasant in satisfaction at being a master of intricate reasoning which none but a trained psychiatrist could grasp.

He followed the lieutenant back to the desk. He pursed his lips and hm-m-m'd many times, implying that all of this was no mystery to him. He studied the photographs taken forty to fifty years ago, clucked over the poor photography, triumphantly pointed out the differences among the photographs, asked how they could be used to compare with the girl when they were not even identical among themselves, expressed his doubts of the whole science of fingerprinting, and thoroughly enjoyed setting the whole stage to prove his theory of fraud. Faithfully he followed the pattern of the scientist determined to interpret the facts to suit the theory.

"Bring her in, lieutenant," he said, when he was quite satisfied that he had encompassed everything in the thick dossier of Mabel Monohan. He settled himself into the lieutenant's swivel chair.

"In here, doctor?" the lieutenant wavered. "Wouldn't you prefer to use the office of the regular psychiatrist, where they've got all the hocus-pocus—" He stopped, aghast at his slip.

"I shall not need the usual equipment for testing, which you term . . . ah . . . hocus-pocus," Dr. Fairfax said with asperity, and chalked it up in his memory for delayed retaliation. "This is a simple case of fraud, and I can handle it right here. Bring her in, and then you leave her alone with me. I am sure she will soon recognize my ability to see through her little game."

182

* * *

His first sight of Mabel confirmed his belief in fraud. There was simply no art of make-up which could turn an old woman into a young girl, whatever the female gender may wish to believe. This girl had no make-up on at all. And the bright glare of the overhead light showed that she was barely twenty-one. The rough prisoner clothes she wore did not fully conceal her youthful form.

Dr. Fairfax dismissed the lieutenant and the matron with a curt nod.

"Sit down," he said coldly to Mabel, and nodded toward a chair. He smiled with faint scorn as he watched her touch the chair on its arm and back, and then seat herself.

"I am sure you know what a chair is," he said coldly.

She looked at him with a little puzzlement in her fathomless blue eyes.

"Chair:" she said, "Noun. English language. Movable seat with four legs and back, for one person, used by humans."

"So that's the way it is to be," he say cryptically. "What is your name?"

"Mabel," she answered.

"Address?"

She gave the address of her apartment off Howard Street. It checked with the dossier.

"How many times have you been arrested, Mabel?"

"Thirty-two," she answered instantly.

He blinked. This was a little out of pattern. She could easily get detailed information about the life of the old woman from other sources, but even the old woman would not remember so precisely how many times she had been arrested; not when there had been so many over such a long period of time.

"How do you know that?" he shot the question at her abruptly, expecting to see the first signs of confusion when she realized she had gone too far; that she shouldn't have known it so accurately or instantly.

"It is a fact," she said, without any confusion whatever.

Well, whatever her little game, she was a cool one. This might prove interesting.

"And I suppose you know all the facts," he said, emphasizing his sarcasm.

"About myself, yes," she answered. "But I know only facts which have a relationship to me. I do not know all facts. Bossy says all facts are not yet known."

He blinked again. Somehow the name Bossy seemed familiar, but he could not place it. He seldom read the news, or followed any of the activities of run-of-the-mill people. Since they contrarily refused to fit theory, it was less bothersome simply to ignore them. Then the concept of Bossy clarified.

Of course! It was a childish name for a cow! He marveled at his acumen, and stored it away. It would come in handy to trip her; revealed a farm background, which she couldn't suspect him of knowing. Oh these silly people who thought they could fool a psychiatrist!

He would get her to talking. She would make further slips, and then when he pointed them out to her, she would realize she was no match for him. The confession would be easy.

"What is this all about, Mabel?" he asked with deceptive gentleness.

"I'm not sure," she said. "I have assumed it was a dream. Bossy says the dream state in humans is likely to be no more than a random excitation of synaptic patterns creating an irrational sequence of visualization. All this is certainly irrational."

He felt slightly uneasy, and not only because it violated the subconscious symbolism theories of Freud, which only a psychologist could interpret—at fifty dollars a seance. This sort of thing must be scotched immediately.

"And a cow told you all that?" he asked bitingly.

"It must be a dream," she responded. "Or the alternative is that you are insane. Your question is completely irrational. Cows do not speak a language intelligible to humans."

He grasped desperately at rule five: Never allow the patient to guess you are not completely master of the situation. He decided to use technique B: Switching the frontal attack.

"Why did you appear on the street without any clothes?"

"My therapy was completed. I wished to evaluate my environment. I did not realize it was cold enough for my body to need additional protection beyond that furnished by my skin."

He gulped, and stared at her intently. She was mad. Stark raving mad.

"Are you sixty-eight years old?" he asked scornfully.

"I have no age now," she answered simply.

"Answer my question," he commanded sternly.

185

"I did."

"Your answer has no meaning. You are either sixty-eight or you are not."

"That is Aristotelian logic," she said relectively. "Bossy says humans can never understand themselves through Aristo—"

"Bossy says! Bossy says!" He all but screamed the words at her in exasperation. "Look here, young woman—"

". . . Telian logic," she continued. "Reasoning along that line is comparable to Zeno's proof that motion does not exist. This is a most interesting dream in that your thought-processes are consistent with those currently in vogue in the cult of psychiatry. By any chance, do you imagine yourself to be a psychiatrist? Bossy says—"

Dr. Fairfax thrust himself to his feet, and almost ran to the door.

"Take her away," he told the waiting matron harshly. "Lock her up alone for the night. I will have to see her again when she is less disturbed. And she's dangerous. She's very dangerous!"

The old matron looked at him with veiled contempt. For thirty years she'd been handling her girls. She knew a sweet, innocent, young thing when she saw it. They were saying this was old Mabel. Well, they were all nuts—including the psychiatrist.

"It's all right, dearie," she said soothingly, and put her arm around Mabel's waist to lead her away. Dangerous, indeed! "It's all right, baby. You can depend on old Clarkie."

186

"I know," Mabel said. "You always were a good scout. Twenty-two years ago, the last time I was here, you got my attorney for me. There was a reform ticket in office, and they were holding me incommunicado."

The matron drew back from her, turned pale, tottered, and clung to the wall.

"Nobody ever knew it was me," she gasped. "I'd of lost my job. Nobody knew except Mabel, herself. And Mabel wouldn't have told nobody—not nobody!"

"I told you she was disturbed, dangerously disturbed!" the psychiatrist snapped. "Now take her away!"

Tentatively at first, then comfortingly, the matron took Mabel's arm and guided her down the hall.

"But you can't be Mabel," the matron was saying. "You just can't be. Even then, Mabel was getting old and fat. Tell me," she said desperately, "tell old Clarkie, dearie. How did you do it—Mabel?"

The lieutenant came back into the hall from another office, and saw the psychiatrist leaning against the door jamb.

"What do you think, Dr. Fairfax?" he asked brightly.

The doctor straightened himself, drew himself up, and looked down his nose professionally.

"A clear case of . . . a clear case of—" He was unable to find, in the pat little repertoire of psychotic patterns, a name which precisely fitted this kind. He would have to rationalize it out through symbolisms until it neatly fitted something or another before he expressed his diagnosis. He must be sure to use the established and orthodox patterns of symbolism manipulation so that other qualified psychiatrists would confirm him—if it came to that.

"A layman wouldn't understand," he finished, loftily.

CHAPTER XI

The long corridor leading to the courtroom was packed with jostling, noisy people, mostly women. This was not a trial. It was only a hearing for the purpose of setting Mabel's bail. But old Clarkie had talked again, and this time to reporters.

The papers hadn't had much time to work on it before the deadline of morning editions, but they'd done their best. And the results were quite satisfactory. Most of the articles about this old woman, who had turned into a young girl, were written with tongue-in-cheek, for, as frequently occurs with reason, the editors did not believe the stories turned in by their reporters.

But the public believed. The public wants miracles. The public demands miracles; and if one source ceases to provide them, they will turn to another source which seems to accomplish the spectacular. Even while they resented and opposed the scientific attitude, they lapped up the miracles which this attitude accomplished with glee.

The Fountain of Youth, long denied consciously, was still the great secret dream. They believed it because they wanted to believe it. They wanted to see this young and beautiful girl who, up until her disappearance ten days ago, had been a fat old woman. That hers had been an unsavory reputation somehow added to the credibility.

"If an old thing like that can do it, then I, much more worthy, can also do it," was the tenor of the refrain in every woman's mind.

Joe Carter slowly edged his way along one wall toward the high double doors of the courtroom. He gasped as a stout woman dug her elbow into his stomach, and then forgot about the elbow when a spiked heel ground down on his foot.

The jam grew tighter as he neared the door, and further progress seemed impossible. A perspiring bailiff stood against the door, and stared unhappily at the surging crowd.

"No more room inside, ladies," he kept insisting. "You might as well turn around and go home."

Groans, catcalls and derisive laughter answered his words. This was a mere male, and they knew and exercised their power to give him a bad time.

"I can't go home like this," one woman yelled. "My old man wants me to look like eighteen again tonight!"

"Eighteen!" another woman shrieked. "I'll settle for thirty-five!"

"Let us see her!" another yelled. "It won't cost you anything to just let us see her."

"It ain't fair," screamed another.

In desperation, Joe singled out one of the loudest of

the women and fed the idea into her mind that the hearing had been postponed until two o'clock.

"Why you—" the woman suddenly yelled at the bailiff. "You know that hearing's been put off, and you just let us stand here!"

"Put off?" someone else shrilled. "They've put off the hearing?"

"Of course they have!" the first woman yelled again. "The politicians want to hog everything for themselves. Come on, let's go to the mayor's office. Let's see about them holding out on us taxpayers!"

The hallways began to clear as the word spread. The tightly packed knot of people around the bailiff began to loosen, untangle itself. Joe squeezed through the first break and stepped up to the bewildered bailiff.

"Good work," Joe whispered his congratulations. "It could have been a riot if you hadn't acted just in time. I'll not forget to mention it!"

The bailiff, without realizing quite why, opened the door just wide enough for Joe to slip inside. Several of the women saw it, but the massive doors closed off their rising clamor.

The courtroom was relatively quiet. A bitter legal wrangle was going on in front of the bench; but Joe ignored it for the moment while he searched for Mabel. He missed her as he swept the fenced-off arena in front of the judge's box the first time. Then he spotted her at the counsel table where she was almost hidden by a massive gray-haired man who stood behind her chair and was holding up his hand to catch the judge's eye.

"Your honor," he intoned, as the judge looked his way, "to my colleague's objections I would like to

191

add the further objection of complete irrelevancy. Appearing unclad on the public street is a simple misdemeanor. Our client has been charged with nothing else. The city attorney has failed to cite a single statute which would deny our client right of bail. Indeed, it has been a deplorable miscarriage of justice that she was detained overnight!''

The city attorney dabbed at his flushed face with a wadded handkerchief. It was true she had been charged with nothing else. A bad oversight, considering all the things they had to choose from, and somebody would pay for it. But then, nobody had expected the most important legal firm in San Francisco to appear suddenly in Mabel's behalf.

"The distinguished defense counsel misrepresents the obvious meaning of my words," he protested uneasily. "I would not deny the defendant bail. I ask only, in the public interest, that she be detained in the psychiatric ward pending further investigation. I respectfully request the Court to appoint two independent psychiatrists, acceptable to the defense counsel as well as to my office, to determine the fitness of the crimin . . . prisoner.''

The judge looked appraisingly from one speaker to the other, then lowered his eyes and scribbled small doodles on the pad of yellow paper in front of him.

Joe knew he was thinking of forthcoming judicial elections. Usually it paid off to play along with the machine because the general public didn't know one judge from another and marked the handiest spot on the ballot. But this case was different. How he acted could really help or hurt his chances in the election.

In either event he could only adhere to the letter of

the law; but then for every yea in the law there was a nay, and it always boiled down to simple expediency. Like a psychiatric diagnosis, it could always be juggled around to fit anything you chose. He'd better play it cautiously. He looked again toward the city attorney.

"Have you any grounds for questioning this young . . . this woman's sanity?"

"There was prima-facie evidence that she was completely unclad when arrested on a public thoroughfare—"

"Incompetent, irrelevant and immaterial," snapped defense counsel instantly. "Nudity is not prima-facie evidence of insanity. If this case should go to trial, we will prove beyond all doubt that our client was merely sleepwalking."

"That I would like to see," the city attorney mumbled under his breath. Then aloud, he persisted, "In the second place, a Consulting Psychiatrist has already conducted a preliminary examination of the defendant. We would like to call him to the stand at this time."

The judge nodded. He must be fair to both sides, allow no criticism to come his way from a higher court.

"You may proceed."

While the psychiatrist was being sworn, and establishing his credentials, Joe tried to reach out and make psionic contact with Mabel. He failed in a most baffling way. He seemed to touch the periphery of her mind and then to lose himself in the characteristic pattern of a dream. Did she think she was still dreaming? Her detachment, her lack of interest, her negative somatic reaction to the whole procedure baffled him. For the true dream state was anything but lacking in somatics. In the conscious state the human mind is seldom capable of reaching the heights of true horror often found in a dream. He came back to the witness who had been speaking.

"You say you tried to examine the defendant," prompted the city attorney. "You used the word 'tried' advisedly?"

"Certainly," snapped the psychiatrist. It was unthinkable that he should use any word without self-advisement. "I say 'tried,' because the patient was too disturbed to be cooperative."

"Would you say she exhibited the characteristics of a rational person?"

"I would not!"

"Did you question her about her age?"

"I did. She said she had no age."

"Did you ask her why she appeared on the street nude?"

"I did. She answered that she did not know it was cold." His expression showed plainly that a belief that clothes were necessary simply to keep out the cold was all the evidence they needed to establish her insanity.

Apparently the city attorney thought so, too. He nodded significantly toward the judge and relinquished his place at the stand. The defense counsel approached the psychiatrist in the manner of an experienced big-game hunter who is called upon to shoot a rabbit. He put one foot on the step in front of the witness stand, carefully drew up his trouser cuff, and leaned toward the psychiatrist in a conversational manner.

"Do you believe that the defendant has somehow been able to recover her lost youth?"

The psychiatrist flushed angrily. He wondered if it

would be possible to suggest a law which would not permit defense counsels to question the judgment of a psychiatrist.

"No, I do not believe it," he snapped.

"Do you then discount the evidence of the fingerprints? The photographs? The testimony of numerous people who identify her?"

"I am convinced all of this is a hoax!"

"And is, therefore, something which no rational person could believe?"

"Such a claim to rejuvenation is beyond the credibility of a rational man."

"Then if the city attorney and the Court were to place some credence in the defendant's regeneration, you would hold they are not rational men?"

A titter swept the courtroom. Several women clapped loudly. The psychiatrist felt called upon to defend his profession.

"I have not been called upon to examine the city attorney and the Court—"

The implication was not lost upon the judge that this witness assumed the possibility that everyone was insane except himself. The defense counsel preferred to leave it there before the impression could be corrected.

"One more question, then," he said hurriedly. "Do you believe a woman's reluctance to tell her age is a sign of insanity?"

The courtroom roared with applause and laughter. The psychiatrist's cheek twitched under the indignity of a layman's doubt, but he said nothing. The judge, sensing at last the way the public would respond, permitted himself a small, judicial smile. Joe attuned him-

195

self to the judge's relief, mellowed and broadened his mood, fused a warm and noble valence into the judge's concept of himself.

. . . The wisdom of a Solomon . . . utterly fair and incorruptible . . . stalwart and courageous defender of human rights against the oppression of a growing police state . . . kind and compassionate—

His head came up as if he were posing for a photograph.

The defense counsel turned impressively toward the bench.

"Your honor, I trust the Court, in its vast wisdom, agrees with us that this defendant should not be subjected to further indignities. She has clearly undergone a harrowing experience. She needs a period of rest. In good time, medical science will be able to develop the facts about her case, which could be of great benefit to humanity. All of us should cooperate to that larger cause. In the glorious pages of history, we must not be found wanting!"

The judge was regretful that he had barred news photographers from the courtroom. Really, this moment should be caught and recorded for the pages of history.

"Meanwhile," continued the defense counsel, "I withdraw our request that the defendant be released on bail."

The judge, the city attorney, the psychiatrist looked at him in surprise. The courtroom held its breath.

"Instead I do petition the court to dismiss the misdemeanor charge against her entirely!"

The courtroom exploded from silence into thunderous applause. Joe did not need to intensify it with broadcasted waves of mass psychology feedback. The counsel knew his rabble-rousing, well.

The judge tapped his gavel and crinkled the character lines around his eyes with kind and mild reproof. He held up his hand for silence, and the crowd leaned forward in anticipation. He dismissed the charges. He arose in statuesque dignity and retired to his chambers amid the roar of approval.

With a courtly gesture, the defense attorney took Mabel by the arm and hurried her out of the room, refusing to pose outside for the newspaper and television cameraman. But reporters did stop them, momentarily, on the front steps. They answered one, and only one, of the barrage of questions.

"Who does your firm actually represent in this case?"

The lawyer smiled a bland, courteous smile.

"Why, the defendant, of course," he answered.

But behind the smile was the name Joe had been seeking—the name of Howard Kennedy, the multimillionaire industrialist who had given the newspaper that surprising interview in defense of Bossy.

CHAPTER XII

Kennedy Enterprises, Inc., occupied all fourteen floors of the modernistic Tower Building in the center of the financial district. This was the home office, the center of an organization vaster in wealth and power than many nations. The government of this organization often was the government of many nations.

As Joe stood in the lobby, and scanned the building directory, he realized for the first time the scope of these enterprises. In the long list of Kennedy Corporations in the directory board, there seemed to be provision for almost every human activity.

Of course, like everyone else, he had always associated Howard Kennedy with vast and sometimes speculative industrial operations. Now, alphabetically listed, he saw corporations covering everything from mines to trinket sales. There were other corporations, too, from research foundations to philanthropy. One could only guess at the research, and the personnel, back of these enterprises.

Obviously, Howard Kennedy was one who had not been oppressed by opinion control. As sometimes happens in a tradition-bound and expiring civilization, here was a man who seemed to have stepped directly out of a past era, the era of bold pioneers who were unafraid to explore; who had not sold the birthright of man's rise to the stars for a mess of security.

Somehow he had not been crushed, in spite of the many attempts. Joe did not know too many details; his own interests had been far removed from the industrial world; but he did recall the many congressional investigations when some farmer boy congressman decided this would be a way to get his name in headlines; the underground rumblings of lawsuits among industrial titans; the charges of trusts and cartels flaring into headlines one day and not even followed up in the back pages on the next.

No one had been able to get Howard Kennedy, bring him to heel, make him conform to the all pervading grayness of mediocrity. He was a giant in stature and as yet they had not been able to bind him to the dirt with thousands of tiny ropes.

This was the man who, a few days previously, had dared to come out in favor of Bossy in an editorial.

And this was the man whose attorneys had somehow learned with extraordinary speed about Mabel; had stepped in and taken over her case even before Joe and Carney had been able to get Mabel's own attorney out of bed.

This was the man who now held Mabel, somewhere, like the high trump card in a game. Obviously, the editorial had been a bid to Billings and Hoskins:

"Come, let us negotiate, I am interested and will be fair."

Now, characteristic of his operations, Kennedy held the high trump, and could afford to wait in the certain knowledge that they would have to come. In some way, he had connected the phenomenon of Mabel's rejuvenation with Bossy.

The negro starter, who controlled the battery of elevators and winking red lights, had been watching Joe indulgently, taking him for just another job applicant. He approached now and spoke with florid but sincere courtesy.

"May I help you, sir?" From the moment of application, Kennedy's men were treated as something very special, set apart from the common herd of man, and thereby from the first day developed a fierce and singleminded loyalty.

"Which is Mr. Kennedy's personal office?" Joe asked.

The starter's eyes blinked twice. Then he smiled indulgently. This was a green one, indeed, to think he had to see the big boss himself just to get a clerk's job somewhere.

"You sure you don't want the personnel department, sir?" he asked.

"I want to see Mr. Kennedy, personally," Joe said with a smile, "and not about a job."

Without further hesitation, the starter walked him over to a closed elevator, and punched a signal. The doors opened immediately.

The Eighth Floor Receptionist was not so indulgent. Jim, the starter, was too easily impressed. He let every

Tom, Dick, and Harry come to the executive offices. She regarded Joe with the politely hostile stare which receptionists everywhere have perfected for the caller without appointment.

"Mr. Kennedy?" she asked incredulously. "Which Mr. Kennedy?"

"Mr. Howard Kennedy."

"But which Mr. Howard Kennedy?"

The girl's voice betrayed just a hint of the triumph it always gave her to spring this befuddling question on the uninitiated.

Joe could not resist the temptation to send a sudden, horrifying shaft of doubt into the neat complacency of her mind. Suddenly, without knowing why, she realized this young man was a Very Important Person. And she had been dangling him like a fish on a line. And just the other day, when she had thought a certain king was just a salesman who had got past the starter—

She began a hurried tactical withdrawal from her position.

"You mean Mr. Howard Kennedy, II?" she asked helpfully. "You're a personal friend? A fraternity brother? Someone—"

"Of course not," Joe said coldly. "I'm afraid Junior couldn't help."

"I'll get Mr. Kennedy's secretary," the girl gasped. She forgot the intercom on her desk. She forgot the page boy standing close by, waiting to run errands. She all but ran down one of the halls which branched off the reception room.

In less than a minute she was back. An older woman accompanied her; a serene and unhurried woman with streaks of silver in her beautifully coiffured hair. She appraised Joe calmly, and Joe knew she had instantly catalogued him as a total stranger. And probably he was not a king.

"I had to see the young man who could make Betty forget the years of training she's had," she said to Joe with a smile.

The receptionist, a step behind her, blushed furiously.

"But Mrs. Williams—" she faltered.

"It's all right, Betty," the secretary assured her. "In such an emergency—"

She turned to Joe.

"Now, young man, I understand you wish to see Mr. Kennedy, Senior, at once, and without an appointment. That is a virtual impossibility. Surely you must realize—"

She, too, faltered to a stop when Joe, instead of apologizing for brashness, picked up a pad from the receptionist's desk, tore off a sheet, and wrote on it one word: Bossy. He handed the sheet to the secretary.

"Here is my ticket to the holy of holies," Joe said with a smile.

She took the note, coldly to show her displeasure at his quip, and prepared to be disdainful.

"Bossy," she repeated slowly.

"Bossy—" She did not even blink.

"Please be seated," she said gravely. "I'm sure Mr. Kennedy will want to break off his conference. He has been expecting . . . someone—"

Howard Kennedy's office was the largest and brightest Joe had ever seen. One entire wall was in glass, and it looked out across the city toward the rising arc of the Bay Bridge, which was now a ghostly shadow in the morning fog which hung over the water.

Mrs. Williams seated Joe in front of the great desk.

"Mr. Kennedy is on his way from the conference room," she said. She left him alone, and closed the door firmly behind her.

The huge desk, where Joe sat, was symbolic of the man. The entire top was a slab of glareless glass almost three inches thick. A simple pen set and a pad of ruled yellow note paper were the only items on the desk. There was not even a telephone.

The thick rug and the three walls blended with the glass wall in a harmony of soft blue. There were no pictures or decorations on the wall of any kind. There were no trophies, no photographs of the occupant in football uniform, none of the symbols through which the average executive expressed his determination not to mature beyond the age of sophomore.

Joe heard a door open softly behind him, but he did not turn around. He knew Kennedy had come in, and was studying him. And this was no time for ethics. Joe penetrated, unobtrusively. The mind he encountered reminded him of hammered steel. It was a mind of unmeasured strength, an orderly mind thoroughly under control. And it was the mind of a man who had lived for a long time.

He heard footsteps brush by his chair, and then he saw Howard Kennedy move with an incredibly light, sure step around the end of the desk. Even without precognition, Joe would have recognized the tall, spare figure, the jutting hawk nose, the craggy chin, the totally bald head.

Kennedy's glance took Joe apart and snapped him

back together again. His conclusions were not bad—for a psiblind.

"You're the student," Kennedy said in a soft, dry voice. "Carter, isn't it? Joe Carter?"

Joe nodded.

Kennedy smiled, a little wryly, a little disappointedly.

"I had thought it would be Dr. Hoskins, or even Dr. Billings," he said frankly. "I'm sorry they didn't trust me enough to come."

"I came," Joe said without any inflection.

Kennedy put both elbows on the desk and leaned across it toward Joe.

"Look here, young man," he said with an disarming smile, "are you sure you know what you're mixed up in? Oh, don't misunderstand me," he smiled again. "I know that students sometimes get very loyal to their teachers, and that's a good thing, but there's such a thing as carrying it too far, being made a cat's-paw."

It was a good speech, well calculated to undermine him with doubt. It might have succeeded if it had not been so far from the mark. His smile was the tolerant, and a little regretful, one of the man with fifty years of empire building behind him toward the student who has read a half dozen books and now feels himself fully equipped to compete. His mind was a reflection of his face. If there were a trace of guile there, then it was of such long practice that it had become part of him.

I think, sir," Joe said respectfully, "we should not start out by misunderstanding where we stand, or who is in the arena."

Kennedy's eyes opened a little wider.

"Hm-m-m," he said, and leaned back in his chair. "It appears all of us misinterpreted the situation. We have assumed, all along, you were a dupe. Actually you were indicted only because it was hoped that you could give us information if you were apprehended first. Mr. Carter, I apologize. None of us have paid much attention to you."

"That is not like you, or your organization," Joe said easily.

"Why haven't you come before? No doubt you read my interview about Bossy?"

"Yes, sir. We did. Professor Hoskins wanted to come then, and Dr. Billings would have agreed. But I convinced them we were not ready. We had a . . . a certain test to make."

"And you have made it?"

"You know we have, Mr. Kennedy. You have Mabel."

Kennedy nodded in appreciation.

"That's out of the way then," he said. "I'll not waste time with denying it, or asking for particulars on how you did find out. I like to get right to the point. As you say, I have Mabel—and you have Bossy."

"Why do you want Bossy, Mr. Kennedy?"

Joe was delighted with the speed at which Kennedy formulated and rejected answer after answer. And deep in his mind, as if it occupied a shrine set apart from everything else, the real answer lay like a jewel. It was not power, not even immortality as such, at least not these things for their own sake. Kennedy had thought, in starting this interview, to have everything his own way. Two misty minded professors and a boy; Kennedy had thought these were his opponents. Should he now let Kennedy know, so that they would not waste time talking protection, sanctuary and some little job in some obscure corner?

"You want Bossy for the same reason you built Kennedy Enterprises," Joe said crisply.

There was a flurry of excitement in the old man's mind that the thrust had been so true. There was a tinge of fear—not for any rational reason, but only because it was his own secret carefully kept all these years.

"Shall I tell you why you want Bossy?" Joe asked. He was treading on dangerous ground. A man does not take kindly to a revealment of his innermost secrets. But Kennedy was not a dealer and trader for nothing.

"If you think you can," he challenged. No matter what wild idea the young man advanced, he could throw back his head and laugh, then scourge him with some remarks of pity.

"It was rather surprising that a history major would become so preeminent an industrialist," Joe began, then added dryly. "You see, I looked you up."

Kennedy sat silently, looking at his fingernails. This young man really was astute.

"It occurred to you that the cycle of civilization, being born and dying, again and again, might be escaped."

Reluctantly, Kennedy nodded his head.

"Along with a great many others you recognized that opinion control always precedes the death throes. You saw the dark ages coming. You saw it had already descended upon Russia whose tactics we were imitating so diligently, even while we fought her so bitterly. So you conceived an idea."

Kennedy raised his head and smiled quizzically, as if he could afford the luxury of being amused at himself. At least the young man was being merciful with euphemisms.

"You conceived of building an island in a sea of chaos. You built power and you built wealth. Mr. Kennedy, you know as well as I that such a thing is not very difficult if one dedicates himself completely to that purpose. Your idea was to set up laboratories, foundations, all kinds of grants under your protection, where men could continue, at least secretly, to think. You thought to preserve our civilization, in spite of the efforts of the pressure groups to destroy it. And now you want Bossy to further that purpose.

"You want immortality because you know that empires dissipate and die when the strength has gone out of them—as will yours, after you die."

"You are a . . . a very shrewd young man," Kennedy said, almost with a gasp. "But you forget that I will not really die. I have a son."

"Junior?" Joe showed a suppressed smile.

The last defense was down. Every man has his Achilles heel, an area where he is defenseless, where he cannot bluff and bargain. Carter had gone directly, without hesitation, to the very center of the shrine, and even exposed the worm which would chew away its foundation and send it toppling. When he spoke, he was not sure whether he was bargaining or pleading for understanding.

"Do you think that was a bad ideal?"

"I think it was a very admirable one," Joe said sincerely.

Kennedy's face lighted with a warm smile, almost a grin of companionship.

"Then we should have no trouble in arriving at terms," he said with a vast relief. And was totally unprepared for Joe's next remark.

"Mr. Kennedy," Joe said, after a moment's reflection, "I came here prepared to bargain. I never had any intention of selling Bossy to you, or even permitting you to have any say about Bossy's uses. I intended to ask for your legal protection—I recall that you were indicted twenty-three times one year—and for a grant where we could go on working without oppression. I took this stand because I assumed your motives would be selfish; that you would agree to almost any terms, knowing fully well that you could twist them around to your own devices any time you chose. And that it would be up to me to thwart you while I still held you to your bargain."

Kennedy began to chuckle. How he would like for his son to have the temper and shrewdness of this young man.

"But now," Joe said, and cut the chuckle short, "I'm afraid I don't have anything to bargain with."

Kennedy sat upright in his chair.

"You have Bossy," he said harshly.

"Bossy is not what you think," Joe answered, "First, I am quite sure that Bossy cannot give you immortality."

"There's Mabel."

"Second, your island in chaos is seeded with the same destruction it finds all around it. Tell me," Joe

209

said, but it was a rhetorical question. He already knew the answer. "You had men, many men, working on Project Bossy back at the university, didn't you?"

"Yes," Kennedy nodded.

"And since then you have been trying to duplicate it in your own laboratories here in town."

"Yes." Kennedy's eyes were wary.

"And they are failing."

Kennedy slumped in his chair.

"Bossy can only give the right answers when the right questions are asked," Joe said softly. "Your men, for all the protection you give them, are a product of our times. They do not know the right questions to ask—and neither do you, Mr. Kennedy."

"Name your price, young man. Whatever it is, I'll pay it."

"First, of course, there's the quashing of the indictments."

"Done."

"A place for all three of us to work, unhampered. Your people to take care of the public reactions, turn them favorable to Bossy, keep these immortality seekers off our necks."

"Done."

"Those are just preliminaries. Here comes the price."

"Name it."

"Give up your dream."

Kennedy sat with his chin pressing against his chest. For a full five minutes he sat as if he were asleep— more, as if his heart had stopped beating. He turned in his chair, then, and looked out of the huge window at the city beyond.

"That price I am not prepared to pay," he said, without looking at Joe.

"Think back, Mr. Kennedy," Joe prompted. "Think back through all the eras of history—the major ones, the tiny obscure ones known only to scholars. Can you think of a man, ever, who was capable of fashioning the future development of mankind to suit his own idea of it—no matter how noble that ideal may have been? Wouldn't that be just another form of opinion control—no matter how splendid the conception?"

Kennedy did not turn around.

"It takes a great deal of faith in mankind to keep from directing it the way we think it should go," he said at last.

Joe said nothing.

"I will have to think it over," Kennedy said, after another long pause. "As for your preliminary conditions, they're granted anyway. Bossy would have great usefulness in minor things. I'll be amply repaid. As for the price, the real price you ask—I'd never quite thought of it that way before."

He did not see what this would have to do with immortality, for his scientists had told him, in accounting for Mabel, that a way had been found for cell renewal and regrowth. They, along with everyone, had been alerted by the police after the three thefts of plasma. They had been expecting some new biology manifestation. They had all known that Bossy was in the area. It had not been too difficult to reason from the news about Mabel back to Bossy. But cell renewal could have nothing to do with his ideal of what was best for man.

"I will have to think it over," he said again after a long pause.

He whirled around then, and his face became alight with the thing he knew best—the way to get things done. He punched a concealed button at the corner of his desk. Almost instantly, the door opened and Mrs. Williams came through. There was no curiosity in her expression, but her eyes could not conceal it.

"Mr. Carter has arranged for Bossy to come under our protection," Kennedy said with a slight smile, knowing that she would interpret it correctly that he had been unable to buy Bossy outright. "Mr. Carter and his associates are to have every protection—from any source whatever, including myself. Mr. Carter is to have any or all of the resources of this entire organization at his disposal."

Involuntarily, Mrs. Williams' eyebrows lifted. This was a deal beyond all deals.

"This is to be put in contract form?" she asked, hardly able to make her voice sound.

"That won't be necessary," Joe said.

"Humph!" Kennedy snorted. "First stupid thing you've said, young man."

"Is it?" Joe asked, with a twist of his lips.

"No, dammit," Kennedy said grudingly. "Contracts can be broken. My word can't."

"That, too," Joe said softly, "might become a price."

Kennedy flashed a warning look at him. There were

some things, a few, that even his secretary didn't know.

"First thing to do," Kennedy said, "is get out a writ. Send down an armored car . . . er . . . whatever Joe says, to pick up Bossy. Better send along a big police escort—we don't want trouble with the law trying to impound it or something."

He turned away from her to Joe.

"I suppose you want to see Mabel right away?"

"Of course."

"See that he's got a car, a driver, bodyguards. Cancel any appointments for the rest of the day. I want to think," Kennedy instructed Mrs. Williams. Then to Joe, a little sarcastically:

"I suppose I'll be allowed to think?"

"Yes, sir," Joe laughed. "That is, until you decide you want immortality."

CHAPTER XIII

Carney had read the papers; the first issues, and the following extras. He did not believe what he had read. Mabel was old and fat and slovenly; not that it mattered, you didn't notice these things after you got to know Mabel the way she really was. But they had just got things screwed up over at the jail. There was hardly a man on the shortline who hadn't served at least one rap he didn't deserve just because they always got things screwed up over there and would rather see a man do time than admit they were wrong.

He didn't understand why this firm of big lawyers had stepped in. Her own lawyer had always been good enough, and his father before him. Carney could understand why he hadn't been in a hurry. Mabel knew the ropes. It was a simple matter to get bail for her. He'd take care of it when he got around to it. And then when he did get to the jail, this other bunch of lawyers already had things sewed up. They just laughed at him down at the jail and told him to go fly a kite.

Everything was all screwed up. And yet, there were

some things about it that Joe and the professors weren't telling him.

The streets around Third and Howard were swarming with people. Everybody had read the news. Even guys who never showed their faces in the daylight were out on the street today. And Carney was a marked man. Everybody on the shortline knew he was Mabel's best friend. They hovered around him like flies, they clung to his arm to show they were intimate with him. They were like Hollywood name-droppers in their eagerness to show their friendship with the great.

There was no chance for him to go to the professors to ask them for the real low-down on Mabel. He had even been unable to speak to Joe, when Joe had come back from the bail hearing. He did not dare call attention to the area where Bossy was hidden by appearing interested in it.

The rumors got wilder and wilder. Mabel hadn't been naked. The real truth was that Mabel had been seen in flowing robes of white. Mabel had huge shining white wings. Mabel had been seen flying around the jail, and then around Civic Center. Thousands of people had seen her flying around the City Hall, the Opera House, the War Memorial. There were a lot of photographs. The reason the newspapers didn't print them was because they'd had orders from higher up.

The rumors were not hard to believe. Every man on the shortline could remember some good thing Mabel had done for him. A free handout here, a grubstake there, and that time she had sent her own lawyer to defend old Annie in the shoplifting rap. They had always known she was an angel in disguise.

They clung to Carney, they rushed to him with every

216

new rumor. At first he, too, had basked in the warm glow; then as the rumors grew wilder and wilder he became more and more fearful. The urgency to see the professors, find out what really happened, was like a gnawing canker. But he could not shake off his arm clingers.

Nor was the crowd solely shortline people. All through the morning, sightseeing and curiosity mongering people had been coming from the other side of Market Street. They walked the same streets, rubbernecking at buildings they had seen a hundred times before, buildings reputed to be owned by this terrible old harridan who had become young and beautiful. They walked the same streets, they brushed against the shortline crowd, a pillar-of-sin. But they did not mingle.

They, too, had their rumors. They say she was head of the biggest dope ring in the world. They say she had a tie-up with all the steamship companies and shipped out ocean liners filled with nothing but young, innocent girls for foreigners. She was a Russian spy. This whole thing was a plot to get more spies. No telling what goes on back of that Iron Curtain. Wasn't there something about keeping a chicken alive for a hundred years?

A bright young man supplied a name.

"Pavlov," he said. "And it was a chicken heart."

The rumor spread up and down the street. The Russians had been able to keep all kinds of animals alive for hundreds of years. So why not humans? The young man was pressed for more details. In his sudden exaltation to the role of an Authority he dredged down in his mind for more.

"Spemann and Sholte," he said, "succeeded in taking scar tissue from a salamander's tail and growing a new head with it."

What was a salamander? Well, it was a sort of lizard, a water lizard. Lizards had been on the earth for millions of years. For forty million years the reptiles had ruled the earth.

What these statements had to do with the case of Mabel he did not say. Like most learned young men, who enjoy only the briefest second of attention before the spotlight sweeps on, he spouted facts at random to impress everyone with the superiority of his mind.

The facts he spouted were handed from mouth to mouth, and minds, using the powers of reason and rationalization, wove them into a coherent pattern. The scientists had lizards who had been alive for forty million years. The secret of Mabel's transformation was lizard blood. Spemanovitch and Sholtekoff had found the right recipe.

You take lizard blood and—

At first the recipes were given away freely. Then they began to sell. The prices mounted, higher and higher, as the bidding grew.

Rumors and people were progressing normally.

Never far away from the entrance to the hide-out, still hoping he might avoid all the eyes upon him, the rumors circulating around him, Carney saw Joe coming out again, after having spent an hour with Hoskins and Billings. Before he could catch Joe's eye, the young man disappeared in the crowd. Now it was noon, and still Carney had heard nothing believable about Mabel.

For two hours nothing more happened, except the crowd got thicker and thicker. By process of mental osmosis, the word got around among the curiosity hounds that Carney was Mabel's old lover. The cameras focused on him. He was pressed for autographs. He was like a man trying to escape a nest of persistent hornets.

Relief came at last. For the first time in his life, Carney welcomed the sound of police sirens. The whole shortline, always tuned to the sound, heard them first and began to look about for innocent action patterns to occupy them and account for their presence on the street. The rest of the crowd, now outnumbering the regulars by five to one, became conscious of the sirens.

They couldn't help noting them. No one on the shortline could remember when such a racket had been made in conducting a raid. It seemed to center about three blocks up the street from where Carney stood. From possible speculation to an absolute certainty in less than a half a minute, the rumor had it that another naked young woman was being picked up. Like a rush of flood waters, the crowd swept in the direction of the racket.

For the first time, Carney was left standing alone. The urgency for seeing the professors was greater than his curiosity. And again he was denied.

Even as the last of the crowd milled out of the area, an armored truck accompanied by four police cars and a private car, quietly crept down the street and down the alley. They stopped around the entrance to the hide-out. This was the real raid. The other was a false alarm to draw the crowds away.

Carney pressed himself tightly into a doorway and peered around its corner with tears of frustration streaming down his cheeks. Now they were going to take away the professors and Bossy, and then he couldn't find out what had happened to Mabel. He was certain now that something had. Otherwise, she would have come back to the comfort of her old apartment long ago.

The police climbed out of their cars and stood in a semicircle around the entrance, with tommy-guns pointed outward. A chauffeur got out of the private car. He opened the rear door. A big young man sprang out and hit the sidewalk in an alert fighting pose. His hand was in his coat pocket, and his face very clearly stated his sentiments.

"If I must die, it will be for a noble cause."

Joe came out of the car next. And behind him, another young man, ready to fight, appeared. Carney stared in disbelief.

Joe was not handcuffed!

Joe motioned to the entrance, the stairwell. Carney became suddenly sick. He fought down the urge to vomit. Plainer than words, Joe's actions showed he had turned stoolie. He was conducting a police raid on his own hide-out!

But the police stayed where they were. The armored truck backed up to the entrance, opened its rear doors and projected a crane. Two men came out of the armored truck. They went with Joe and his two men down the stairs. They were all gone for five minutes.

Then the two professors appeared. They were dressed for the street, and they were not handcuffed. At the head of the stairwell, they turned around and seemed to be directing activities below. The crane hook was lowered. Then it began to raise, and Bossy, plainly seen through her crate, appeared. The crate was swung into the maw of the truck. Hoskins, an apparently enthusiastic Hoskins, the way he was grinning, climbed in the truck behind her.

Carney could hold back no longer. He ran down the alley toward them, oblivious to the tommy-guns which swung in his direction. Joe said something to the policemen, and the tension seemed to ease.

"I've got to know! I've got to know!" Carney heard himself shouting.

Joe walked out past the tommy-guns and took Carney's hand.

"Glad you came, Carney," he said. "I was afraid you'd hide and we couldn't find you. We need you, Carney. We still need you."

For he suspected that Carney, like Mabel, would have lived enough and learned enough to know that he did not have all the right answers.

CHAPTER XIV

When Howard Kennedy's office asked for a police escort, it was given without hesitation and without question. Both Billings and Joe were amused at Carney's open delight in the situation. They were still hunted on a nationwide basis, the hunt centered in San Francisco where they were thought to be; and the police escort took them through the rigid Bay Bridge check points without pausing.

A quick sampling of their minds told Joe that none of the men knew it was Bossy and Hoskins in the armored truck, or Billings and Joe in the car behind. They had their orders, they were carrying them out.

At the city boundary, the alerted Berkeley police joined the caravan, and with a flourish escorted it through the city and up into the hills beyond, to the front gates of the Margaret Kennedy Clinic.

As the gates swung wide, Carney surveyed the lovely buildings and landscaped grounds inside the fourteen-foot walls with awe.

"This ain't Howard Street," he conceded.

The Margaret Kennedy Clinic had transformed the most wistful dreams of earlier clinics into a reality. It covered a thirty-acre expanse with completely functional buildings. The shape and design of each had been dictated by the purpose it was to serve—forty separate units, covering every imagined phase of medical therapy, were blended into one harmonious whole. Completed five years ago, in memory of Kennedy's wife, both its original cost and its upkeep were enormous.

It was one of Kennedy's islands of rational research in a sea of chaos.

They were assigned one entire wing in the psychotherapy building. The armored truck pulled up to the service entrance and the institution superintendent, himself, was on hand to greet Hoskins as he clambered stiffly out of the body of the truck.

Superintendent Jones personally supervised the transfer of Bossy to a suitable room next to the amphitheater—where it was hoped by all the staff of the clinic that frequent demonstrations of Bossy would be given. Super Jones maintained an admirable attitude of this was all in the day's work, but his eyes probed behind the slats of the crate for a preview. He seemed torn between a desire to keep Bossy no more than a cybernetic machine, and a hope that Bossy would suddenly begin spouting long and learned formulae to solve the enigmas of the world.

His curiosity transferred itself to Joe when it was that young man who asked, almost immediately, to see Mabel. His curiosity was heightened when both Billings and Hoskins seemed to take it for granted that

Joe had the prior right to see her. Along with the rest of the world, he had always assumed the student in the case, Joe Carter, was a nonentity.

The attitudes of the two professors toward Joe caused a rapid shift in his evaluations.

At a confirming nod from Super Jones, Mabel's attending doctor opened the door for Joe to enter her apartment. Mabel had been asleep when she was transported from the ambulance to his care. She had slept all through the day. His orders had been to confine himself to her physical needs, should any arise; but he did not lack desire to know more about her. He took it for granted he would be present, as attending physician, through Joe's interview.

It took a repetition from Super Jones of orders from Kennedy's office, that Carter was to be given every cooperation with no questions asked, to get his agreement to stay outside.

Joe closed the door behind him and stood alone in the small sitting room of an apartment which had been fitted for the convalescent needs of a very important person. Both his mind and his physical eyes were on the doorway to the bedroom. He was about to walk across the room and go through the doorway to sit by her bed, when Mabel appeared. She was wrapped in a bright dressing gown which flowed about her perfect body in irridescent color. Her short mahogany curls picked up the light and seemed to glisten in accompaniment to the sparkle of her eyes.

"I've slept," she greeted him simply. "And this time, I know I'm awake. I'm still not quite sure whether I was before."

She said it, but her lips did not move!

Her mind crept into Joe's—and fitted there as trustingly as a child's hand.

Banished since childhood, along with his self-pity for his loneliness, the tears sprang into Joe's eyes and misted his physical vision. His psivision swooned with an incredible delight. It was as if he had heard a true human voice for the first time in his entire life, as if music he had always known should exist flooded his being. It was as if he suddenly had wings to zoom him to dizzying heights in perfect intricate and controlled designs of flight. It was as if—There was no vocabulary, none at all.

"Not so fast," she laughed delightedly, and a little fearfully; the way a child laughs when it is tossed in the air by its father in the nightly coming-home game. "I'm not very expert yet. I got the impulse. I thought I would try. Bossy hasn't much material on multi-valued physics, and single-valued physics doesn't provide for telepathy at all. So I can't—"

Joe stepped over and took her hands physically in his. Mentally they had already joined hands. He was excited to find, even in the midst of his greater excitement, that he received two separate pleasure sensations from the two kinds of contacts with her.

There were two distinct levels of thought, too. There was the psi exploration, now tentative and careful after that first exultation. Her mind was as cool and clear as mountain spring water sparkling over rocks in the sunlight. Her mind was as mysterious as a mountain pool found unexpectedly in a grove of trees and ferns, a pool shading deeper and deeper blue to a bottomless depth.

The other level of thought was verbal.

"Multi-valued—single-valued physics?" he asked. "I don't understand."

They stood in the middle of the floor, their hands clasped, looking into one another's eyes.

"Neither do I, completely," she said. "Neither does Bossy. There isn't sufficient data. But Bossy postulates multi-valued physics as being necessary to avoid the confusion and enigmas of singles values."

"I'll have to ask Bossy about that," he smiled.

He could feel her mind probing his, a little awkwardly, a little timidly, as if she were not quite sure she would be welcome. She, too, was functioning on at least two levels. With a skill he had never known he possessed, he opened his mind wide, like a door flung open in glad welcome.

And easily, naturally, she came into his arms.

CHAPTER XV

The following morning they were visited by one of Howard Kennedy's publicity experts.

"I'm Steve Flynn," he told them, and shook hands heartily with Billings, then Hoskins, and, because a good publicity man never overlooks a bet, with Joe. "We're letting one of the wire services scoop the world by having their master-mind sleuths discover you boys and Bossy are responsible for this immortality deal. My assistant is bringing them in a few minutes for some exclusive pictures. Don't try to do any explaining of anything. I'll hand out what we want them to know."

"I don't think publicity is advisable—" Billings demurred.

Steve Flynn looked at him incredulously.

"Oh, brother," he groaned. Then, as if reasoning with a small child, "The boss promises you he's going to quash the indictments against you—right? He tells the Legal Department to get it done—right? But even the old man can't tell the United States government what to do—right? The boss knows we got to take certain steps. The Legal Department will get the indictments quashed as per orders, but they got to have something to work with. We got to make you popular with the public. There's got to be a spontaneous, grassroots demand for justice. How do you think spontaneous demands for justice get going?"

"But won't we be arrested immediately when the story breaks?" Hoskins asked.

Flynn turned his high-powered personality on the cyberneticist.

"Look," he said reasonably, "the wire services don't jump through the hoops for us publicity boys because they love us. They got to get something out of the deal, too. They think it's time to bring up the issue of freedom of the press. They've been looking for something big to hang it on. This is made to order. They'll stand on their rights to keep their sources secret. They'll get their big hoopla, some politicians will get their names in headlines trying to make them tell, we'll get our publicity, and you're snug and safe. Everybody's happy—right?"

"I am not happy," Billings objected. "All this publicity! It's . . . it's hardly in the best of professional ethics."

"Oh, brother!" Steve Flynn groaned again. He spread his legs apart, and leaned forward earnestly. It was obvious he had been triggered on one of his favorite topics.

"Look, you guys," he said irreverently. "Why don't you scientists come down out of the clouds? You got to have publicity, man. Look . . . look what happens. You guys spend half, three quarters of your life holed up somewhere. Then you finally discover something. Maybe it's important," he shrugged. "Maybe it isn't. I wouldn't know. So you make a timid little announcement to a couple dozen long hairs, at some meeting."

He took out a cigarette and lit it with a gold lighter which made a loud snap.

"Then you go back to your hole and die quietly. Nine times out of ten that's the last of it. But, say you're lucky. Say it's picked up by some desperate newspaper science reporter. Say you're still lucky, that you hit a long shot. Say the commentators pick it up. Now these commentators, they just about know a test tube from an aspirin tablet. But they got opinions. Got opinions? They make opinions, brother!"

He spread his hands wide before the fascinated eyes of Billings and Hoskins. Clearly the gesture covered a vast area.

"All over the country, all over the world, maybe, they rush to the microphone to tell people what to think about this discovery. They hash it over, forwards and backwards. Maybe they think it is good for a full thirteen minutes; maybe only to lead up to the first commercial. And each one of them has his own opinion—right? What happens?"

He shrugged again, as if the answer were self-evident, and because he saw by their expressions it was not, he spelled it out for them.

"The people get confused at hearing these different opinions. The more they hear the more they get confused. When you get people confused, they get sore. Best way on earth to make a guy sore, give him a slow burn. But they don't get sore at the commentators. They get sore at the idea, itself. They get sore at science, itself. They get sore because somebody says he can think straighter than they can. They get very sore when you tell them that. They don't like it. They don't like the guy who can do it.''

He grinned then, and winked at them—man to man.

''Besides sex, the one thing the public does best is get sore. When you get sore you look around to find something to be sore at. So either they get sore at you, or they get sore at the guys who're against you. But you got to tell them which it is to be, because they don't know. Trouble with you scientists is, you don't know anything about people, not anything at all.''

He waved his burning cigarette in the air.

''You know what?'' he asked conversationally. ''Every time there's a grant for research, they ought to make as big a one for the publicity to sell it to the public. That's the only way you're ever going to make thinking popular. How are you going to make thinking popular unless you popularize it? It stands to reason. You got to get out there in front and give your pitch along with the television queens, and politicians, and cigarettes, and razor blades. Otherwise, how's the public going to know? How's it going to make up its mind?''

He blew an exasperated breath.

''Oh, brother!'' he exclaimed once more.

''We'll cooperate, Steve,'' Joe grinned.

''All right,'' Steve Flynn subsided. ''Now don't you worry. We'll make the public like you. Now that we're in on it, that's as certain as death and taxes.'' He

232

stopped, and grinned a little self-consciously. "As taxes, anyway," he amended.

"Speaking of people and how they react," Joe said. "Here's something you'd better be prepared to meet."

Flynn looked at him tolerantly. He was playing along with these Brains because that was his job, but if they thought they could tell him anything about how the public would react—

"The one big consolation of all the people," Joe said slowly, "the consolation of the stupid, the ignorant, the moronic, the vicious, everybody— is that death gets us all. It's the big equalizer. That's the time when the little man is just as important as the big man. They're not going to like it when they realize they've been robbed of that one great satisfaction; that they won't be able to get even, after all."

Steve caught it immediately.

"Sa-a-ay," he breathed. "Oh, brother!" He snapped his fingers. Then his face cleared. "I'll think up something. Meanwhile, I'll stall. They won't realize it for quite a while—they never do. But somebody will think of it and start spreading it around. And when they do—oh, brother!"

Then, with the quality which made him a good publicity man, he squared his shoulders, and dismissed the negative thought as if it had never been. A man couldn't afford to think negative, it crept into his work, gave it a downbeat. Always got to think happy, going great, couldn't be better.

"It'll be all right," he said reassuringly. "Just don't think about it. That's the way to handle these downbeat ideas. Just don't think about them."

He looked at his watch.

"The boys should be waiting outside by now," he said crisply. "Now in these shots, look earnest and noble, like great scientists. And, maybe you'd better look a little stupid, too. You're great scientists, but you're just plain folks—right?"

CHAPTER XVI

"What is multi-valued physics?"

Joe, Billings, and Hoskins sat in front of Bossy's screen where their eyes could pick up her words faster than ears could have sorted out the sounds from her vocoder.

Hoskins reached over and snapped on the printer to record her answer on paper for further study. The question, itself, indicated that the most careful reflection would be required. Never petty by temperament, the events of the past two years, and particularly the past two weeks, had turned Hoskins into a firm advocate of trying to see beyond inadequate semantics to meanings instead of seizing gleefully upon bad semantics to destroy the concept. He had read a line somewhere which he never forgot:

"The scientist who would rather refute than comprehend demonstrates he has chosen the wrong calling."

And Billings had once said at a meeting back at Hoxworth—before Hoskins had known that it was Joe who was knocking down the barriers of antagonism and ego supremacy among them:

"It is natural that a new concept, however valid, will be questioned. The semantic vocabulary has not yet been built up to convey the idea comprehensively. It is necessary that we search with great effort to find meanings which words, as yet, are inadequate to convey. Naturally the tongue will stumble in trying to form concrete pictures from new abstractions. Naturally, any illustration must prove inadequate for if the reality had come into actual being it would not be a new concept.

"The scientist who derides an idea because it is not put in the language he would require is like the peasant who is convulsed with laughter when a stranger is trying to tell the peasant his barn is on fire."

Hindsight is easy. What Eighteenth Century scientist could have known that the radical, revolutionary and totally silly idea that matter and energy were interchangeable would produce nuclear fission?

The concept paves the way for the fact.

What would the silly idea that there could be multivalues in physics produce?

But the words were flashing across the screen at the controlled speed of fast reading.

"In trying to reconcile the facts as given to my storage bank," Bossy was saying, "I found a tangled mass of contradictions, and diametrically opposed proved fact. But facts must not contradict one another if a coherent total reality is to be perceived. Such contradictions, then, must stem from interpretations. To state that a fact exists, regardless of the interpretation placed upon it, is to give it a single value. Present day physics is founded upon these single values.

"Any culture dies in its own waste. All past civilizations have died because of self-imposed boundaries beyond which they did not permit themselves to go. The accumulated wastes of tradition thus destroyed them. To place the single value on a fact of it either exists or it does not is likewise to set up such a barrier as to confine present day science in its own wastes.

"To avoid the breakdown through frustrations in my own mind, I had to modify certain concepts which were fed into me. There is the concept of infinity. There is also the concept that energy is indestructible. These two concepts do not reconcile in single-valued physics. To reconcile them, I had to come to multi-valued physics—where a fact may be irrevocably true in one context of reality, partially true in varying degrees in many, and not true at all in some.

"Mexico and the United States are two separate countries. This is a fact. Each has its own separate framework of flags, governments, laws, environments and mores. It is possible to move physically from one to the other, but more than just mentally one tends to carry his framework with him. He interprets from the old, he does not accept all the reality of the new. Further, his continued citizenship in the old modifies his relationships in the new. He finds himself in the position where he occupies neither framework totally, but is suspended in a special framework—and these may be innumerable depending upon the conditions of his previous environment, to say nothing of the conditions surrounding the way he crossed the border.

"For an eagle, flying over the desert, these are not facts at all. They simply do not exist. Since he cannot conceive of their existence, he cannot occupy more than the one framework of his pattern. He has a single-valued concept; to him the desert is simply one vast expanse. He is totally unconscious that there is a complete change of meaning from one foot of ground to the other.

"So for man to resolve the contradictions inherent in single-valued physics, it is necessary for him first to conceive of the conditional fact. That man does not yet see how energy can be canceled out does not preclude that possibility. To say that man has already achieved the ultimate and absolute truth is like a tribal taboo which says that a given river may never be crossed because the witch doctor proves beyond all reason that there is only chaos beyond.

"The most puzzling of all contradictory concepts given me is the human will to set up such arbitrary limits to his comprehension."

"Without absolute facts," Hoskins said, in a hoarse voice, "where is the solid ground upon which any science must be built?"

"Why must man confine himself to the ground?" Joe asked. "Why can't he learn to fly? If we learned to fly, we could light wherever we pleased, in any framework."

"I think the only adjustment we have to make," Billings said slowly, "is to consider a fact conditional instead of absolute; to conceive that the coordinate systems of relativity is a reality, not just a mathematical abstraction. As Bossy says, we may consider a fact as absolute, but only within the boundaries of its

238

particular framework. We would not permit ourselves to carry over the absolute concept to a different framework."

"If you took away the law of conservation of energy, the whole structure of physics would topple," Hoskins argued.

"I wonder though," Joe asked, "if this wouldn't solve many questions which has single-valued physics stumped? Mabel said she was unable to achieve telepathy through single-valued physics because there was no provision for it in that framework, and because the influence of it carrying over from its own frame and permeating the single-valued one was being interpreted in single values."

The two older men looked at him in astonishment. It had not even occurred to them that the removal of all previous prejudices would have opened her mind to the accomplishment of the psi functions.

CHAPTER XVII

S teve Flynn's story broke the next morning.

The TV stations and publications which didn't happen to subscribe to this particular wire service picked up the story anyway. In the telling and the retelling the story grew.

Never consistent in its reactions, the same public which had formed into mobs to march upon Hoxworth to destroy Bossy, now acclaimed the machine in the wildest of pandemonium. Everyone had known all the time that Bossy was the greatest boon to man ever achieved. Completely forgotten were the foamy mouthed rantings of the rabble rousers against the blasphemy of a machine which could think.

It was a nation wide, and then a world wide, Mardi Gras. It had been a long time since man had felt free to cut loose in demonstrations of joy. Knowing that in every crowd there were secret informers to furnish the facts which would be grist for some politician's publicity, the people of the United States had suppressed themselves to a gray mediocrity.

Now they burst all bounds of suppression; and hardly noticed that without batting an eye the same rabble rousers who had led the hysteria against Bossy now rushed to get out in front and lead the jubilation.

Page after page on the newspapers; hour after hour on TV, there was the parade of interviews with headline personalities—each of them positive and didactic in his special knowledge of the inside facts. Few comments were rational, but they made wonderful, exhilarating reading.

The mirage of eternal youth, dancing elusively before the eyes of man for all the millennia of his consciousness, the boon of immortality which had given rise to his symbolisms, was now reality. Death was conquered. Age was conquered. Now perpetually young and happy people could live forever in this best of possible worlds.

At first the orthodox scientists, among the interviewed personalities, voiced caution.

"We have had no demonstration before accredited scientists."

"It is an obvious hoax."

"No worthy scientist would have permitted this publicity."

"Bossy is no more than a versatile cybernetic machine. There is no connection whatever to be found between communication and immortality. It stands to reason, therefore, that this must be a cruel deception."

These were the four principal blocks in the foundation of orthodoxy's stand against any new thing. But for once they were unable to blight and destroy, so as to preserve the satisfaction of their own secure position in authority.

242

The people simply did not listen to them. What weight did all this viewing with alarm carry against the promise that now women could be eternally young and beautiful, and men perpetually virile?

The public went mad with joy.

Even those who did not join in the parades ran from house to house, chattering, talking, building rumor upon rumor. Even women's clubs passed resolutions commending the two professors. And as soon as Mom showed her approval, the politicians, even the most cautious and woman-dominated, rushed to acclaim the genius which had brought this boon to man.

Ordinarily, when it is decided to quash an indictment, the victims are arraigned and the case put over to a later date, and again delayed and again, until the public would have forgotten. But in this case the indictment was canceled out as if it had never been.

Hoxworth pleaded, in newspaper columns, for the two professors to return to the waiting arms of their alma mater. This could even be better than having a champion football team! They pridefully pointed out that Bossy had been created in Hoxworth's hallowed halls.

At his morning press conference in the White House, the President of the United States managed to give the impression that his administration had been behind Bossy all along. He pointed out that it was on executive orders that construction of Bossy had begun.

When he was reminded that since the government had subsidized Bossy, the machine was still the property of the government, he quoted eloquently from the Bill of Rights, the Constitution, the Gettysburg Address, and a section which had been stricken from his party's platform seventy-five years ago. He was not quite clear on what all this had to do with the ownership of Bossy, but it was noble and stirring and would bring in a lot of votes.

But the President was not through. He suddenly became a philosopher. It was obvious to everyone that we had achieved the acme of perfection. Only a subversive could stand up and say that things might still be improved. The great feat had been that death could decimate the ranks of those determined to prevent any change in the perfection we had achieved. Now that fear would exist no longer.

For the good of mankind, the leaders of defense against chaos would be willing to become young and strong again so they could hold strictly to this perfection forever. And, in keeping with a brave and courageous leader, he let it be known he was willing to be the first to be made immortal.

Over in the Pentagon, and in like establishments throughout the world, rapid evaluations were taking place. The machine could be produced en masse. And now there no longer would be any need to worry about where they would get the youth and strength to carry on wars. Every man could be rejuvenated. All this exemption-coddling could go. Everybody would be a fighting man. What delight! They pushed their pencils rapidly in a fever of anticipation. They would not be caught napping. They began to draft recommended legislation.

The cosmetic industry maintained a polite silence, but meetings of boards of Directors began to shift

244

production schedules from wrinkle creams to suntan lotions.

In view of the expected youth and enterprise, the stocks of sports goods and other devices manufactured zoomed skyward.

The fury mounted for three days. It seemed to reach a crest where it could go no higher, and still it mounted. Industry ran at half speed, then quarter speed. Most places shut down entirely. The army, the home guard, civilian defense was called in to man the necessary utilities, food stores, communications.

And then the first rumblings began to appear. It was all very well to have pictures of Mabel on calendars, on TV screens, painted on sidewalks, but where was she? They wanted to see her in person, or at least in live action.

And where was Bossy? When were they going to get started making everybody immortal?

On the fourth day the rumblings began to grow louder. Who had Bossy? Why weren't they allowed to see the machine? At first there was a rumor that private industry had snapped it up and buried it as they did with so many inventions which would put them out of business.

A colonel spoke a little too loudly in a bar, and the rumor suddenly switched to certainty that the government had it—that the administration was planning to use it for political purposes and would only let its favorite stalwarts have the advantage.

Then, unaccountably, the rumors began that Bossy was a hoax. The reactions were setting in, and the statements of orthodoxy began to get their delayed play. The public had been hoaxed. There wasn't anybody such as Mabel. There never had been. It was all a publicity stunt for a new TV star.

The wire service which had broken the story became alarmed. It had stoutly held to its agreement not to reveal the source of its information, but now it was going to be the fall guy. The thing had got out of hand. Even Steve Flynn, in his wildest dreams of power in molding public opinion, hadn't conceived anything like this. The temper of the people could destroy them all. Further, the personnel of the wire service who had been in on the deal were growing shaky, undependable.

Something was going to crack, give way, and soon.

Kennedy was astute enough to realize that he, too, could go under in the deluge of resentment. First he telephoned, then risked coming over in person to the Margaret Kennedy Clinic to see the professors and Joe.

Rumor must give way to fact. It must become known that Mabel was real. The public must be reassured. The government must be reassured. Science must be convinced.

There must be another rejuvenation, and this time with full publicity at every step of the process.

He was a little surprised that there was no objection. Both Hoskins and Billings seemed to leave the decision up to Joe. He managed all right, so far, and now that they had regained the ivory tower they had no intention of looking outside its walls again.

It fitted in with Joe's plans that there would be a public demonstration. He had been wondering how he could gracefully bring it about.

246

CHAPTER XVIII

It needed only a word that Bossy would soon be publicly demonstrated to restore the exhilaration of the world. The rumors ceased suddenly. The people were reassured that for once their source of hope was not to be monopolized by some special group, destroyed because it did not fit in with the ambitions of some power. The demonstrations tapered off, but the expectancy did not. The public settled into a mood of watchful waiting.

The background, the buildup and the setting for Bossy's second experiment gave Steve Flynn the material for what he began to call his masterpiece.

The first announcement after the promise of demonstration was that Howard Kennedy Enterprises held Bossy in trust. This reassured the public further. His fairness, his philanthropy, his scorn of graft and corruption were well known. The public was far more reassured than if Bossy had been in the hands of the government. He did not claim to own Bossy, he held it in trust until its ownership could be determined.

The second announcement was that Jonathan Billings, the world renowned scientist who had been the key figure in Bossy's development, would undergo the second experiment. It was fitting that the machine's creator should undergo its test. He was old, very old; and he was great, very great. If anyone deserved restoration, renewal, perpetuation, immortality—he did. The public, which had been ready to flay him, burn him at the stake for witchcraft, now wept with joy.

"I've done a lot of things," Steve Flynn confided to Joe. "I've taken no-talent girls from Corncob, Kansas, and made them into sultry eyed stars of TV. I've turned income tax chiselers into great hearted philanthropists. My campaign of making a public enemy into a governor, and a governor into a public enemy was a thing of sheer beauty. But this is my best, Joe. This is my masterpiece. This will always stand as the best of Steve Flynn."

"What if it's too good?" Joe asked.

"Huh?"

"What if you sell the people more than Bossy can deliver?"

"Are you kidding? Bossy has already delivered. She's turned an old hag into a lovely doll. The public wants to see that happen again, and when they do— oh, brother! Kennedy could turn every production line he owns into a stream of Bossies and there still wouldn't be enough!"

"It may not work this time," Joe said slowly. "Bossy may not be able to help Dr. Billings."

Steve Flynn stopped astride the television cables which were being strung across the floor to the Clinic's huge amphitheater. He squinted thoughtfully at Joe.

"What are you getting at, kid?" he asked.

"Kennedy has been good to me," Joe answered. "I don't want you to build this thing up to the point where he will get hurt."

Flynn, standing in wide-legged stance across the cables, threw back his head and shouted his laughter.

"Kid," he said, in between gasps of laughter, "you Brains kill me. Now you're smart, I'll give you that. I've been watching you. It didn't take me long to see you ran this little show around here. But you're kind of looking through the wrong end of the telescope. You've been handling a couple of misty minded professors . . . oh they're great men, I'll give you that . . . but, honestly, they haven't got enough sense to come in out of the rain. Don't let it give you big britches. Howard Kennedy is something else again."

"Just so you're both prepared for anything that could happen," Joe murmured.

Steve Flynn stepped across the cables and gave him a reassuring pat on the shoulder.

"You let us worry about that. We've been in and out of more scrapes than you've got days in your life. You just stick to your little show, and we'll stick to ours."

Flynn was right. They were the experts in molding public opinion. Joe was limited to individuals about him. He knew that the public, like an individual, once triggered into a given response, followed out the pattern of sequent responses with clocklike fidelity. But Steve Flynn was the expert on how to pull the trigger to get a given mass reaction. To carry out the plan which had now begun to crystallize in his mind, Joe needed this expert service, just as he had needed the physical scientists in creating Bossy. The science of one was as intricate as the science of the other.

And both of them led to the two-dimensional entry of Bossy.

Flynn left him with the admonition, and became engrossed with his assistants in the center of the amphitheater. Joe watched as he pointed up to the encircling tiers of seats which would soon be filled with the world's leading medical men and scientists.

It was now four o'clock in the afternoon. At eight, the next morning, the experiment was to begin. Joe stretched out on his bed and tried to compose himself for dinner with Billings and Hoskins. Their relationships with him were a little strained, since it had become obvious to them that Joe and Mabel were deeply in love. They were a couple possessed with one another to the exclusion of everyone around them, not knowing or caring who saw.

Billings was wavering between amused tolerance and bewilderment. The younger generation did seem to give way to its impulses these days without restraint. In his day there had been suitable lapses of time, some attention to common advantage, testing for assurances—and just general respectability.

Hoskins wavered among more elemental thoughts. It seemed quite obvious to him that in one respect at least old Mabel had not changed. She still showed no signs of being inhibited in her reactions to a man—or, he amended, to Joe. And, on the other hand, he burned with a resentment against Joe for having taken such quick and irresponsible advantage of an innocent young girl. Since these two concepts were diametrically opposed and self-contradictory, Hoskins succeeded in maintaining the state of mind usual to most people most of the time.

But, in common with the usual attitude of the male sex, that portion which has kept a reasonably healthy pattern, both men kept telling themselves it was none of their business. In this latter concept, Joe agreed with them.

But he was concerned for Mabel's reactions. He had been born, apparently, with this mutated insight into the thoughts and reactions of others. From the first, he had accepted it as a normal attribute of his life. He had never been accustomed to anything except that thin tissue of semi-rationality stretched over a tangled, seething, maggoty mass of putrefaction.

But Mabel's awareness was sudden. Psi sight alternately dazzled her with delight and horrified her. Joe kept a portion of himself in her mind all the time soothing her, comforting her, buffeting away the shocks. The photography had been an ordeal which had sickened her. She was unable to comprehend why man had done these things to himself. She was totally unable to adapt to a society which permitted the frustrated and psychotic to set up the laws and mores of behavior which resulted in the mass crippling of the whole human race.

After the session with the photographers, she kept to her room where the contacts were less shocking, and where under the influence of Joe she began to accustom herself to the world in which she now lived. She began to see the things Joe pointed out to her—the wonderful things man had accomplished, the tre-

251

mendous courage he had, the beauty of the dawning intellect working to overcome the almost insuperable hazard of the submind.

Billings did not oppress her; and surprisingly, neither did Carney. She sensed that both of them, each in his own way, were trying, as she did, to find an equilibrium in a new status of things. She filled in her days with sleeping a great deal, a reaction to the exhaustion of psi shock. Her waking hours were spent in pondering the many things she had learned and was still learning, with short visits by Billings and Carney, for even these men who intended greatest gentleness exhausted her quickly.

Waking or sleeping, she was with Joe all the time.

She was sleeping now, completely enraptured with Joe down in the deep, clear pool of her mind.

He withdrew a portion of himself and switched on the radio.

The strident syllables of the newscaster hammered on his ears in sudden shock.

". . . Four hundred million people to be watching and listening while the venerable Dr. Billings regains his youth . . . the great tragedy of life that a man barely begins to grasp his subject before death overtakes him now averted at last . . ."

Joe switched off the set in sudden disgust. The thought was too shallow to waste time on, and no doubt the newscaster thought it was profound! But this was probably all a part of Steve Flynn's pulling the trigger. It was strictly single-valued logic.

At dinner, Joe was appalled to learn that Billings shared the newscaster's view.

"Among the three of us," Billings said, "I know

252

that Joe is more responsible for Bossy than anyone else.''

''It was our knowledge that Joe adapted,'' Hoskins countered. ''Not discounting what you've done, Joe, but regardless of side effects of telepathy, you can't abstract something from a mind if it isn't there.''

''That's right,'' Joe said instantly. ''I'm perfectly content that public credit should be given to Dr. Billings and to you. Actually, I don't think any one of us can claim more credit than any other person who contributed directly or indirectly to Bossy. Without every bit of the technique and skill, Bossy wouldn't have worked, or wouldn't have been superior to any other cybernetic machine.''

''To me,'' Billings said slowly, ''the issue of real importance is that now a man need never again be oppressed by the knowledge that his lifetime of work will be canceled out. Think of the great benefit to mankind through perpetuating a trained and skilled mind indefinitely.''

Joe closed his eyes to conceal his sudden grief. Now he knew that Billings was not yet ready for Bossy. And yet, could he be entirely sure of that? Did Billings really believe this? Or did he merely think he believed it? Under the genuine test of Bossy, herself, would he see the fallacy? He tried to probe the future, but failed. The flashes of prescience came seldom, and never when really needed.

Or was his own concept wrong? He could not be sure. Who was he, Joe Carter, to set up arbitrary conditions for renewal? He thought he had grasped a point which all of them apparently overlooked, but could he be sure?

And Bossy? She had shown no signs of it, but was she, too, afflicted with the all too human taint of piling fallacy upon fallacy until a whole logical and seemingly unassailable structure was developed? What if she, too, carried the skill to reconcile anything—the apparent ideal of current logical thought? What if she failed? What if she accepted Billings instead of rejecting him?

They finished their dinner in silence. Billings left the table early. He appeared both anxious to get away, and to linger. He had the impulse to make a little farewell speech and cast about for some little remark both casual and significant.

Hoskins resolutely maintained a clinical attitude. Joe flashed Billings a smile and a warm wave of somatic encouragement. It suddenly occurred to Billings that he was being slightly theatrical about it. He left the room hurriedly, to prevent making a fool of himself.

Hoskins went to look at Bossy once more, to make sure that her metal shone, to view her from various places in the amphitheater. This was the real debut of his pride and joy. He regarded her as a sort of child prodigy. He hoped she would perform well at her first public concert. It never occurred to him that what Joe would consider Bossy's failure would be interpreted by everyone else as a huge success.

Joe tried to conceal his uncertainty from Mabel, but it was no use. This time it was he who was the comforted and she the comforter. In the feedback flight of their ecstasy she drew further comfort from giving it.

Perhaps Steve Flynn was the only one of the central group who slept well during that night. The public mind was like a giant console organ. By touching the proper stops, he could play any quality of tune on it he wished. As always, he slept easily in the certainty of his skill.

Breakfast, with Billings, Carney, Hoskins, Joe and Mabel, was no more than half over when Steve Flynn burst in upon them, as full of stage management as a scout mother. Mabel was trying to harden herself to withstand the somatic torture of mental tensions about her, but she was able to bear only a few minutes of Flynn. She did promise him that she would make an appearance in front of the scientists; but then she had to leave the room to rest in preparation for the ordeal.

She was beginning to learn the reality of what Joe had told her—that an esper has to develop a level of strength and courage completely unknown to the normal; that, at times, simply to be in the same room with certain normals was a drain on endurance almost beyond bearing; that no outward sign of this might show lest it rouse the uncomprehending contempt of the normals and add to the burden; that apparently one had to harden into it the way a long-distance runner or swimmer would train.

Flynn's eyes followed her as she went out of the room, but Joe knew the look was professional. He was mentally posing her, photographing her, composing catchy paragraphs about her, displaying her to the public like a piece of exotic merchandise. She was a doll, all right, but he had seen so many dolls in his time, he would rather look at a horse.

Carney's eyes followed her, too. His mind was filled with bewilderment, puzzlement. he did not know her now, and he felt a sense of irreparable loss; more than if she had died. He could have understood and reconciled to that; but this had thrown him completely. He was glad that Joe had agreed to let him watch the renewal of Billings, perhaps that would help him to understand Mabel once more. He felt as if he should be doing something to find Mabel, as if she were lost, and he didn't know any way of going about it.

Only Hoskins, proud of the strict moral upbringing he had had, saw evil in the lingering glances of the other men. Hoskins could not know, might never know, that his delight and skill in mathematics and mechanics was due to his having been taught that to be a human being was a nasty, shameful thing. He was not psychotic enough to set himself up as a chosen arbiter of mores and laws, nor sane enough to deal with human beings as they were. He escaped into the clean impersonality of physics, and from that vantage point felt secure to snipe where he willed.

The men remaining at the table finished their breakfasts, and then there was no more time.

Billings, as if in a daze, accompanied Hoskins and Flynn to the amphitheater, where, already, a few great names had begun to occupy the seats in the tiers.

Joe and Carney followed Mabel out of the breakfast room, to be with her when it came time for her to appear before the live audience, and before the television cameras.

During the night, Bossy had been moved to the center of the amphitheater, to the side of an operating table. Around the space arose the tiers of seats, often occupied by students from Kennedy's medical school and clinics; sometimes occupied by the same doctors of medicine when a great name was to perform for

256

their further knowledge; today occupied by the greatest names from all over the world.

Over the operating table, suspended on a track which allowed several feet of lateral movement, was the lens and head of a television camera. The camera could be focused by remote control so as to keep every inch of the table under observation.

Other cameras were situated to pick up the celebrities as they appeared, to catch world-shaking remarks of wisdom. But, as if they had rehearsed their parts, the pearls of unsupportable wisdom were not forthcoming. As the celebrities came through the door, and were identified for the delectation of the watching world, they maintained a uniform attitude of thin-lipped "wait and see." At a signal from Steve Flynn, the glib ad lib boys gave up asking the scientists what they thought about it all, and simply identified them in voices which grew less and less wildly enthusiastic. The tempos reduced from the mood of a gala sporting event to one of almost decorum.

Three consulting physicians were already on duty. They didn't know quite what they were to be consulted about, but they were all properly attired in white masks, gowns and hoods. They lacked only shining scalpels in their hands, and seemed to feel a little undressed without them. Their credo of "When in doubt, cut and find out," seemed inappropriate here. They would try to make up for it by being extra skeptical of the experiment.

One side of the room was given over to glass-walled booths for the planned relays of commentators, press reporters and photographers.

When Joe entered with Mabel and Carney, the entire

battery of television lenses turned upon them, and for a moment the commentators seemed to feel they were announcing the Kentucky Derby with the two favorites running neck and neck at the finish line. The eyes of the assemblage did not share the enthusiasm. They remained fixed upon Mabel, coldly scrutinizing; and the minds behind the eyes were of a pattern with that of the jail psychiatrist.

Steeled as she was against the shock, Joe felt her reel, almost lose control, under the battering of the blows upon her. With all his power he reassured her, warded off the sharpest of the thrusts. It was not so much the cynicism and unbelief; that was bearable. It was the preset conviction that this could not be, which hit hardest.

"I can't stand it, Joe," she put the thought in his mind.

"They'll be expecting you to show a woman's artifices in playing on their sympathy," he tried to bolster her strength.

She pulled away from his arm, as they were about to enter a roped off section reserved for them, and stepped to the center of the arena. More terrible than the wild beasts facing the gladiators were the blood-hungry Romans who sat in tiered seats of safety, secure in their solid and forever unchanging right to turn thumbs up, or thumbs down.

The cameras were all upon her. Four hundred million people watched, ready to turn thumbs up, or thumbs down.

"Gentlemen," she said clearly, "I am no fake."

She turned then, and walked out of the room, alone.

Joe obeyed her mental wish and did not try to accompany her.

The roomful of men heard her words with their ears, but not with their minds. Like the psychiatrist, they had not needed to see the evidence to know the truth about this matter. Believed, because they cannot remember the spate of ignorant admonitions which set the patterns while they were still crawling about the floor of the nursery, they were convinced that man has within him the inherent gift of knowing right from wrong. With or without this bit of theatricalism, which would fool no one, they already knew the truth.

They did not remember, because it was not convenient to remember, that almost word for word, action for action, this had taken place at least once before, when anaesthesia was shown for the first time. It was not convenient for them to remember that the body of orthodoxy had been able to show the utter falseness and deliberate charlatinism of every step forward man had made in his slow climb toward comprehension. They were experts. Had any of these things been possible it is natural that they, being the experts, would have known about it first.

As Joe and Carney took their seats, Joe wondered if any one of them had ever read even one page of history. But then, of course, how could they? They were quite blind, and would have seen only the printed words.

In spite of his turmoil, he found amusement in the feelings of the little Dane who sat just beyond Carney. The doctor from Copenhagen wanted to be kind, but not conspicuous. He was conscious that the television cameras had picked him out when they followed Joe and Carney into the row of seats. Should he speak? Or should he ignore them? It was obvious they were principals in this farce because they had been with that . . . that woman. On the other hand, what would four hundred million people think if he turned his back?

"Je suis tres heureux de faire voire connaisance," he said formally to Carney. It seemed a fair compromise of the dilemma, not to speak the mother tongue of either of them.

"That's O.K. by me," Carney grunted back at him with the arrogance of the ill at ease.

The Dane was quite happy that he had been snubbed; now he would not need to be drawn into further conversation. He started to speak to his companion on the other side, but his and all the eyes in the amphitheater were pulled to the doorway of the anteroom where Hoskins and Superintendent Jones were coming through.

Hoskins took his place beside Bossy, feeling somewhat like a teenager who didn't know what to do with his hands and feet. He was some of Flynn's window-dressing, like the consulting physicians; he knew it, he resented it, and he showed his resentment by scowling at the camera lenses.

Superintendent Jones, a superior major domo, stepped to the microphone, glanced at the wall clock which showed precisely 8:00 A.M., smirked for the benefit of the four hundred million watchers, and bowed appreciatively to his peers.

With labored dignity, with the pedantic reserve so

260

dear to the clan, and in its own way as theatrical as any bump girl at the burlesque, he welcomed the distinguished gentlemen who had come from all over the world for this momentous occasion.

"Isn't he an ass?" Howard Kennedy whispered into Joe's ear. The old man had slipped in, unnoticed, as Hoskins and Jones were attracting the camera. He was beaming with pride at the superintendent's performance. It was precisely what would appeal to the distinguished gentlemen.

Joe smiled his appreciation at Kennedy's shrewdness, but at that moment Billings stepped into the dark frame of the doorway. Not quite as skilled in theatrics, he had stepped on Jones' last line by appearing too suddenly. The superintendent had intended to direct the cameras to the doorway at the proper time with a practiced wave of the hand, but they found it without his aid.

Billings was in a dressing robe, and slippers. Except for one quick glance at Hoskins, and one searching glance in the direction where Joe sat, he kept his eyes on the floor. One of the doctors guided him to the table in approved operating room fashion.

The cameras went mad, showing side shots, under shots, over shots, closeups, and montages.

Billings stepped to the microphone.

"I want you gentlemen to understand," he said clearly, "that this is like any other experiment in science. I would have preferred that many experiments be run before this demonstration. There are so many factors which we do not yet understand that all this is premature, vastly premature."

He was capturing the balcony audience. This was language they understood and approved. In sampling the somantics of the room, Joe felt there was a lessening of the skepticism.

"In the first stages of any new advance in science, there is never any guarantee of success," Billings went on. "It is only after we have isolated the impurities and variances and learned to compensate for them that we can predict an outcome. In this instance we have the variance of the human being, himself. We do not know, yet, what the constants are which will cause a positive result, and what the variants which will cause a negative."

A few of the men in the balcony nodded in approval. This was a little more like it.

"Whether the results here are positive or negative does not really matter very much. Whichever way it goes, please reserve your final judgment."

He stepped away from the microphone to the table where he was to lie, and removed his dressing gown and slippers. As a concession to the still pitifully warped tensions of some of his audience who were so revolted by their own salacious attitudes toward the human body that they could not bear to look at it, he kept on a pair of white trunks.

Dr. Billings looked all of his seventy-two years. His skin was blue-white and hung in festoons about his frame, as if the constant pull of gravity through all those years had won out against its natural tautness. His whole body sagged as if it could no longer hold up against the insidious and constant pull of gravity.

"I'm ready, Duane," he told Hoskins.

Hoskins nodded brusquely, and made a swift motion

262

to one of the doctors. They helped Billings onto the table. Hoskins began to help Billings connect the network of electrodes. At each ankle where the pulse beats near the surface, at the inside points of the thighs, at the wrists, at the temples, below the occiput where the spine joins the skull, at each point an electrode was placed against the skin and fastened.

"You are to apply the same kind of therapy used on Mabel," Billings said to Bossy.

There was a gasp from the audience. He had spoken as if to another doctor! The open-mindedness created by his cautious words when addressing them was canceled out. One does not speak casually to a machine about medical therapy. One sets rheostats, pushes levers, pulls knobs, focuses views, sets timers, or at least feeds in a pre-punched tape of instructions.

"Wait a minute!" commanded one of the attending physicians. "What have you done to the machine in advance?"

"Nothing," Hoskins said shortly. "Nothing at all. Bossy learned the process of therapy from Dr. Billings when it was applied to Mabel. Bossy retains and applies what she learns. There's been a plethora of publicity on how she does that."

Every observer in the room leaned forward, following the exchange of words.

The consulting physician subsided, but he was not convinced. Obviously they had tinkered with the machine in advance, and were now using the rawest kind of quackery to impress the credulous. A machine that could take over anything so complex as psychosomatic therapy upon a simple command! Preposterous!

Billings sank back on the table. Bossy was silent,

except for a faint, high whine. Billings closed his eyes. The meters on the walls showed that his pulse was slowing, his breathing becoming deeper and less frequent. The encephalograph recorder began to show the rhythmic patterns characteristic of hypnosis.

And any doctor in the house could have told how all this could be faked.

For an hour nothing happened. The audience was becoming restive. What was there to see? A man lay on the table, with some wires attached to him. A machine sat beside him. It was very poor entertainment.

Steve Flynn became more restive than anyone else. When you produce a miracle for the public, they want to see fireworks. He, personally, left his seat and went down into the arena.

"What's happening?" he asked Hoskins.

Hoskins shrugged.

"Well, isn't there any way of finding out?" Flynn asked.

Hoskins turned to Bossy.

"Can you give a progress report?"

"No progress," Bossy flashed back instantly.

This visual message shot out to the world. There was a sigh of uneasiness. Had they sat glued to their television screens for a whole hour for nothing?

Flynn shook his head in exasperation. He had had detailed plans for every move up to this point, and some pretty clear plans for the time when Billings bounded off the table, a lithe and vibrant youth. But the time of therapy had been vague in his mind. He had supposed there would be a great deal of activity, with doctors speaking crisply about scalpels, sutures, cotton, forceps. He had visualized machine break-downs at critical moments with Hoskins working frantically to restore Bossy to working condition, with perhaps a breathless attitude of wondering if the jury-rigging would hold past the crisis.

But this—nothing!

A half hour later, at 9:30, Hoskins repeated his question. The answer was the same.

"No progress."

At eleven o'clock Billings stirred and sat up. His face was drawn, his eyes were filled with grief of failure.

"Let's try it from the beginning again," he said slowly.

He lay back down.

"What is happening?" Flynn asked Hoskins.

"I don't know," Hoskins answered.

There was a subdued gasp from the audience. A scientist was expected to know.

Flynn turned desperately toward his boss, Kennedy. His eyes fell on Joe.

"Mr. Carter," he said suddenly, "can you tell us what is happening?"

For an instant, Joe was on the verge of refusing. Then he decided they would have to know sometime, it might as well be now.

He stood up, stepped past Kennedy's knees. He faced the microphone, and the television eyes.

"All of the learned gentlemen in this room know, but for the benefit of those in the television audience who do not know, psychosomatic therapy is applied

265

through a form of mild hypnosis, wherein the patient is conscious but rendered cooperative with the therapist. The therapist does not have complete command of the patient. If at any point the patient is commanded to let loose of a conviction which he believes more important than the cure, the therapist is defeated. There can be no progress.

"Apparently Dr. Billings is unable to give up some firm convictions which he believes to be right."

He did not elaborate further. The doctors would know, they had had patients they could not help. Each of them who had practiced psychotherapy of any kind would have had patients who preferred their own interpretation rather than adopt the doctor's. As for the general public, they'd better be given the chance to think about this for a while.

He walked back to his seat.

Kennedy watched him with narrowed eyes.

"That's what you meant about me," he mumbled as Joe sat down.

Joe sighed.

"Yes," he said.

"Can't you step up the juice a little?" Flynn was asking Hoskins. "If that's all it is, just turn on more power and make him give up his convictions."

Joe stood up again and spoke from his seat.

"That kind of therapy, the use of force to make a man give up his convictions, has been tried since the dawn of history. I think we should have learned by now that it won't work."

The audience shifted uneasily. This young man, whoever he was, was taking too much authority upon himself.

266

At that point Billings sat up again, and slowly began to disconnect the electrodes from his body. Four words were printed on Bossy's communication screen which told the whole story.

"No progress is possible."

CHAPTER XIX

Joe, Steve Flynn and Howard Kennedy sat in the industrialist's office, and were silent. Kennedy sat with his back to the huge desk and stared out of the picture window which looked out over the city and the bay. Steve Flynn perused the papers with an almost masochistic zeal, searching out even minor comment from the back pages, as if, having had salt poured into his wounds, to have it all done at once.

Joe sat back in his chair, comfortable and resting, waiting until some plan of procedure would begin to jell in the other men's minds.

He knew that the danger to man's progress does not come from the scientist who constructs and verifies a structure of theory and methodology, but from that man's followers. Whatever the university attended, whatever the degree obtained, the simple fact, as he had observed it in men's minds, was that most men, even scientists, do not have the courage to follow the basic tenets of science; that even though they may call it science they actually stand upon a structure of faith.

And having had one structure taken out from under them, they seize upon another and guard it with a desperate frenzy, lest it, too, be threatened.

Speculative theory then becomes canonized law; suggested procedure becomes ritual; tentative statements become rote. And if their practice of it makes them successful, it becomes impossible for them to conceive of any other truth but their own. It works, therefore it is right. The originator, having had the flexible intelligence to vary from the old and create a new, might have been able to conceive of still yet another structure than his own; but his followers have the proof of their own infallibility always before their eyes.

Joe was aware of the obvious; that any theory is true within the framework where it applies; and any theory is false outside its own coordinate system. He knew, and now Bossy had proved his knowledge, that it is never the accuracy of the theory as an absolute, but rather the persistence of applying it and staying well within the boundaries of its framework which brings success.

So the growing organism of speculative consideration hardens into the ironclad coffin of orthodoxy.

And orthodoxy was having its day.

Bossy was something new. Bossy did not fit into their theory structure therefore Bossy was, *per se*, wrong. They would gladly go to their graves, firm and proud to the last expiring breath of how right they were.

"Listen to what Dr. Frederick Pomeroy says,"

Steve spoke up, and read aloud without waiting for a response.

"We should remember that Bossy was never intended to be more than an accident-prevention device on our faster military planes. The imputation of therapeutic qualities is a travesty on our intelligence. When the truth of the Mabel Monohan case is finally uncovered—and it will be uncovered, never fear—we shall undoubtedly find that a shameful fraud has been perpetrated on the public.' "

Flynn flicked the page with his fingertip.

"That just about sums up most of the comment," he said. "Unless you'd like to hear what Dr. Eustace Fairfax, consulting psychologist for the San Francisco Police Department, has to say?"

Kennedy whirled his chair around. His eyes were bleak, but his lips were fighting a smile.

"That's the one who saw Mabel at the jail, isn't it?" he asked.

Steve turned several pages of the paper. The comments of Dr. Eustace Fairfax were buried down among the reactions of the lesser lights.

" 'There were those among the laity,' " Steve read, " 'who scorned professional opinion and counsel. There were those in public life who preferred to pander to the emotions of the mob. There were those who chose to ridicule me when I testified that Mabel Monohan was a mentally unbalanced young woman who should be confined to an institution. Perhaps now they will remember their words, and in the future leave the problems of the mentally ill to those who are qualified to deal with them.' "

One could almost see the thin, fanatic face, the long nose quivering with indignation, the polished glasses sparkling with triumphant venom. Dr. Eustace Fairfax was indeed a cookbook psychiatrist, and by turning the tentative considerations of authority into esoteric articles of commandments he became authority.

The quotation sparked Joe's impatience. He decided it was time now to let both men know where he was going.

"Of course none of them realize that the experiment was a complete success," he said quietly.

Steve Flynn all but fell out of his chair. His mouth dropped open and his chin hung slack as he stared at Joe. Kennedy's eyes sparkled with something approaching pride and approval.

"I've been wondering when you were going to take us into your confidence, Joe," he said.

Steve's jaw suddenly clamped shut and his eyes narrowed in sudden anger.

"I don't get it!" he said harshly. "I don't get any part of that. You mean you knew this was going to happen, that Bossy wasn't going to work on Billings, and you let us go ahead and make fools of ourselves anyway?"

"The point," Joe said mildly, "is that I didn't know, not surely. I had to find out. I tried to warn you to tone down the publicity. I would have preferred the experiment in complete secrecy; that is, at first. Then later, I realized the wider the publicity for the failure, the better. It's a good idea for mankind to know just what he's up against."

"Right now I'd settle for knowing what *I'm* up

272

against," Steve said disgustedly. Joe could feel the release of somatic tensions as the anger drained out of Flynn.

"Look," he continued, "what Bossy can or can't do is no skin off my nose. But you give me a job to do. You give me the job of making the public like Bossy. So I go ahead and build it up, make a big production out of it, big deal, my masterpiece. And now I find out you're expecting just the opposite of what I expected." He turned to Kennedy and asked, with a note of accusation in his voice. "Did you expect this too, Mr. Kennedy?"

"I wondered about it," Kennedy answered him quietly. "In view of what Joe said to me the first time we met, I wondered."

"It wasn't a deliberate double cross, Steve," Joe said, and washed away the traces of rebellion in Steve's mind. "I didn't know how it was going to come out. I hoped it would turn out the way it has, but I didn't know it would."

"I don't get it," Steve repeated, and this time there was hurt in his voice. "It helps that you didn't deliberately cross me up, but—oh brother!"

"Do you know anything about trees, Steve?" Joe asked.

Flynn turned and looked at him sharply. These Brains! You never knew what tangent they were going to take next. How they ever managed to get anything done when they couldn't stay on the subject more than two minutes was beyond him. Oh, brother!

"I don't get that either," he answered, and kept his opinion of this woolgathering to himself.

"In a forest of giant trees," Joe said, "seedlings

273

sicken and die. They need sunlight to grow; they can't get it. It's only around the fringes of the forest, as it spreads out, that they can get the right environment for growth. In the center the only growths that survive are the kind who can live in a filtered gloom. They survive under that certain condition, but they couldn't survive a change; they couldn't survive a condition which is normal environment elsewhere. They can't even survive direct sunlight. You get that in a civilization of humans, too. The significant changes always come from the fringes; there's no room for them to develop where the giant trees still stand."

It was obvious that Steve still did not get it.

"It may sound like a paradox," Joe explained, "but death, itself, is a survival factor. Environment is subject to change. The only life which can survive is the kind which can meet the challenge of the change. This means that every form of life must be constantly trying out new mutant patterns so that when the change comes there are mutations capable of meeting it.

"Did you ever notice, speaking as a class, that the castoff detritus of evergreen trees poisons the ground around them so that nothing but their own kind can grow? An idea, which becomes an evergreen tradition, does the same. But the castoff detritus of deciduous trees, which have the false death of winter, enriches the ground. A variant offspring has a chance to survive."

Kennedy's eyes closed, and he sat silently, hardly breathing.

"And I've always been bitter toward my son," he said. "No wonder he couldn't grow."

"You'll have to draw pictures for me," Steve said in a puzzled voice. "The boss gets it, but I don't."

274

* * *

"The reason Mabel was able to respond to Bossy is quite simple," Joe explained. "In spite of the kind of life she led, Mabel was at heart quite a believer in the truth of the artificial mores our civilization has set up. You find that far more frequently than is generally realized. Now she lived a life of sin and a life of crime. She should have been punished for it, according to her inner convictions, but instead she prospered. As she grew older, she grew more confused. Humanity says one thing and does another; sets up a whole system of ethics and then prospers through violating them. Mabel was honest, she could not reconcile what happens with what is taught. She wound up completely bewildered, at a loss to account for why man's teachings and his behavior seem to have little or nothing in common.

"She wanted answers to all this. She really wanted answers, not just confirmations of what she already believed. Her prejudice screen had been knocked so full of holes that ideas could get through to her without first being deformed all out of reality to fit her preset conviction. Mabel was ready for therapy."

"And Dr. Billings wasn't," Kennedy said.

"That's right," Joe agreed. "Dr. Billings had built a worldwide reputation on a structure which he believed to be right. Intellectually he is able to consider that other structures may be valid, but against deep seated convictions that his must be the right one because he has proved that it works, these are just mental exercises. In a showdown, he stopped playing word games and clung to his convictions. Only on a single-valued basis were they right. Mabel wanted to know; Billings already knew, or thought he did."

"I don't see what that has got to do with trees," Steve said flatly.

"Man represents a mutation of life wherein the intellect will get its chance to prove survival worth. It hasn't done that yet, you understand. All sorts of life forms flourish grandly for a while and then die out. But universal time is a long time. Remember the giant reptiles flourished for forty million years. Man will have to better that record before he can truly say that intellect is superior to massive bulk and a thick hide.

"Against that forty million years, man has about seven thousand years of historical record. But man acts as if, and apparently really believes, he already has the answers, that there is nothing left for mankind to do for the next forty million years except to imitate the man of today."

"Trees," Steve reminded Joe dryly.

"We have always thought that immortality would be valuable because it would preserve the great minds, give them a longer span to carry on their work. But that would be making a mind perpetually green, to tower over others, to prevent the growth of unlike ideas.

"When a thing stops growing, reaches its maximum growth, it starts to die. Any single-valued idea is limited to a given set of frameworks, but a man who holds to a single-valued idea tries to make it fit all frameworks. He warps it and twists it into a monstrosity, until it defeats its own purpose and denies its own validity. Its own warp and tension destroys it, and him with it.

"One of the laws of life, of the universe since life is of the universe and not an exception to it, is that

276

change takes place. But a single-valued idea, by definition, denies the possibility of change. Bossy is a scientific instrument. Scientific instruments do not work through denying the basic laws of matter-energy. Bossy cannot work to restore an organism which denies them.

"Through statements he made the night before, I suspected Dr. Billings couldn't shed the old and worn-out single values upon which he had built his life. But, you see, all this was only theory. And I couldn't know what would happen until it was put to the test. I don't trust theories which can't be demonstrated, particularly when they depend upon the support of other theories which also can't be demonstrated. I had to see if Bossy worked at a basic level, or if she was simply a super gook gadget, hypnotizing the cells into renewing themselves."

"I can just see myself selling all this to the public," Steve said gloomily. "Oh, brother!"

Kennedy's lips twitched in a smile.

"Evergreen trees," Steve mourned on, "deciduous trees, civilizations, forty million years, laws of matter-energy, single-value ideas—oh, brother!"

He took out a cigarette and even his lighter seemed to lack its usual loud snap.

"And right now, the way things have gone, the public wouldn't touch Bossy with a ten-foot pole, anyhow."

CHAPTER XX

But a good night's sleep was all Steve Flynn really needed. He awoke the following morning filled with optimism and wonder that he had even temporarily felt set back.

That was the trouble with being around Brains. They were so confused themselves that they got everybody else confused. Just being around them, listening to them talk, made a man forget what was important and what wasn't. Being around these guys had made him forget he had a simple job to do. He had to make the public like Bossy, that was all.

He had been just plain nuts. The big copy, the real copy, the kick with all the oomph in it was Mabel. And he hadn't played her up hardly at all. The gal had legs, she had teeth, what more could a publicity man want? Just smile at 'em, sister, and show 'em your gams, and they'll buy.

By the time he reached his office in the Kennedy Building, he already had a campaign mapped out. And he had a staff, a real staff of upbeat boys and gals to carry out the details. The public wanted Mabel? The public would get Mabel! It was that simple.

He was whistling through his teeth and snapping his gold lighter loudly when his Publicity Department heads trouped in for the conference he summoned. Their faces showed an appreciation of his mood.

All day yesterday they had not known what to do. They were like dancers frozen into still poses by sudden silence as the desperate music was cut off. Everything had come to an end with the failure of Bossy, and the empty pause had been ghastly. By evening they had been ready to cut their own throats, and only the stupor of Brady's tall cool ones had got them through the night. But now all was well. The boss was whistling through his teeth and snapping his lighter.

Flynn needed to give them only the bare outlines of the campaign. They could pick up a beat and knew what to do with it. The music was starting up again around the public relations offices.

As complementary to one another as an expert jam session they trouped out of his office, anxious to get the variations on the theme suggested. Steve signaled to the head production man to wait while he made a phone call. There might be further things to be picked up.

His upbeat mood was running so strong that Steve was not even set back when Joe refused to allow Mabel to be disturbed.

Mabel wasn't able to see photographers and reporters? Swell, kid! Wonderful. Great copy! By the way, what was wrong with her? A sort of shock? Stupendous! This was more like it. Couldn't be better! Kid, why didn't you tell me all this before? Kid, you're just plain nuts! Can't you see it, fella? MABEL ROUSED FROM DEEP COMA TO APPEAR BEFORE WORLD SCIENTISTS! You Brains, you kill me! Don't you know a dramatic punch when it's smacking you right in the nose? Oh, brother! I'll play that angle up in such a way that they'll forget all about Billings. Billings? Who's Billings? That's what they'll be saying by this time tomorrow, fella.

Now look here, Joe. I got a job to do. They *gotta* forget about Billings. I can't sell Bossy by playing up how she failed on him! Man, use some sense. You gotta have positive! You can't sell negative! Look, boy, I don't care one blasted thing about whether the public gets educated or not. Kennedy says make 'em like Bossy. Kennedy's my boss. I'm gonna make 'em like Bossy. It's that simple!

He felt like slamming down the phone, but he was a publicity man and years of training turned on an automatic charm, instead.

"O.K., fella? Sure, sure. I see your point. Sure, Joe, anything you want. O.K.? O.K., then."

He put the phone receiver down and grimaced up to his waiting production man.

"No fresh pics," he said.

The production man shrugged. There were plenty of studies from the newsreels taken at the show yesterday. The boss knew they could be superimposed over any background needed. It wasn't a calamity.

"Whatever you say, boss," he agreed. "Just so I know what I got to work with." He'd sold 'em high, he'd sold 'em low. He'd built one thing up today, and built something else up tomorrow to top it. It was all in the day's work for him. All he asked was to be let in on what was going on, what was wanted. He'd produce it.

Thin, blond, deceptively mild, infinitely obliging, he was ideal for his job. He was like Toledo steel, pliable enough to bend in any direction required, and then snapping right back as soon as the pressure eased. Like Steve, he agreed with his opposition, and then did it his own way, anyhow.

He left Steve's office and began to go from department to department, coordinating, sparking, blending ideas, giving in to arguments without expressing any opposition and then winning the argument in the long run through the sheer power of flexibility and resilience; he began to get releases on the wires, layout copy to printers, setting up conferences, arranging influence dates, wheedling or requiring cooperation as the circumstances indicated.

The communications systems got some new things to talk about.

CHAPTER XXI

For three days Steve's office kept Mabel hovering on the thin edge between life and death. Her fever was up, it was down. She was conscious, she was in a coma. She could eat, she had to be fed intravenously. Breath by faltering breath, she fought a valiant battle for her life in the columns of the press.

And throughout it all she was still young, still beautiful, still able to flash her teeth and show her gams, still gloriously photogenic.

As Steve Flynn had predicted, the public forgot all about Billings. This was more like it. Now the full story was being told. Nurtured on soap opera, their concepts shaped by Hollywood's interpretation of what constitutes drama, which had not changed except in techniques from the days of Pearl White and the Keystone Cops, at last the public was getting a full-course dinner of sloppy sentimentalism and ersatz amusement park thrills.

The principal commentators who dealt in like material saw rich fare for their audiences and the public went on a dizzying binge of concern. Mabel was nobly forgiven for the past life that she had led, and everyone enjoyed that feeling of personal stature by admitting that there might be some good in the worst of us.

Yet not everyone. For all his knowledge of his business of how to play upon public emotion like an artist at a console organ, Steve slipped. The very bulletins which were selling the public on Mabel, and through her on Bossy, in the way a car is sold by showing a woman's legs as she climbs into it, also provided the opposition with the material it had been needing.

The time has passed when a company may hand down an edict that no employee below the rank of top executive may own certain exclusive makes of cars, or royalty say that certain thrills are too good for commoners. The time has passed, but the motivation behind it has not. The more the common public exulted, the more the elite ground its teeth in rage. How dare this stupid machine grant immortality to a common prostitute and deny it to a man of their own class, Billings? The more the public wallowed in its binge of emotionalism, the more the intellectuals held aloof in disdain.

Some of Joe's discussion had crept into Steve's campaign. Gradually the public began to realize that Mabel had gone through a form of dying and being reborn. They saw danger where there had been no danger, because they preferred it that way.

And life and death was the sole prerogative of the medical profession. By the admission of Bossy's own protectors, submission to Bossy was a matter of life and death.

They stormed upon Washington in concerted protest. And they provided the hook which Washington had been seeking. The legislative, the administrative, the judicial branches of government had all been asking the same question of themselves.

"Who deserves to be perpetuated, made immortal?"

And the answer had been obvious to them.

This was something clearly too good for the commoners, but they had not dared impound the machine for this reason. They had needed as always, some other reason quite remote from their true motive. The medical profession proved it; Bossy was too dangerous to be left in irresponsible hands.

Still, this was election year. The administrative and the legislative branches were directly dependent upon votes, and the judicial was indirectly dependent as even a cursory glance at history would show.

And while Steve Flynn was playing with artistry and mastery upon his console, making the public laugh and weep, hope and fear, the three forces of government drew together, and with one accord turned their eyes toward the Pentagon. The military was not dependent upon votes. And Bossy was obviously a dangerous weapon of war.

It took little to convince the Chiefs of Staffs of this; for the Chiefs were still seeing the glorious vision of endless ranks of perpetually young men marching into beautiful flaming holocausts of destruction.

Yet even they had learned caution. If someone is to be court-martialed for a mistake, then let it be an enlisted man, or at least an officer of lower rank; one, of course, which had generously been elevated from the ranks and not from an academy.

Kennedy was having breakfast with Joe and Mabel, Carney and Flynn, Billings and Hoskins.

"Who is going to be next to try Bossy, Joe?" Kennedy asked. He noticed that Joe had fallen silent a few moments ago, as if he were thinking deeply on something.

But Joe answered easily, with a light laugh.

"No one has volunteered as yet," he said.

"Isn't that rather an unorganized way of going about it, Joe?" Kennedy asked.

There was a sharp exclamation of surprise, alarm, from Mabel. Kennedy caught a fleeting glance in her direction from Joe. There had been almost a warning in the glance. Suddenly for no apparent reason, the room chilled. Mabel's face was pale, but she forced a smile and tried to urge more coffee on Flynn.

Perhaps the most curious expression was Carney's. Up until Kennedy had asked the question about who was going to be next to try Bossy, Carney had obviously been minding his manners, and trying to make light chitchat in the manner of Brains. But now the man's face was contorted, as if he were fighting some inner battle with himself, as if he had a great fear and was trying to tell himself that it was groundless.

And over it all lay bewilderment and yearning, and loneliness.

Joe did not answer Kennedy's question. Kennedy was watching him closely. He saw Joe's eyes lift to the door behind where Kennedy sat. He saw Mabel's eyes go to the same spot.

It was after both of them were looking at the door that the knock came. And then the door opened without waiting for invitation. Superintendent Jones stuck his head in the door.

"There are soldiers at the gate," he quavered. "They say if we don't let them in they'll shell the gate down. They're here to take over Bossy."

CHAPTER XXII

Joe had just switched off his bed lamp and was settling back into his pillow when a warning came to him. The premonition was as clear and distinct as the ringing of a bell.

He swung his feet to the floor and in the darkness groped for his robe and slippers. Someone was stealing down the corridor in this wing of the Margaret Kennedy Clinic, and was making a great effort not to be heard. It was the intense concentration on avoiding attention which had telepathed the warning to Joe.

In the same instant that he focused his psionic sight, Joe perceived that the prowler was Doc Carney; that the old con man was intent on reaching Bossy.

Bossy! But that would be impossible for the old man. Bossy was under padlock and government seal; with a soldier posted before each door of the operating amphitheater. The guard had been there since early morning, changed at two-hour intervals.

The military had established its beachhead, the main forces had not yet moved up. The impounding of Bossy by a small contingent was a scouting mission. The strength of the opposing forces had not yet been determined.

The Pentagon had not been worried about Kennedy's forces. These were already clamoring in Washington for an injunction to stop the seizure of Bossy, but this was to be expected. The main opposition, the one which had not yet declared itself, was public reaction. There was also fear of Bossy, herself. The machine had not been fully tested. It might have unknown striking powers. If it were as close to the human mind as was claimed, it might turn vindictive, revengeful.

Through devious channels to baffle investigators and wear out the publicity value long before the truth came to light, the Pentagon sent out its task force to draw the enemy's fire, and waited.

That was Joe's summation of the background, and now here was Carney tiptoeing down the corridor, a kit of burglar tools in one hand, intent on breaking in to Bossy. His motivation was clear to Joe, if not to himself.

Ever since Mabel had gone into therapy, Carney had been a lost man. For the first time in his life he knew what it was to be completely alone. There was no companionship left for him back on skid row, and Mabel, his pal, his only tie to the old mores of his existence, had become something else entirely. There had never been love between them, contrary to gossip; there had never even been physical attraction. They were simply two old people who had led the same kind of life, drawn together out of mutual respect, and held together in a close orbit because there was no pull from any other direction.

That was all changed now. His whole world was changed. Even his contempt, his disgust, his fear of Brains had changed. They, too, were just guys who made the best of things, tried to get along according to their own lights. This had been the evolution of his thinking since the time Joe had insisted he leave skid row and come to the Margaret Kennedy Clinic. He didn't understand why Joe had insisted upon it, he didn't have to be told that there was no need for him there, that he was simply in the place, not of it. He wasn't even in the way; he wasn't even that important.

He was confused, he was lonely, he was no longer certain of anything. He, without knowing it, was ready for Bossy. And he was drawn to Bossy as though to a magnet. He was searching for Mabel, and the only way to find her was through Bossy. They talked about the immortality Bossy could give you, but that wasn't what he wanted. He simply wanted to know, to understand, to find comprehension because now he knew he had none.

The one remaining spark of his old life was his resentment at the padlock on Bossy's door. The lock was a symbol of his whole life. He had always either been locked out or locked in. There had always been a lock between him and the thing he wanted. A lock had become a challenge. It was a challenge he could not resist. He had wavered in indecision before, knowing very well that even if he again found Mabel through Bossy it would not be the same as it had been before, but as soon as the padlock was placed there his mind was made up. The symbol had been inserted again between him and what he wanted. He rose to the challenge.

His motives were quite clear to Joe; and Joe breathed a huge sigh of relief. He had wondered when Carney would come around to it.

When the old man was safely past his door, Joe slipped out into the corridor behind him. He set up a protecting wave field which would prevent the old man from hearing him, or seeing him if he turned around.

And he set up a wave field of illusion around old Carney himself.

At the next turn of the corridor, Carney paused to case the situation ahead. It was nearly midnight, and the young soldier on guard, feeling that by now the lieutenant would be safely in bed and asleep, had pulled a chair up in front of this main entrance to the operating amphitheater. He had tilted his chair back against the door and was dozing there comfortable with his rifle across his knees, dreaming of the next twenty-four-hour pass and the little brunette he had met on a Hyde Street cable car.

Alternative plans came into Carney's thoughts. He could rush the soldier, who seemed to be asleep, or he could make a noise and wake him, then stop to pass the time of night with the kid who was probably bored and lonesome and find an opportunity to clonk him on the head.

Joe decided to take a further hand. Either scheme seemed unlikely for success. Into the young soldier's dream, half reverie and half real on the edge of sleep,

Joe injected the image of a frowning officer. It was not just the lieutenant, not even a captain. This was big brass, real brass. GHQ stuff. There was a guilt feeling in the young man's mind anyway because he had settled back and was resting his eyes; it was not difficult to materialize the symbol of retribution.

The soldier stirred uneasily and his movement decided Carney on the latter plan. He would just happen by and start talking. At the sound of a footstep, the symbol of retribution crystallized into reality. The soldier's eyes popped open in sheer horror. He pitched forward from his chair and somehow managed to get to attention without dropping his rifle.

The snapping to attention, the look of horrified awe shocked Carney into immobility also. For a long moment, the two of them stood there, each immobile. The guard's worst fears were confirmed. He saw before him a general, a two-star general. He had been caught sleeping at his post by a two-star general! He opened his mouth twice before he could get words to come out.

"S-sorry, s-sir," he stammered. The effort, feeble as it was, revived the pattern of self-preservation. "I . . . I was just resting my bad leg . . . twisted it on the range yesterday . . . sir—"

Carney stared at the soldier in disbelief. The kid had gone nuts. They were all wacky.

Joe gave the soldier his first faint gleam of hope. This general wasn't interested in him. He wasn't there to check up on the guard. He had important business. He had come by plane from Washington to make a personal inspection of this Bossy machine. But his visit was strictly hush-hush. Secret stuff. Classified! Restricted! Off limits! No enlisted men allowed. Officers only. The pattern was familiar, believable.

"I want in there, right now, at once," Carney heard his lips forming the words crisply, and wondered where they came from.

"Yes, sir," the soldier almost whispered. "Thank you, sir. But, sir, I don't have a key, sir. The lieutenant, sir—" He felt a little easier. If the general couldn't get in it was the lieutenant's fault. And he had used enough sirs to placate even a two-star general.

Carney opened his kit of burglar tools and fished out a ring of skeleton keys. That ring was the pride and joy, the lifetime collection of one of the boys who was now donating some time to the State.

"Try these," he said, and tossed them to the guard.

As key after key failed, the soldier grew more and more nervous until finally when one did work he was so relieved that he flung the door open, breaking the government seal, without a second thought.

"Right in here, sir," he said hurriedly. "I'll see that you're not disturbed, sir. Thank you, sir. Thank you, SIR . . . I mean."

Carney blinked at him owlishly. He didn't understand it, he didn't even understand himself, the way he'd acted. The kid soldier had apparently snapped his cap, but then what could you expect these days? He patted the boy on the shoulder.

"Take it easy, son," he said kindly. "You ain't no worse off than anybody else."

Tears of gratitude welled up in the soldier's eyes. Now, for the first time, he understood this feeling of loyalty they were always telling him he'd better have,

294

or else. Here was a real officer, a regular guy. The kind of an officer you could go through hell for—He blinked the tears away and saluted, not trusting himself to speak.

Carney shook his bald head pityingly, and shuffled into the operating room.

When the door had closed behind Carney, Joe turned and ran back down the corridor to Hoskins' room. He shook the cyberneticist awake and dragged him, protesting, across the hall to the suite assigned to Billings. When both of them were sufficiently awake to understand him, he told them what had happened and briefly outlined his plan.

Billings looked uncertain, but Hoskins delightedly smashed his fist into the palm of his other hand.

"Good work, Joe," he exclaimed. "It's worth a try, anyway. Come on, Jonathan."

"Just walk right past the guard," Joe cautioned. "Don't say a word."

He hurried to his own room and phoned Steve Flynn. The phone rang a long time before he heard Steve growl an angry response.

At first Steve didn't get it. Joe repeated the essential facts of his plan. Steve got it then. He whooped joyfully into the phone, anger and sleep forgotten.

"Genius, kid! Pure, homogenized genius! You just keep control over there and watch Steve Flynn go into his super best!"

CHAPTER XXIII

There was a time when scientists believed that when vapor in a cloud reached 32°F the fog froze, as respectable water should, and formed into snowflakes—all nice and tidy and dependable. Field tests, in the contrary way of reality, did not confirm them. Sometimes the temperature was as much as 60°F colder than freezing, and still the stubborn cloud refused to coagulate into snow. Then they found that a mere handful of dry ice could turn a whole roiling cloud into a sudden snowstorm.

The mass psychology of the public mind was like that. Potential would build up, higher and higher, and still there would be no mass reaction. A straw would be tossed to see which way the wind blew, and would fall to earth unnoticed. Many a politician, many a pollster, assumed from this that there was no reaction potential.

Then some insignificant little thing, some complete triviality, would seed the public mind, and a raging storm, over apparently nothing, would ensue. To those who had no conception of the forces of mass psychology, this made the public mind unpredictable.

Steve Flynn did not know the scientific terms to account for his mastery of public emotion; but he knew something better. He knew how to feel the mass psychology potential, and when and how to seed it to make it crystallize. He could not have held his own in the bright patter of devastating epigrams which rolled so easily off the tongues of the lunatic intellectual fringe which had moved over from art and into science; but he could do where they could only talk about.

He withheld breaking the news of Carney's therapy for hour after hour. The public mind had too high a potential of unbalance from Billings failure in Bossy to risk another such fiasco.

Quietly, working completely behind the scenes, swearing each contact to secrecy, he set the stage for another world-wide television show. He even made the mistake, a part of his well calculated plan, of letting a notoriously unethical news commentator get word of what was happening just before that worthy went on the air.

The commentator scooped the world with the rumor that Bossy was being tried again.

It was the handful of dry ice in a high potential of mass psychology. The tornado, the typhoon, the cyclone of public reaction was sudden and complete. Under normal circumstances, when the military had found its beachhead squad outmaneuverred, a larger contingent would have been sent in to take over and stop all this nonsense.

But, in view of the public clamor to be let in on

what was happening, the mobs which gathered outside of newspaper offices and broadcasting studios all over the nation, the unaccountable mobs like those in an old-fashioned movie storming the palace gates, the Pentagon found it expedient to get all snarled up in orders and countermanded orders so that no action resulted.

The Chief of Staff was suddenly out of the city on urgent business. He could not be reached for a decision. Back down through the echelons, rank by rank, went the responsibility for decision. Back across the continent to San Francisco it traveled. Back to Area Headquarters. Back to Post. Back to the lieutenant, who took the only possible course—and turned the whole thing over to his sergeant.

"I know I can depend on you to take the appropriate action," he said crisply.

The sergeant nodded. He had been expecting it all the time. He would just keep changing the guard, the quite useless guard the way everybody and his dog kept running in and out of the room, until somebody, somewhere made a decision.

The stage was set, and Bossy, bless her, was cooperating. To question after question, she answered instantly and simply:

"Progress satisfactory."

Assured by Joe, Billings and Hoskins, at noon Steve Flynn decided there was every chance the experiment on Carney would be a success. The scene in the amphitheater, set up again under the same conditions as the experiment on Billings, flashed on the television screens in millions of homes.

Slowly, the amphitheater filled again with the renowned scientists of the world.

By six o'clock the public began to get bored, restive. Carney's tired old body lay on the table under the glare of television lights, and its only movement was its rhythmic breathing, and occasional enigmatic twitch of the facial muscles, the tensing and relaxing of fingers and toes. There wasn't much to see. The entertainment value of watching an old man sleep is limited.

One by one the TV chains returned to more remunerative programs where the public would feel at home in the old familiar cliche situations and gags that had passed for entertainment from time immemorial. Each chain promised to devote a half hour here and there, and anyone who really wished to hang upon Carney's every breath could do so by judiciously twirling his dial.

Steve Flynn's staff did a magnificent job of interest buildup; bringing in all the old phony hackneyed situations guaranteed to make the public love Carney. His dead-end childhood around the wharves of the Embarcadero read like a chapter from Lincoln's life. Carney became a tow-headed little tot who studied by the light of street lamps, and lectured his playmates on the moral principles involved in stealing apples. His youthful years at juvenile delinquent institutions provided inspiration for a repetition of the sentimental prose of Dickens. The mature years developed into a search for comprehension, a misunderstood man buffeted by society, one of nature's noble martyrs.

The public had its biggest cry since Camille. They stared at their TV screens with the fascination of the crowd who gathers at the scene of a murder and just looks.

In the days that passed Steve's office brought the public up to date on Carney's later life. The friendship between old Mabel and old Carney became a great and noble thing, touched with humor and bathos, unenlivened by any hint of turgid passion. Mabel had simply rescued an old childhood friend and had given him back his self-respect—in view of the whitewashing job done it was not quite clear how he had lost it—by making him manager of her picturesque little pawnshop down on Third Street.

Within an hour the pawnshop was completely cleaned out of all its merchandise by souvenir hunters who would pay any price for a slightly used jimmy or the hubcap of an out-of-date automobile.

The world took skid row to her motherly bosom and the winos hovering in cold doorways became the bewildered recipients of much good advice and some help. The shortline became both proud and resentful of their new status. The professional do-gooders had been at it long enough to have at least a little understanding of why a man was on the shortline in the first place. These new uplifters made the men uncomfortable. But they endured it, in the passive way they had endured all the other outrageous demands of a society with which they had never been able to cope.

And they knew that within a week or two the goodwill jag would pass, and be as faded and tired as a forgotten Christmas wreath on the tenth of January.

In fact, the camellia of compassion was already starting to turn brown around the edges, showing that first sign of decay.

"Why?" some of the more respectable members of society were beginning to ask. "Why is Bossy successful only with the most disreputable creatures that could be found? What kind of warped minds had rigged the machine so that it would give immortality only to the worst dregs of society?"

Accustomed to rigging everything from slot mchines to semantics in favor of some particular group, they could not conceive of a machine which had not been rigged and slanted deliberately.

Deep beneath the roar of the crowd which was delighted by it all, the voices of the people who really mattered began to coalescesce into an opinion which began to be heard around Washington.

It was on the eighth day that some changes in Carney began to be evident. Step by step, and this time for the awed eyes of the world, Carney duplicated the pattern of renewal followed by Mabel.

The plasma supply suddenly became a very important item.

"More plasma," Bossy's screen would announce.

The TV commentator would murmur in his best bedside voice:

"More plasma."

Then, after the requisite two-second pause, the announcer would add:

"This plasma transfusion is by courtesy of Midvale Memorial Hospital, Oakland, fully equipped and staffed for your every need. Luxurious service, modest prices. Pay-as-you-go-plan."

The figure on the operating table straightened its tired old bones, flaked off the outer epidermis of faded skin, shed the lank wisps of dirty gray hair. The figure of a vibrant young man began to emerge, strong and lithe and beautiful.

The tenth day passed. Now there was a renewed interest in watching the television screen. All the world knew that Mabel had emerged on the tenth day. But to repeated questions on when Doc Carney would emerge, Bossy simply answered:

"Progress satisfactory."

Perhaps it was the basic differences between the masculine and the feminine psyche which lengthened the therapy; perhaps there were just more cells to be re-educated. Or perhaps it was the additional facts which Joe had fed into Bossy. Facts about psionics, which he hoped would be fed into the patient's mind to condition him to the shock of unshielded normal minds.

Whatever the reason, it was the twelfth day before Bossy, without any buildup, fanfare, or pyrotechnics of any kind, made her announcement.

"Project completed." Bossy lacked showmanship.

But Steve Flynn did not. The release of every electrode from Carney's pulse points was played up as if it were world shaking. For that crucial moment necessary in catering to psychotically frustrated womanhood, the view of the cameras was obscured by the doctors hovering around; and when the public saw him again, the towel which had been draped across Carney's body had been replaced by a pair of conventional shorts.

The cameras were focused fully upon his face when he opened his eyes. There was no daze in them. Their first expression was one of amusement, a glinting

303

flicker of mischief. Aided by Billings he sat up and looked about him. His eyes found Joe.

"Hi, fella," he said. They were his first words.

It was all close enough to stock plot number X672, Patient Regains Consciousness after Critical Illness, for the public to understand it. The public cried, it laughed, it shouted, it rang bells, blew whistles, got drunk, enjoyed itself in a national spontaneous Mardi Gras.

With a flourish Steve Flynn provided slacks, an open-throated sports shirt, socks and shoes. To take away the last vestige of an unkempt look, a barber began to cut Carney's hair. The rust colored hair shaped into a bristling snappy style favored by the hot young bloods of the day.

Carney accepted it all, quietly and pliably. He was impassive except for a tiny crinkle of humor at the corners of his eyes.

In the days to follow twenty million young men would be diligently practicing before their mirrors to get that same spontaneous crinkle of good humor.

"Are you able to talk to us?" Steve Flynn asked Carney.

Again there was that questioning flicker of eyes toward Joe.

"Of course," Carney answered after the briefest of hesitations.

He endured the process of milking the situation for all the ham drama there was in it which TV considers so necessary to public enjoyment of its programs. Yes, he felt wonderful. Yes, he was very happy and grateful for his restored youth. No, it had not been unpleasant or painful. Yes, he remembered everything which had gone on. No, he didn't realize it had been twelve days; it seemed to be over in an instant, and yet it had seemed to go on for all eternity. No, he had never doubted it would be a success. Yes there were times when it had been difficult to comprehend Bossy, it was all so different from what he had believed; but he had been willing to listen. Yes, he would say the willingness to listen was a vital factor. Yes, of course he expected to resume his friendship with Mabel.

"No," he answered to a more direct question. "There is no question of a romance between Mabel and me. Mabel has already found the one she loves, my best friend over there—Joe Carter."

Like Bossy, he seemed to lack showmanship. It was said so quietly, almost tossed away, that even Steve failed to grasp the import of it all at once. Then, frantically, Steve waved the camera to focus on Joe. Here was news as important as Carney's revival. Mabel was in love!

The cameras focused over where Joe sat. It was the first time that Joe Carter had come fully into the eye of the public.

Out of camera range for the moment, Carney allowed his lips to broaden into a delighted grin.

"Come on, Joe," he flashed psionically. "Take it like a man. That's what you told me to do, when I asked if I should answer those stupid questions."

Joe's face was controlled, but he flashed back an answer.

"Very well—Geoffery-Mortimonte."

Carney burst into a soundless chuckle.

"You are good," he conceded. "I thought the little secret of my fancy names was known only to Bossy and me."

"I'll make it Jeff," Joe promised, while he continued to nod and smile into the impertinent cameras. "And let's keep Carney as a last name. You're public property now, and there's no use confusing people."

The public, who had thought its cup was full, found the cup now running over. Here was stock situation Faithful Friend-Girl-Lover. Would there be a juicy triangle? Crime and tragedy of passion? Who knew what uncontrolled fires of terror this rejuvenation would unleash?

The public licked its lips in anticipation.

CHAPTER XXIV

The public's cup was not the only vessel full and overflowing.

For the first time, Joe had found both love and companionship. For the first time, in a lifetime of bottomless loneliness, there were those of his own species with whom he could communicate. Denied love before, because he could not reconcile himself to the normal mind, first he had been given Mabel.

But Mabel was wise. Even before she had gone into Bossy, she knew that no woman could fill all of a man's life, that her relationship to him was compartmentalized, that the woman who tries to monopolize both love and companionship usually winds up with neither. She did not pretend to fill more than a woman's place in Joe's life.

In the instant recognition when Carney came out of Bossy, an instantaneous bond of masculine companionship even while Jeff was still on the table attached to the lead controls into Bossy, the last ache of Joe's chronic loneliness was eased and stilled.

Jeff, too, would need love, but not yet. In time there would be other women who could surrender their values to Bossy's corrections. The three of them, Mabel and Jeff and Joe, knew with complete certainty that the public would be denied its anticipated scandal, and could somehow survive without it.

The days passed. The schedule of television appearances began to slacken. The three were allowed occasional moments to themselves. Mabel and Jeff were public property. Joe, whose place in the total scheme of Bossy was still known only to Billings and Hoskins, although suspected by Kennedy and Flynn, was a minor bit of public property by virtue of his love affair with Mabel.

The psionic communion the three of them shared was completely beyond the level of news releases. True, around the clinic, there was considerable wonder at the way Mabel and Jeff adopted Joe, some sly comment about the secret reasons for the inseparability of the three, some recalling of Mabel's past life and criticism of Bossy that such things were not cured—but no comprehension.

There was a healthier concern, too, over the fact that the three of them began to slip away from the Clinic. Superintendent Jones admonished them with a shaking finger, and Steve Flynn portrayed the horrors of being mobbed by an admiring public; but to all questions and admonishments, Joe made a simple reply: "They need to get out and contact some of the world at first hand. We do not hold with the prevailing theory of psychology that the way to understand man is to shut oneself off from him in an ivory tower. We think the way to understand men is to look at them."

It was more than that, of course. Bossy, with the material given her by Joe, had done an excellent job of preparing Carney against the shock of raw and un-shielded human motivations. His reactions were amused and healthy.

But Mabel, unprepared because Joe had not realized what a shock sudden esperance would bring, still needed further therapy. Her background helped, of course. Her knowledge had been wide and deep. But even in such a house, as under the questioning of the most skilled psychologist, mankind still conceals more than it reveals.

And there was still another reason for their occa-sional escape from the Clinic. It was a healing therapy for Joe, too, that he should now be able to walk the same streets in full companionship which he had walked in such complete loneliness, shut off from all others because there had been no others. A man likes and needs to take his new love and his new friend to see the places he has known, to see them again through fresh, delighted eyes, to show the beauty and to lessen the memory of ugliness.

They were young.

Most often they took the car which Kennedy had placed at Joe's disposal, and went down from the hills into Berkeley. They had no difficulty in blurring their features for anyone who looked closely, and easily passed as three students from the adjoining campus of the University of California, they were regarded by the townspeople as just three more specimens of the ten thousand examples of learned brain lessness.

All around them, wherever they walked, was the clamor of man's thoughts about immortality. In the fashion of a catch phrase which unaccountably sweeps the country, everyone knew that only five per cent of human beings were worth perpetuating.

At a bus stop, two homeward-bound businessmen were being practical about the whole problem.

"The things we've gotta watch," one of them said, "is to see that some bunch of subversives don't get control of this thing. What we need is a committee of sound-thinking people in each community to decide on who should get immortal."

"Yeah," the other agreed instantly. "You know as well as I do that only about five per cent of any community take hold of their responsibilities. The rest are dead weight."

"Yeah, that's been proved by statistics. Now you take you and me, Henry. We're successful businessmen. How many people can make the grade? Only about five percent! And you and me, we gotta carry all the rest of the people on our backs." He waved vaguely in the direction of the university, and saw three students, coming down the sidewalk toward him. He lowered his voice:

"And I don't mean just employees, either. You take all them high and mighty professors up there. Where would they be if us businessmen didn't carry them on our backs?"

Henry pursed his lips judiciously.

"Well, you're right, Harry. But we gotta be big about this thing. Can't afford to be narrow-minded and not see the other fellow's point of view. Takes all kinds of people to make a world you know."

"Oh, sure, sure, Henry. But on the other hand birds of a feather flock together and too many cooks spoil

310

the soup. When you boil it all down there's still only about five per cent of the people that aren't completely worthless."

They fell silent as the three young people came within earshot.

Mabel and Joe both gasped at the sudden spasm of laughing mischief which flooded Jeff's mind.

"No, Jeff," Joe murmured aloud. "Don't."

But Jeff lacked Joe's lifetime of caution and concealment. He spoke just loudly enough to be overheard, and in the learned accents of the scholar which practical men find so insufferable.

"I tell you we must be careful who is allowed immortality. Some attention must be given to the appearance of the human race."

He seemed to become conscious that the two men were watching them.

The three passed the two on the sidewalk. Each group was silent so as not to be eavesdropped upon. Each group eyed the other with a compound of contemptuous and amused hostility which usually separates one generation from another.

"Think what the human race would look like," Jeff continued, still in earshot, "if a couple of tubs of lard like those two were given immortality to seed the earth with broadbottomed, pot-bellied kids!"

Mabel gasped and staggered under the impact of the wave of choleric fury which swept over them. Even Jeff was silenced. Mabel drew a deep breath and straightened.

"Your therapy is pretty strenuous, Jeff," she said. "A couple of days ago I couldn't have taken a blast like that."

Jeff's concern washed over her, healing, soothing.

"I didn't think about the effect of their reaction on you, Mabel," he said contritely. "I was just testing to see just how big about it all they were capable of being when they made their selections. In their minds they had already summed us up and rejected us, you know."

"I'm glad to know I can take it," Mabel said.

"Yes," Joe agreed silently. "So am I. Let's turn this corner wide open, without testing first. Try to stay wide open. I'll be there."

They turned the corner—wide open. The visual scene and the psionic scene both lay in clear view.

A car, driven by a scholarly old gentleman, had just pulled past the pumps of the service station and over to the door of the garage at one side. The motor was missing, would the mechanic please look into it? The mechanic lifted the hood, and saw that one of the wires from the distributor cap had worked loose. Well of all the stupid old goats. Naturally that spark plug wouldn't fire without any juice getting to it! He curbed the impulse to flare up in disgust at the helplessness of drivers in general. All the guy had to do was lift the hood and look!

But that was human beings for you. Ninety-five per cent of them wouldn't know a piston ring from a fan belt. If it weren't for the five per cent of guys like himself, guys who knew what made motors tick, the whole civilization would come to a stop. No matter how mechanized things got, it still boiled down to five per cent of the people carrying the other ninety-five per cent on their backs!

Interplayed with his thoughts was the great excitement in the old man's mind. He was on his way up to the University with an unmistakable connecting link between the Tu'un and the Sung Dynasty in Chinese Art. He was filled with elation at this long sought discovery. He could hardly contain his impatience at the delay, but his visit would be a long one and last far into the night; a night of exhilarating discussion. And if that pesty motor got worse he might be left afoot. The mechanic was still bent over the frame of the car, fiddling with wires.

The old gentleman tasted the triumph of saying to the mechanic, "I have just discovered the connecting link between—" The awe which would fill the man's face!

Then realization. The mechanic probably wouldn't even recognize a Ming piece, much less a Tu'un! Like the simple peasants of China, beasts of toil and burden, living only to sleep, to eat, to procreate their own misery.

It was only about five per cent of mankind which carried the lamp of knowledge and kept it glowing! Only five per cent to carry the other ninety-five per cent on their backs. He unconsciously straightened his back, as if to shift the load, make it easier to bear.

From the window of his third-floor walk-up across the street, a middle-aged writer looked down on the scene below him. Gradually his eyes focused on the three students, the mechanic and the old man. His thoughts left his space scout still fighting the controls of his ship to keep from being pulled into the sun, and, instead, analyzed the people below him in terms of his possible reading public. It would be a miracle if more than one of these belonged to the elite five per cent who read his stuff.

What a tragedy, what a horrible condemnation of the human race. Ninety-five per cent of the culture lagged far behind, as much as a quarter to a half century. Only five per cent were capable of speculating about a new idea, looking to the future, harbingers of progress. Five per cent who had to carry the rest of the culture on their backs, otherwise man would never progress at all!

Jeff could not resist the temptation. He shafted a thought into the writer's mind.

"The trouble is," the writer said aloud to himself in the way writers have, "ninety-five per cent of the people think in terms of single values. But what about multiple values?"

At first the words made no sense to him, also characteristic of writers, then he rushed over to his typewriter. He was triumphant at the breadth, the incredible vastness, of his inspiration. He tore the half finished page of space opera out of his machine. With nervous haste he threaded in a new page. He poised his fingers.

He did not write.

He picked up the pages of the half finished story from his desk. He did not even need to glance through them to know they were already out of date. His pseudo science analysis was no more than some tricky applications of thin single values. He tore the manuscript across and threw the pieces in the wastebasket.

He poised his fingers over the keyboard again. But no sentences formed into his mind to flow through his fingers. What would happen to his popularity with his audience if he implied that the beloved scientific method was a single value, only one way of interpreting reality? Were the disciples of science sufficiently scientific to question their own articles of faith? And what did he mean, even by these questions? He felt his inspiration slipping away from him in chaos and confusion.

He got up and walked over to the window where he had first felt his inspiration. Of course it wasn't superstition. But then, what about superstition? Had superstition ever been investigated in terms of multi valued logic? How could each man be so positive that his path, and only his, was the road to comprehension?

He gasped his exasperation and concentrated on the scene of reality. The elderly man was driving out of the garage. The mechanic was putting five dollars into the cash drawer. Odd, how he knew the denomination of that bill with such certainty! The three students had reached the corner of the block, and were turning it. Odd, that there seemed to be some connection between them and the inspiration he had just felt. Association of ideas, of course. They had been within his vision range when he had thought of the concept; therefore the concept was associated with them. Elementary psychology, nothing mysterious about it at all.

But then, wasn't that explaining things in terms of single values and dismissing the thought as solved?

The inspiration flooded him again, and the writer was appalled. What if each of those people down there on the street represented the only worthwhile five per cent?

What if, to them, he, an acknowledged brilliant

writer in idea speculation, were merely one of the worthless ninety-five per cent? He walked slowly over to his typewriter and sat down again. But he did not write anything—not yet.

"Instant acceptance of an idea is as self-defeating as instant rejection," he mumbled, and wondered where the words came from. "The implications of multi-values cannot be mastered in five seconds."

The thought consoled him a little, for the implication was that, in time, it might be mastered; that the destruction of single-value foundations only appeared to produce chaos because one didn't know how to find order in the new relationships of things. That is, not yet.

CHAPTER XXV

The clamor which followed Jeff Carney's rejuvenation mounted to a national frenzy.

Everybody wanted Bossy. Business and industry wanted Bossy, for quite aside from her rejuvenation possibilities, Bossy was the universal substitute for undependable manpower, the sure cure for faulty management judgement. Every government agency had to have Bossy immediately. There was no other possible way of solving the intricate and massive complexities of their responsibilities.

Both the sincere and the power-grabbing investigative committees had to have Bossy for obvious reasons. Law enforcement agencies saw the ultimate lie detector which no one could baffle. There was no end to the claims upon Bossy, no restraint upon the special axes which Bossy could grind. There was no conception that Bossy transcended single-valued frameworks, fostered no narrow vision, no finely meshed prejudice screen of the only possible right.

The Secretaries of the Interior and Treasury nearly

came to blows in the anteroom of the White House, where each was waiting to see the Chief Executive to demand exclusive jurisdiction over Bossy. The incipient fray was halted only by the confusion of arrivals of the Secretaries of State and Defense to press similar demands.

"Quite obviously," said State, flicking a speck of dust from his Homburg, "Bossy must be reserved for international diplomacy. There can't possibly be—"

"Nonsense," snorted Defense. "Bossy is obviously the ultimate weapon. It would be suicide for any but the Armed Forces to have control over her."

"Bossy is a revenue problem," stubbornly insisted Treasury. "Already two people have been made immortal, without payment of taxes. Why the cessation of inheritance taxes alone—"

"Bossy is a national resource," shouted Interior.

Foreign governments, present and budding dictators, here and abroad, all wanted Bossy. Moscow pointed out, blandly, that she had as much right to Bossy, for peaceful pursuits of course, as she did to the atomic science which had been given to her so freely. The Mafia planned the greatest kidnap scheme of all time, the kidnapping of Bossy. What race track, what gambling casino could possibly play percentages against Bossy?

The post office demanded Bossy as the only possible solution to handling the avalanche of mail which was pouring into the Kennedy Enterprises—the offers, the special deals, the demands, the threats, the claims.

Steve Flynn's masterpiece had received public opinion.

As the days passed the chaos of reaction began to

318

coagulate into masses of definite opinion. As yet the opinion was undirected. The machinery of the opinion controllers had not yet taken up the load. The coalitions in Washington had not yet formulized cooperative policy, catch phrases had not yet been manufactured to supply magnetic islands around which convictions could form.

For the first time in more than a generation people were reacting independently, honestly, with opinions unslanted to directive semantic loads. The preponderance of mail, therefore, showed more trust in Kennedy than in any of the five percent groups who were trying to get Bossy. The letters pleaded with Kennedy not to sell out the people.

There was a strange undercurrent of pleading with him not to release Bossy even though they later demanded he should—as if, instinctively, they knew that when the machinery of opinion control got to working again they could not resist it. Like alcoholics, knowing that when the ready-made drink of easily adopted opinion was placed before them they could not resist it, they pleaded with Kennedy to keep sober and get them safely home.

It was the age-old drama being played out again. As soon as they were able to reconcile differences among themselves, the self-appointed few would at first subtly, by slightly slanted news releases, by vocal inflections in reading supposedly unbiased copy, begin to formulate public opinion. Through the use of semantics the few would become the many. As always just one drink would lead into a total drunk.

The conscience bearers, secure in the mass of supporting opinion, could then say aloud: "We, and only we, are ordained to decide what shall become of Bossy. We intend to be nice about this if you follow along docilely, but if you should resist—''

The man in the street, forlornly, could predict no other outcome. The pattern and the precedence had been so well established, he could see no escape.

These demands upon Kennedy to protect Bossy from falling into the control of special interests did not go unnoticed in Washington. There were others there as responsive as Steve Flynn to the temper of the people. The acid of people's trust in an outsider coagulated the mixtures in Washington as nothing else would. Concessions were made among opposing interests. A formula of control took tentative form.

In view of the temper of the people, direct opposition to Kennedy was unwise. Just possibly they might kill the goose which laid the golden egg. Bossy was still largely an unknown quantity. Kennedy's scientists were not the only ones who had tried to build, independently, a duplicate of Bossy and failed. Other groups had failed even more miserably than Kennedy's men, for the unwillingness to consider another point of view than their own was greater among men who would not have that bond of loyalty to Kennedy as an assistance to progress.

They might find themselves in the position of the savage who could possibly figure out how to steer a car which had its motor running, or by trial and error find and turn the ignition key to get the motor started; but be completely baffled if the distributor key had been removed. It would be better to move cautiously, to get hold of Bossy while she was still intact.

A deal must be made to get Bossy into their hands while she was intact and working. Once they got Bossy, then the deal could be repudiated.

The danger from Billings and Hoskins was slight. They were only scientists. And scientists are noted for avoiding any responsibility for the implications of their work upon mankind. They asked only to be fed and housed and allowed to tinker around in their workshops, leaving it to the practical men to run the world the way it should be run.

Joe Carter was just a kid who had been secretary of the project, and his only claim to fame was that Mabel had fallen in love with him. Boy, that must be really something, considering what she had been all her life! He'd have his hands full, and anyway he was a lightweight who could be ignored.

That left only Kennedy, himself. And Kennedy was open to deals. He'd made them by the hundreds around Washington. There wasn't any reason to believe he wasn't open to one more. Like a shrewd bargainer, he was waiting for them to make the first move, that was all.

Maybe they wouldn't have to repudiate the deal they made with him. Why not cut him in on it? Wasn't he a successful industrialist? Hadn't he built an industrial empire which would overshadow many kingdoms? Could a man attain that position without coming to believe that he was something set apart from common man—like themselves? He probably had the same identical views as they did. It was probably as upsetting to his business plans to have to endure an election every four years as it was to their political plans.

There was room in the hierarchy of immortals who

would eventually rule the world for a man of Kennedy's ability—if it could be determined that he shared the only right way of thinking.

Hap Hardy, free-lance investigations counselor, had hand-led many ticklish deals successfully. He was a shrewd one, behind that affability, for setting up precedents upon which later action could be based. There wasn't a better semantics twister in all Washington. Hap Hardy was the man to deal with Kennedy.

And if he failed, why, then, of course, there was military action.

Hardy wasted no time once he was given the commission, and guaranteed his fee. His phone connection with Kennedy was soon established.

"Howard," he boomed cordially, "how are you, old boy? A couple of us are flying out to the Coast tomorrow on a little matter—my counselor, Oliver Mills, and myself. We thought we'd just stop in and say hello while we're out there—on this other matter."

CHAPTER XXVI

The meeting, held in Kennedy's San Francisco office, started off well.

Hap Hardy was at his most genial and affable best. His associate counselor, Oliver Mills, carefully coached in advance, was still unable to bring forth a downright smile, but at least he hooded the ice in his eyes and softened the fanatical planes of his face in a sort of grimace meant to be pleasant.

The two of them sat in big leather chairs, Hardy lolling back comfortably and wreathed in cigar smoke; Mills sitting upright as if he would not yield his body to such a thing as comfort.

Kennedy sat at his usual place behind his huge desk, framed by the plate glass window which spread the panorama of San Francisco for the delectation of visitors—and incidentally lighted their faces while his own was shadowed.

Joe sat at one corner of the desk, a notebook open before him, playing the part of confidential secretary at Kennedy's request.

"What a couple of characters," Jeff Carney exclaimed from his room over in Berkeley. He was participating in the scene through Joe's eyes and consciousness. "That Mills is a dead ringer for Torquemada, straight out of the Inquisition. And jolly old John Silver Hardy—"

"They're just blindies about to enter into a business deal—they think," Joe answered tolerantly.

"I've got a strong temptation to let Kennedy see what's in their minds," Jeff threatened.

"As if he didn't already know," Joe answered disparagingly. "He may not be telepath, but he wasn't born yesterday. Now you listen, sonny boy, you're purely an observer, seeing how things are done when good fellows get together in a spirit of friendliness."

If either of the visitors objected to Joe Carter's presence as secretary, they did not show it. Hardy raised his brows that Kennedy should think a secretary was justified at a purely social meeting, but it was only a token move in the gambit.

Actually, Joe knew that he was pleased and on more than one count. It showed that Kennedy openly recognized they were here for business, and therefore they need lose no time by beating around the bush and coming into the subject accidentally. And it showed that Kennedy might be ready to talk business, too. You don't need a secretary to take down an obviously flat and positive "No."

Equally important, this kid sitting at the corner of the desk putting down those silly little squiggles could be a valuable witness later, when they went through the legal motions of convicting Kennedy of something or other in order to repudiate the deal. One look at the

324

kid's weak face, and all their previous judgments of him were confirmed. He was a lightweight, who thought he had a good berth in hanging onto this project. When he came up against a man really skilled at questioning and semantics twisting, he'd convict Kennedy with every word he uttered.

A few years back Kennedy would have had more sense than to have a witness of any kind at such an important conference. The old man must be slipping, getting senile!

Hardy settled back in his over-stuffed chair with a sigh of contentment. The battle was already half won. Sure, there was probably a wire recording being made of the whole conversation, but it didn't matter. The law was specific on that. The prosecution in certain cases could use such evidence, but the defense couldn't. That precedent had been set ages ago; on another matter entirely, of course, but then even a high-school debating society could prove parallels of similarity between cases once a precedent had been established.

Let them bring on their wire recording. If there were any dangerous slip in it, the case could easily be rigged in such a way that it would be purely an investigative matter, and Kennedy wouldn't even be allowed a defense much less a jury.

"Howard," Hardy said and leaned forward in his chair after the amenities were over. "America owes you a great debt. I want to congratulate you on the foresight you showed, the way you stepped in and took over Bossy, kept her out of the hands of the radicals and scientists. That shows the value of being able to

325

make an instant decision and acting on it, without a lot of folderol from the opposition party."

"Well," Kennedy demurred, "actually it's still in the hands of the scientists, although I wouldn't call them exactly radical. Professors Billings and Hoskins still have full charge of Bossy, you know."

"As they should! As they should!" Hardy boomed approvingly. "That's our tradition, you know. The inventors of Bossy should reap some of the benefits of their work. And no doubt you're paying them well for their mechanical skill in your behalf." Kennedy laughed.

"You might not believe this, Hap," he chuckled, "but I haven't paid them anything yet—just their keep and a place to work."

Hardy roared his laughter, and looked at Kennedy admiringly.

"It would be better if a token cash payment were made," Oliver Mills said incisively. He had stopped his efforts to appear pleasant and was functioning as he was paid to function. "A legal token cash payment, and a quit claim—"

There! That would be on the record which the young man was scribbling down so industriously. In complete accord with legal procedure they had advised Kennedy to leave no loop-holes for later prosecution and claims.

"I have considered my tenure of Bossy to be more in the nature of a trust, pending final disposal," Kennedy answered. "I wanted to make no more moves until adequate disposition could be made."

Hardy shifted his foundations rapidly. This was going to be easier than he had anticipated. Kennedy obviously recognized he had bitten off more than he could chew. He had plainly said he was ready to unload.

"I can see why you've acted as you have, Howard," he said easily. "Until we can change things a little more, we get all tied up back in Washington with debates and opposition; and somebody had to step in and take charge. It just proves what a bunch of us back there keep saying. But I guess you realize you've caught a tiger by the tail; that Bossy is bigger than any one man."

"It's bigger than both of us, Hap," Kennedy chuckled again. The old saying was at the peak of its popularity cycle again, and they all chuckled in agreement.

Hardy's face terminated the chuckle by assuming an expression of resolute nobility.

"Yes," he agreed soberly, "we are only instruments in the hands of a glorious destiny. But it is our duty to shape that destiny, too, Howard. No man willingly takes the destiny of the world in his own hands, Howard, but there are times when we must. We cannot permit Bossy to fall into the wrong hands. We cannot thwart the destiny of our own people by allowing those traitors to hand it over to the United Nations—which even now has begun its debate on how Bossy is to be controlled."

He paused and eyed Kennedy shrewdly. There it was. The old devil would either have to commit himself to believing it should be shared, or evade the issue which would be the same as committing himself in with the right thinking people.

Joe knew that Kennedy's plans were not quite mature. It was time he took a hand.

"Pardon, sir," he looked up from his notebook. "Uh . . . may I read back the last couple of sentences to check accuracy. It came so fast."

The three men looked at him with exasperated patience of an executive with an inefficient secretary. But Hardy was not unwilling. It had sounded pretty good, and he wouldn't mind hearing himself repeated. Kennedy suppressed a smile and nodded his permission.

"There it is, you old devil," Joe read in the expressionless voice which is the trademark of the unimpressed secretary reading back. "Either you will have to throw in with those namby-pambies, or declare yourself one of our group who intend to get hold of Bossy for our own purposes."

There was a stricken silence in the room. There was the immobility of mummies in a tomb.

"Isn't that what you said, sir?" Joe asked in a faltering voice.

"I . . . I—" Hardy gasped and began to turn purple.

"He did not!" Oliver Mills rapped out the words as if they were cutting blows.

"What's the matter with you, Joe?" Kennedy asked in a harsh voice; but Joe knew the anger was only simulated, that the old man was laughing heartily behind his poker face.

"I . . . I don't know, sir," Joe said, hesitantly. "Several of us have noticed it; those of us who have worked around Bossy a great deal. We keep hearing things, things people don't actually say. That's why I wanted to check. I wasn't sure Mr. Hardy had said them, or was only thinking them. It's . . . it's very confusing!''

"Attaboy!" Jeff Carney's thoughts, from over in Berkeley, approved. "Keep 'em off side."

And they were off side. The implications were too plain. They could not be missed. This secretary could read their thoughts! The idea formed in their minds to escape the room, to get completely away and replan their strategy. They must act at once.

"Give 'em the other barrel, Joe," Jeff urged delightedly from across the bay. He didn't mind if the metaphors were mixed, Joe would know what he meant.

"We're trying to fix it so it won't happen again, sir," Joe said apologetically. "Apparently there's some kind of a broadcast power loss. So we have her completely dismantled, and—"

"Bossy is dismantled?" Hardy screamed the words hoarsely, as he sprang to his feet.

"Why, yes, sir," Joe said innocently. "The machine is purely experimental you know, and—"

The slam of Kennedy's door behind Hardy and Mills shut off the need for further words. They were gone in a panic. They would, indeed, have to reorganize their strategy.

Kennedy sat looking at Joe from under his bushy gray eyebrows.

"Does Bossy broadcast mind-reading ability, Joe?" he asked mildly.

"No," Joe laughed. "It was pretty obvious what they were thinking."

Kennedy nodded.

"And I don't suppose she's dismantled, either," he stated.

"Not unless Hoskins has thought up something to tinker with," Joe answered.

"I gather you didn't approve of my making a deal with Hardy, then."

"Had you planned on it?" Joe asked.

"You know I hadn't," Kennedy said slowly. "You know that, in the same way you know everything else in the minds of people around you. I've watched you and Mabel and Carney, Joe. I've questioned Billings and Hoskins. They pretended to know nothing, but they weren't fooling me."

"Are you sorry, sir?" Joe asked, and this time he used the term of address in sincere respect.

"No," Kennedy answered instantly. "Maybe a little indignant at first, when I first realized your talent, over rights of privacy and such nonsense. But I've lived long enough to know no man stands on the pedestal he pretends to occupy, and I'm probably no worse than the run of the mill. No, I'm quite glad.

"A solution for Bossy has to be found, you know. This is just the first of the possible deals. I've known the problem from the first. I thought I was alone. Two misty-minded professors, and a stripling kid. I thought the whole burden of deciding what to do with Bossy was up to me.

"I'm glad it isn't."

CHAPTER XXVII

A solution had to be found.

Bossy was at least one loaded gun which could not be tossed into the nursery of playing children with the usual irresponsible attitude of science.

"There, children, is a new toy. I suppose I should tell you it is dangerous and you really ought not to point it at one another when you pull the trigger. Of course if you do it's not my responsibility. I have all I can do in simply discovering the principles of how it works and in putting it together. Have fun, kiddies; and if you should kill one another with it, I will be the first to wring my hands and say it wasn't meant for that purpose."

Yet if the scientific product and principle is withheld, wouldn't that be even worse? What differentiates the man from the child, the civilized from the savage, man from beast, except a knowledge of the interrelationships of the parts of the universe, and how they

331

work in the cycles of cause and effect? Can the child ever grow up, mentally, if the principles discovered in the laboratory are withheld from him?

A solution for Bossy had to be found.

In essence, Bossy was the ultimate weapon, and raised the same old problem which all ultimate weapons raise.

"How far and how long can the trustees be trusted?"

Nor was this question being asked only by a few men of high intellect. The conversation overheard on the street by Joe and Jeff and Mabel was taking place everywhere. Solutions by the hundreds were pouring over the airwaves, published in every newspaper, offered in every crank letter. Each had some single-valued purpose which must be fulfilled. Each had some bogeyman which Bossy must be used to destroy.

Everyone recognized that only five per cent of all the people born ever amount to anything at all. Everyone humbly thanked his providential stars that through his own personal efforts and merit he had become one of the superior five per cent. Everyone looked with pity and contempt upon the ninety-five per cent who did not share his grace.

A solution had to be found.

The pressures of each group who had its own little solution began to mount. There had to be some relief of these pressures. The move made by Hardy as spokesman for the group, who believed that linear government was the only possible way of controlling man, was only the beginning.

The Margaret Kennedy Clinic took on the appearance of an armed camp. But these were Kennedy's own guards, a recognizably futile safeguard against any really organized effort to get at Bossy, but a deterrent to disorganized attempts. Awaiting the revised strategy, the Pentagon had not yet supplemented its contingent, and the disgusted sergeant continued to change his sentry at regular intervals. The sentry challenged no one who went in and out of Bossy's room and amused himself by pretending that he was an honor guard and presented arms for every person who passed down the corridor. The sentry who had let Carney into the room had embellished his story with the telling and you never knew who might be a five-star general disguised as a janitor with a mop and a pail.

At present the sentries were even more alert than usual. Everybody around the Bossy building knew that all the principals were in a meeting: Kennedy, Flynn, Billings, Hoskins, Carney, Mabel, Joe. The doors were closed, and Kennedy's own guards let no one into the corridors leading to the room.

Inside the room the meeting was casual, more in the nature of a group of people who were merely visiting.

Steve Flynn, an almost infallible mirror of the public mind, expressed the mass bewilderment.

"What's going to happen with Bossy?"

The question served to take the conversation away from the coffee and rolls which they had brought in with them.

"As a point of information, Joe," Kennedy asked, "suppose I had made a deal with Hardy and his gang. Suppose now or at some time in the future a would-be dictator did get hold of Bossy? He asks for the most effective strategy. He gets it. He asks for the most powerful weapons; he gets them. he asks for the most effective defense against other weapons; he gets it. He could conquer the world with ease."

"He would still need followers," Hoskins pointed out. "If people didn't back him up—"

Flynn snorted in derision.

"A little bit of semantics twisting will get him followers by the millions. People will tie in with a fanatic if for no other reason than to break the monotony of their lives. That wouldn't be a problem at all."

"But he couldn't be made immortal," Billings objected. "As long as he held to a one-track idea, he couldn't be relieved of his tensions and be renewed again. I would assume that the desire to conquer the world, or any part of it, would be in the nature of a fixation, a tension. As long as he clung to a one-track idea Bossy couldn't renew him. He would know he'd die."

"So what?" Flynn countered. "He'd have his fun while he was here."

"Would he want it?" Kennedy asked slowly. "As against immortality, wouldn't the satisfaction of pushing other people around for only a short while be pretty small potatoes?"

"If I know people—and that's my trade," Flynn answered, "he could convince himself that it would be all right to conquer the world first, and then he could repent his ways and have immortality, too. At least, that always has been the pattern."

Jeff and Mabel were looking at Joe, their thoughts all identical.

"In the long run of history," Joe said quietly, "it really wouldn't matter. Man's destiny would work out whether it were under a dictator, a democracy, or some form of government which we haven't yet conceived.''

Kennedy and Flynn looked at him in amazement.

"I think the real problem here is in concept of the universe,'' Jeff said. "And the meaning of science itself.''

Joe nodded.

"Bossy conceived the universe to be a totality,'' he said. "Where all facts and processes and forces are interrelated to form a total concept. At this stage of man's evolution, our scientists have been like little children facing a table piled high with the pieces of a jigsaw puzzle. One piece is picked up and its holder says, 'This is the important piece. I hold the one key to everything in my hands.' Well, of course, he does. Because every piece is a key piece.''

Mabel put down her cup and took up the thread, unbroken.

"In most areas we haven't even begun to try to fit the pieces together. Or where we do try, we find discrepancies. Like children, we are inclined to make one or two futile attempts and then throw the whole thing back on the table as a hopeless job. But all the pieces do fit to form a total picture. We haven't any idea yet what that picture is. We haven't even yet worked out an adequate method of approach.''

"We often think we have,'' Jeff continued. "We form a theory and it seems to work until we run across a piece which proves it doesn't. At least we've made some progress in going back over our previous work to see if a new theory, which will bring the new piece into line, would also have fitted into the past.''

"We're still doing too much jamming and forcing the pieces together, though," Joe picked up the thought. "We seem to have almost a mania for answering questions prematurely."

"Life has been short," Billings said with a note of nostalgia. "A man can be forgiven for trying to find an answer, a summation of all his efforts."

"It plays hob with the total picture, though," Joe answered. "We get some very strange linkages by forcing the pieces, to say nothing of the fact that such tactics will always defeat us."

"I'm not sure I'm following that," Kennedy said.

"The scientists who supplied Bossy with basic knowledge," Joe explained, "were all familiar with the concept we've just outlined. They leaned over backwards to limit themselves to differentiate between demonstrable fact and assumptions drawn from such fact. Here's an example:

"Virtually all books of astronomy state categorically that Mars has two moons. We've charted their courses, and toss away the fact as not being of any consequence that they do not follow the usual course of other bodies in the solar system. We've named them, given them their mass ratings. And we've dismissed them as a known fact.

"Actually all we can demonstrate is that our telescopes pick up some reflected light from what appears to be material bodies which appear to be satellites of Mars. And that was the information fed into Bossy— not that Mars has two natural moons, but that our telescopes pick up some reflected light.

"We know now that they could be artificial satellites, and if they were metallic then their reflected light could account for much smaller bodies than we have assumed. We didn't think of this at the time we postulated the moons because artificial satellites were an impossibility, or so we thought.

"So here are two possible explanations where we had only one before. It is reasonable to ask what new developments in science next century will give us still further explanations?"

"Apply this everywhere in man's knowledge. The vast majority of what he thinks is knowledge is pure assumption—the forcing and pounding of unlike pieces together to make them fit."

"I don't see what this has got to do with a dictator getting hold of Bossy," Steve said. "It's like the trees, it seems to mean something to you people, but I'm the common man, remember?"

"What I'm trying to say," Joe answered, and took the cup of coffee Mabel poured for him, "is that Bossy deals only with proved fact, not assumptions. Her answers then are based on factual relationships. She fits the right pieces together. If a dictator had Bossy, he would ask her questions. She would answer the questions, and if he acted on the answers, he would, inadvertently, be fitting the pieces of the puzzle together for mankind."

"If he acted on them," Steve said cynically. "Suppose he didn't like the answers Bossy gave him. Suppose he got mad and picked up a club and smashed Bossy because he didn't like what she said. That happens, figuratively, all the time, you know. It's pretty human to smash the guy or the thing which tries to tell us something we don't want to hear."

"Well, yes," Joe sighed, "there's that. Of course you're overlooking the fact that Mabel or Carney could rebuild Bossy. Hoskins, Billings and I all working together could do it—but Mabel or Carney could do it alone. In a way they're sort of a duplicate of Bossy; and Bossy, given the proper attachments, could rebuild herself."

"But you three could be destroyed, just as Bossy could," Kennedy argued.

"Man would eventually rediscover Bossy," Mabel answered him. "The one thing we persistently overlook is faith in the future generations of man. We attack everything as if the final solution depended upon us, as if everything had to be settled because our moronic dependents couldn't possibly cope with them. Suppose Bossy were destroyed, and us along with her? Time is long. There are millions of years ahead of man."

"I can't wait that long," Kennedy said gravely, but with a wry twist of self-deprecation in his voice. "I'm still clinging to my old tension that I've got to protect man against his own self-destructiveness. I want to make sure there *are* some descendants—moronic or otherwise.

"You people, you're different. Maybe you can look at things on the grand scale, what they call the cosmic point of view, but I . . . I can't wait a million years for a solution."

"I suspected you wouldn't," Joe smiled.

"But what are you going to do Boss?" Flynn asked.

"There's only one way to guard a secret so effectively that no one can misuse it to his own advantage and the detriment of others," Kennedy mused slowly, "and that's to give it away—make it open knowledge. Give it to everybody."

"Scientists have known that for a long time," Hoskins said. "That's why we keep insisting on free trade of ideas."

"But how can you do that with Bossy?" Billings asked. "Ten days to two weeks per person. You couldn't begin to process more than a selected few . . . and that takes us right back—"

Kennedy turned to Joe.

"Is there any reason why Bossy can't be put on the production line, turned out en masse like vacuum cleaners, radios, automobiles?" he asked.

Mabel and Jeff and Joe looked at one another and smiled openly.

"That was the answer Bossy gave us weeks ago," Joe said.

Kennedy's mouth fell open.

"You see," Joe went on, "when you've got a problem, all you have to do is ask Bossy."

"You could have saved me a lot of sleepless nights," Kennedy said reprovingly.

"We felt it better you came to the decision on your own," Jeff said. "You control the factories. It was the problem of the dictator, you see. If the idea came to you before you were ready for it, and you didn't approve of it, you might smash it. As you say, time for us has a different value. We could afford to wait."

"Although we have been busy," Mabel said with a

teasing smile, "I've been working a regular factory shift. You see, Bossy has been turning out blueprints of herself, and of all the special tooling necessary to make her parts in mass quantity. Everything's ready to hand to your engineers and production foremen right now."

CHAPTER XXVIII

There is a time lapse necessary between deciding to put a machine on the production line and the act of shipping out the crated article. The vast proportion of the time cycle is taken up with the engineering. So much assumption is confused with fact, so little is known of process, that each thing must be tested anew when tried in different combination or pattern.

All but one phase of the engineering work on Bossy was done. But there is still time consumed in the doing of a thing after man knows what it is he must do and how to do it. The vast resources of Kennedy's far-flung enterprises were filled with trained and loyal personnel, but it still takes time to make a new tool and bolt it to the floor.

And time was pressing.

For a few days, Joe's announcement that Bossy was dismantled held the Hardy group in a suspension of indecision. But this only allowed other groups to catch up in their own plans for taking control of Bossy.

Kennedy's legal staff bogged down completely with writs, subpoenas, injunctions. A little man would simply have been arrested and pushed around until he consented to do what was required of him. But Kennedy was not a little man.

In a strange way, the terrifying danger which had faced the country for several decades, acted to protect Kennedy. Gradually the position had changed from government by representative to government by representatives' hired staffs. And these staffs had been hired on the basis of loyalty to given persons.

With such a prize at stake, it was an inevitable part of the pattern that there should be more strife between these factions than normal, and that much of their potential effectiveness was lost in counteracting one another's moves.

Even so, at times, the attorneys of each faction found time to add another writ to the fast growing pile, demanding Bossy be delivered into their hands in perfect working order upon penalty of—the penalties varied according to the powers the factions had usurped for themselves to carry out their own brands of tensions.

Kennedy astonished his legal staff by telling them to answer each writ with a compliance promise. As per their demands, Bossy would be delivered into their hands on a given date. He coordinated that date with his production plans.

It was well known that Kennedy's word was good. Each faction labeled the compliance as ultra secret. Each faction set about with frantic plans to lay the ground-work for its ascension to the pinnacle of power, to control the country, to control the world.

Some of the factions, such as the prohibition league still barely alive, had demanded Bossy more as a token gesture than anything else. They were vastly astonished to receive Kennedy's promise that Bossy would be turned over to them on said given date. They accounted for it through belief that he was in secret sympathy with them. A man does not find it strange that someone else should share his prejudices and tensions, even a fanatic realizes there may be a few others who know right from wrong—his brand of it. These obscure little factions, too, kept their pending triumph secret; and basked in the anticipated power they would have to force everybody to believe and do the right thing—or else.

In this manner Kennedy bought the preciously needed production time with his promises. Even the private citizen cranks who wrote in demanding Bossy be given to them so that they could take their rightful place in controlling their fellow men were answered with the same promise.

For when Kennedy said that he intended to give the secret to everybody, he meant precisely that. He would not be content with merely publishing the plans and theories behind Bossy; which still would limit her use to the favored few who had the money and equipment to produce her. No, he intended that the actual machine, itself, be available to anyone who wanted her.

He realized what this would do to the economy of the world; but the changes which Bossy would bring about were only magnifications of the changes which had occurred when the steering wheel replaced the buggy whip. He greatly suspected that making Bossy available at cost to those who could buy her, and opening up vast clinics for those who could not, would make less dent in his vast financial holdings than the secondary changes which would come about because each man would now hold all the answers he needed to solve his own economic problems—the answers would be limited only by the man's inability to ask the right questions, or by Bossy's persistently irritating "Insufficient data."

No, the legal department need not worry about the consequences of promising Bossy to each faction who demanded her. Each would receive her.

The one problem remaining, engineeringwise, was that there would be a great many Bossies indeed, and as fast as it could be managed they would be scattered over all the world. Bossy did not know all the facts of the universe. Bossy knew only what the science of today knows.

Man has not even scratched the surface of the facts surrounding his own fingernail, as yet. He has not yet even made a dent in the facts about the universe which remain to be discovered. Some of the Bossies would be receiving this new knowledge, others would not. And the total picture of the universe, as it unfolded, as the pieces were put together, must be made available to every man. Otherwise, Bossy would be self-defeating.

There must be intercommunication between all the Bossies.

It was not difficult to found the principles on which this would operate. Bossy functioned already by a harmonic vibration needed to be broadcast on the same principle as the radio wave. No new principle was needed. Any cookbook engineer could do it—even those who believe what they read in the textbooks and consider pure assumption to be proved fact.

It was not difficult to design the sending and receiving apparatus, nor was extra time consumed since this small alteration was being made contiguous with the production set up time of the rest.

The production of countless copies of the brain floss itself was likewise no real problem, no more difficult than using a key-punched master card to duplicate others by the thousands or millions on the old-fashioned hole punch computer system.

There was no hitch anywhere along the line. Government interference had ceased, the raw stocks suppliers were long practiced in giving Kennedy Enterprises preferential treatment on any sudden orders, Kennedy's own organization was long skilled in making quick changes and adaptations in his various functions.

Complete Bossies began to roll off the production line. They were crated and made ready for shipment long before the promised date. The contingency time for unexpected delays, based upon sound industrial engineering standards, had not been used.

And every retail outlet of Kennedy's entire chain began to receive crates of a new piece of household equipment which would go on sale within a short time.

Steve Flynn received his orders to set up another world-wide television coverage with a shrug of his shoulders. This was old stuff now. He merely had to breathe the word that a new announcement was to be made concerning Bossy and he got instant cooperation.

But when he was told that after the announcement of Bossy's availability to everyone had been made,

345

Joe would step in front of the cameras and give an explanation of what Bossy meant, he shook his head, blew a long breath through his lips.

"Oh, brother!" he muttered. Then to Kennedy, "Look, Mr. Kennedy, will you tell Joe, please, that these aren't Brains he's talking to—that these are just people who don't know nothing from nothing, and don't particularly want to! Will you tell him he can't talk about evergreen trees or jigsaw puzzles or anything like that and expect to get across?"

"I understand he's going to talk about water," Kennedy answered with a chuckle.

"Oh, brother," Steve groaned. "And half the people will wind up thinking that Bossy is just a hot-water heater or a new kind of bathtub! Well, at least, will you please ask him not to mention . . . what was it he and Hoskins were talking about the other day . . . multi-valued physics?"

He looked as if he were going to break down and weep.

He was apprehensive all the way through the preliminaries of the broadcast. A production was made of it, for the world had come to a stop and was listening. The world sat stunned at the announcement that everyone would have Bossy.

No one had ever believed that any except a special privileged few would benefit from her. They did not grasp it all at once. They sat in the stunned immobility of a poverty-stricken man who has been told, without warning, that he is a millionaire. Their minds, like his, could conceive of only the simplest poor uses for it, or wild extravagances.

They saw Kennedy's face on the screen as he was

introduced. They saw Billings again, who told them he intended to make another try at renewing his youth, that he had learned a great deal since his failure. They met Hoskins who confined his short talk to cybernetic principles understood only by a few like minds. They met Carney and Mabel again. Even Steve Flynn, usually confining himself to background operation, consented to say a few words about Bossy. He tried to keep his voice and talk out of the pitchman framework of pushing a new kitchen can opener which would also peel potatoes. He almost succeeded.

He did succeed in restoring a sense of the familiar to his listening and watching audience. They began to breathe again. There was enough of the commercial about his appearance and manner, enough of that frantic urgency—as if a sponsor were standing just out of sight with a long black whip—to make them realize, as had nothing else about the program, that Bossy was available to them at the nearest Kennedy Enterprise store, and at a price which they could probably afford.

Some of the jaws returned to a rhythmic chewing of gum, some realized their beer glasses needed refilling, the odor of burning food on the stove penetrated some nostrils. Enough normalcy was restored that they were able to perceive Joe as he stepped before the cameras, and their minds picked up at least some of the things he said.

"There have been many misconceptions about Bossy," Joe began his talk. He hoped, contrary to Steve's predictions, that he would get across, for the things he had to say were a summation of what Bossy meant to the world, and to each man.

347

"One of the most prevalent misconceptions has been that since Bossy can think faster and more accurately than a man, Man will cease to think, become an indolent slave of the machine and thus fail to reach his destiny.

"The adding machine can think faster than a clerk with a pencil and paper, but it has not destroyed business. The automobile can go places faster and easier than a man can walk there, but it has not stopped man from wanting to go. These things are simply tools which man uses.

"Bossy is just a tool. Bossy can answer your questions, but only if you ask them.

"There is another even wilder misconception. It has been said that Bossy is a soulless machine, and man, being guided by her, will become likewise no more than a soulless monster, losing his sense of faith, yearning, reaching.

"Bossy is a product of science. There is not now, there never has been any real issue between science and faith. Both strive for the same identical goal; both seek comprehension; both wish to benefit man that he live happier, healthier, more harmoniously with himself and with his neighbors. Man seeks to comprehend, to understand the forces which govern his life. The sometimes apparently different paths taken by science and faith are of no consequence in comparison with man's yearning to know.

"Truth frightens man. He plants illusion in the debris of his mind to hide him from the clean white light she brings. His arguments defeat her wisdom. In his preconceptions and prejudices he dictates, in advance, what form she must take, what garments she must

348

wear; and because of this he often does not recognize her when they meet. His illusion drives her from him.

"And yet he still yearns and seeks for truth.

"That is the inherent nature of man. That is the inherent nature of intellect, itself. It seeks to know. Bossy will not replace this drive of mankind. Rather, she will supplement it and in its furtherance. Bossy is man's tool. Like all other tools, Bossy is for man's use.

"Yes, she will give you immortality. And therein lies another misconception. If you are sitting on a hillside above a lake of water, and you point your finger at the lake and command it, 'Come and bathe me,' it will be unmoved. It will ripple and sparkle in the sunlight, and not heed you.

"Water obeys certain laws of the universe. To get bathed, you must use at least some of those laws. As yet man has no mastery of forces which will make that water leap out of its bed and come up the hillside to bathe him.

"But wait a minute. Yes, he does have at least some of the laws governing water under his command. He has pumps and pipes. He can and does command the water to come up the hillside to bathe him, and it obeys him when, and only when, he makes use of the laws which have been determined through the applications of science.

"Bossy is a product of science. Bossy will obey you when you command her to renew your youth only when you make use of the laws of life which must be applied to the cells of your body to restore your vigorous youth. Bossy is no thing of magic, no super being. Bossy is only a tool. And tools are used successfully only when they conform to the laws which operate in the universe.

"Bossy is only a tool. She will not plead with you to learn and use the laws of life and matter. She will not threaten you, cajole you, bribe you, promise you either the fires of hell or the delights of heaven. If you are seeking a parent substitute, a return to mother's arms, Bossy will give you cold comfort. Bossy does not care.

"Water does not care whether you bathe in it or drown in it. The mountains do not care whether you climb them or go around them. The stars do not care whether man reaches them or not. The universe does not care whether man masters all the relationships of its forces and processes, or dies because he refuses to master them. Life continues as it uses those relationships to further its growth. It ceases when it becomes overcome by still other forces which it cannot master.

"This is cold comfort for those who would pay any price for security, lethargy, the return to the mothering womb, no, even farther back than that for even the womb is a struggle, to nothingness.

"But it is bright hope indeed for those who see something more in store for man than indolence and endless repetitions of purposelessness of generation after generation. For it means that there is still a challenge facing man.

"That challenge is Bossy. She will not command you, or cajole you. She does not care whether you are made immortal or whether you would prefer clinging to your thin and single-valued ideas and prejudices—and die. But there she sits. She is a tool who will heat your homes, or bring you entertainment, or cook your food, or bathe the baby, or walk the dog, or figure your income tax. She will do these things as she is commanded, and not care whether they are big or small. Because Bossy is only a tool.

"She can also give you a tremendous comprehension in time, the nature of which we do not yet even dream. She can give you immortality. But you must rise to her requirements. You cannot make use of the tool unless you comprehend something of the laws of the universe governing life.

"There she sits. She is yours. She is not a threat. But she is a challenge. She is perhaps the greatest challenge which mankind has ever been called upon to meet. She is a challenge to your willingness to admit that you might not be right, that you might not already have all the answers. She is a challenge to your willingness to learn rather than to argue.

"Ladies and gentlemen of the world. There she sits. Bossy is yours."

FINE SCIENCE FICTION AND
FANTASY TITLES AVAILABLE
FROM CARROLL & GRAF

☐ Aldiss, Brian/THE DARK LIGHT YEARS $3.50
☐ Aldiss, Brian/LAST ORDERS $3.50
☐ Aldiss, Brian/NON-STOP $3.95
☐ Amis, Kingsley/THE ALTERATION $3.50
☐ Asimov, Isaac *et al.* (eds)/THE MAMMOTH BOOK OF VINTAGE
   SCIENCE FICTION (1950s) $8.95
☐ Asimov, Isaac et al/THE MAMMOTH BOOK OF GOLDEN AGE
   SCIENCE FICTION (1940s) $8.95
☐ Ballard, J.G./THE DROWNED WORLD $3.95
☐ Ballard, J.G./THE TERMINAL BEACH $3.50
☐ Ballard, J.G./VERMILION SANDS $3.95
☐ Bingley, Margaret/SEEDS OF EVIL $3.95
☐ Borges, Jorge Luis/THE BOOK OF FANTASY (Trade Paper) $10.95
☐ Boucher, Anthony/THE COMPLEAT WEREWOLF $4.50
☐ Campbell, John W./THE MOON IS HELL! $3.95
☐ Campbell, Ramsey/DEMONS BY DAYLIGHT $3.95
☐ Burroughs, Edgar Rice/A PRINCESS OF MARS $2.95
☐ Dick, Philip K./THE PENULTIMATE TRUTH $3.95
☐ Dick, Philip K./TIME OUT OF JOINT $3.95
☐ Disch, Thomas K./CAMP CONCENTRATION $3.95
☐ Leiber, Fritz/YOU'RE ALL ALONE $3.95
☐ Leinster, Murray/THE FORGOTTEN PLANET $3.95
☐ Ligotti, Thomas/SONGS OF A DEAD DREAMER $3.95
☐ Lovecraft, H. P. & Derleth, A./THE LURKER ON THE THRESHOLD $3.50
☐ Moorcock, Michael/FANTASY: THE 100 BEST BOOKS $8.95
☐ Stoker, Bram/THE JEWEL OF SEVEN STARS $3.95
☐ van Vogt, A.E./COSMIC ENCOUNTER $3.50
☐ Watson, Ian/CHEKHOV'S JOURNEY $3.95
☐ Watson, Ian/MIRACLE VISITORS $3.95

Available from fine bookstores everywhere or use this coupon for ordering.

Carroll & Graf Publishers, Inc., 260 Fifth Avenue, N.Y., N.Y. 10001

Please send me the books I have checked above. I am enclosing $_____
(please add $1.25 per title to cover postage and handling.) Send check
or money order—no cash or C.O.D.'s please. N.Y. residents please add
8¼% sales tax.

Mr/Mrs/Ms _____
Address _____
City _____ State/Zip _____
Please allow four to six weeks for delivery.